THE WAY OF THE RIVE[illegible]

Pamela Street was born in W[illegible] only daughter of the lat[illegible] educated at the G[illegible] Her first book, [illegible] *A. G. Street*, wa[illegible] reprinted severa[illegible] 1971 by *Portrait of* [illegible]plete-ly updated in 1980, [illegible]on of an-other of her books: *A*[illegible]*–Portrait of a Historian*. This is her f[illegible]el. Her first, *Light of Evening*, is publish[illegible] by Pan under the Pavanne imprint and *The Mill-Race*, to which *The Way of the River* is the sequel, is also available in Pan.

Also by Pamela Street
in Pan

THE MILL-RACE

in Pavanne

LIGHT OF EVENING

The Way of the River

PAMELA STREET

Pan Books London and Sydney

First published in Great Britain 1984 by Robert Hale Ltd
This edition published 1985 by Pan Books Ltd,
Cavaye Place, London SW10 9PG
9 8 7 6 5 4 3 2 1

ISBN 0 330 28685 4

Printed and bound in Great Britain by
Richard Clay (The Chaucer Press) Ltd, Bungay, Suffolk

For My Encourager

1

"When will you make Greta's dress, Aunt Chip?"

May Lodge momentarily laid down the crêpe de Chine camisole that she was hem-stitching and regarded her seven-year-old niece, gravely.

"When I've finished Lady Fairfax's order, Emily. If you like, you can fetch that old rag-bag in the corner and see if you can find something pretty you would like her to wear."

Eagerly, the small girl got up and did as she was bidden. Then she sat down on the floor of the workroom again and, extracting a mass of material of all shapes, sizes and colours, she proceeded, oblivious of her aunt, to address herself to her doll, holding up this and that against the stiff, pink, scantily-clad form, as if she were a couturier advising some particularly important client.

May watched her covertly as she resumed her sewing. She thought her a beautiful child, not nearly so thin and frail-looking as her mother had been at the same age. With her dark curly hair, enormous brown eyes and rosy cheeks, Emily disproved all her grandmother's forebodings about London not being a proper place in which to bring up children. If only Sarah would admit that she might be wrong; but then, May reflected, she had never done that in all her life. Besides, with Emily's mother now so ill in hospital, and all the other tribulations which had recently overtaken the small family, May felt that perhaps some of Sarah's condemnation of the capital seemed almost justified.

"This is nice, Aunt Chip." Suddenly the child held up a piece of midnight blue taffeta. "Greta would look lovely in blue."

"Let me see." May held out her hand. "Why, I do believe that's a scrap from the very first dance dress I ever made your mother."

"Is there enough?" Emily was standing now, looking at May anxiously, one hand still clutching the doll, the other placed, almost in supplication, on her aunt's knee.

"I think so, my dear. We might put a few lace frills and flounces round the bottom, just to help out."

"Oh, *yes*. Thank you. Will it be like the ones Mummy used to wear when she danced at the theatre?"

This time May's response was a little more reserved, but Emily appeared not to notice as, with her imagination roused, she produced a sudden spate of further questions.

"Where was I, Aunt Chip, when you made Mummy's first dance dress?"

"You?" May could not help smiling now. "Why, you weren't born, Emily. It was just before your mother married. Let me see, over eight years ago. The end of 1920."

"Where was the dance? In London?"

"Oh, dear me no. It was here, in Wilhampton. In the town hall."

The child looked puzzled. "Did Daddy come all the way from the bookshop to take her?"

"No, dear. Now, put all those other scraps back where they belong, will you." May felt that the conversation was getting a little out of hand, and that it would be as well to steer her niece's thoughts in other directions. But she had reckoned without Emily's persistence. Although the little girl obediently began to refill the rag-bag, she obviously had something on her mind and did not intend to let the matter rest.

"Who did Mummy go to the dance with, Aunt Chip, if she didn't go with Daddy?"

May broke off some silk thread, removed her spectacles and began putting her sewing things away methodically in the work-basket at her side. "What a lot of things you want to know, Miss. Your mother was very pretty. Indeed, she still is. She happened to have more than one young man in those days. She went to the dance with the doctor who called to see your grandmother yesterday about her rheumatism."

"The *doctor*? But . . . I heard you and Granny talking about his wife after he'd gone, Aunt Chip."

"Did you? Well, little pitchers shouldn't have such long ears. Dr Fitzherbert and your Mummy went to the dance before *either* of them was married. Now, that's enough chattering. How about showing me those steps you were on about."

This time the child's attention was immediately diverted.

"Oh, *yes*! Have you got a comb and a piece of tissue paper, Aunt Chip? Then you could blow a tune for me through it like

Mummy does. Play *Bye, Bye, Blackbird*, extra fast. Do."

May searched in her handbag for a comb and then got up to fetch some clean tissue paper from the store which she kept in the bottom drawer of the big deal chest of drawers. She felt that it did not really seem right to be going in for such frivolity at a time like this, yet Katy had expressly said in the letter she had written to her sister asking if she thought Sarah would agree to having Emily at the Mill House while she went into hospital: "Whatever happens, May, if she does come, don't tell her too much. She picks things up so quickly. I want her to be happy. Don't let Mother talk about the operation in front of her. I'll be thinking of you, imagining you dancing with her and singing *Here We Go Looby-Loo*, like you used to do with me, once."

Apart from a few unfortunate remarks which had slipped out, May felt that, on the whole, they had complied with Katy's request, even if it had meant Sarah constantly reiterating her doubts and fears as soon as the child was in bed, forcing May to listen, night after night, to a tirade about how they should never have allowed Katy to marry Philip Mason, that she should never have gone to London and that, certainly, she should never, ever, have got in with all those shameless, wicked, stage folk.

With the latter sentiment, May could not but agree. It had definitely been a shock when, three years ago, just after the General Strike, Katy had written to say that a certain Mr Marcus Kreiger, a distinguished and regular customer of Philip's, had offered her the chance of appearing in a musical he was backing in the West End. The letter had not mentioned that it so happened Mr Kreiger, a rich and successful entrepreneur, had also offered to lend Philip a considerable amount of money in order to help him over the financial difficulties in which Mason and Son, the booksellers, like many another business at that time, found themselves.

"When are you going to begin, Aunt Chip?" Emily's voice broke into May's reveries, somewhat plaintively.

"I'm sorry, dear." May sat down again and, with comb and tissue paper poised, added, "I don't expect that I shall be as good at this as your Mummy is."

"Never mind. You can just start me off."

After a few moments, May did, in fact, find to her relief that there was little need for her continued and somewhat breathless accompaniment. Emily was well away, humming to herself and now kicking her heels up sideways in a most spirited execution of the Charleston. The whole performance was so accomplished, yet so natural, that May could only sit back in fascination and wonder until, suddenly, the door of the workroom was thrown open and Sarah Lodge stood on the threshold.

"May I ask what is going on?" Her mother, in her long black moiré dress with the customary tucker of snow-white lace at the throat, made an imposing, intimidating figure. May, although thirty-eight and used to Sarah's vagaries, seemed far more embarrassed than her niece who, although awed by her grandmother, was, as yet, more perplexed by, than actually frightened of her.

"Emily was showing me how she does the Charleston, Mother."

"The *Charleston*!" No Sarah Bernhardt could have invested the word with more meaningful odium. Although Sarah Lodge had never witnessed the dance since the craze for it had swept the country a few years earlier, she knew enough—through reading the papers and listening to 2LO on their crystal wireless set—to have formed her own uncompromising opinion on the subject. As far as she was concerned, even if the Prince of Wales did dance it, the Charleston was not suitable for *ladies*. It made them look vulgar and corrupt. It was far worse, in fact, than the Cancan. As for her own grand-daughter doing it, that was not to be countenanced.

A flash of memory suddenly jerked May back ten years to the time when Sarah's intense displeasure had been incurred over a vaguely similar incident: how she had mercilessly dressed them all down after hearing that Katy had got up on the stage at the local fair and sung *Our Lodger's Such A Nice Young Man* to the whole of Wilhampton. May could see the scene quite clearly in her mind's eye: the lamplight flickering over the five faces round the tea-table in the living-room of the Mill House. Even poor dear simple Neil had seemed to register his mother's anger and indignation. As for Katy, she had been in tears while Flo, quite gently and kindly, had tried to find out exactly what had happened. Of course, what had made it seem so much more deplorable to Sarah was the fact that she herself was then still in mourning for her late husband. Sidney Lodge, the manager of the Felt Mills for thirty-two years, had scarcely been dead three months. And today, although her youngest daugther was not dead, she had undergone a serious operation and therefore, in Sarah's eyes, it did not behove any member of the family to be seen enjoying themselves, even a small seven-year-old child.

"You will not dance the Charleston again, Emily, here or, I trust, anywhere else." Her pronouncement was made with the same compelling sepulchral intonation that May remembered so well and against which no member of the Lodge family had ever dared to argue. "I came to tell you both that tea is ready." With that, Sarah turned and left the workroom as abruptly as she had arrived.

"Hurry up, dear. Best pop round into the closet before we go." May gave Emily a gentle push and busied herself collecting up the various items she would need in order to continue working in the Mill House that evening. Then, when the child still seemed to dawdle, she began chivvying her. "There, run along. We don't want to keep your grandmother waiting."

"But Aunt Chip . . ." The bottom lip had turned down. Emily was not exactly crying, but she had begun to look very near it. "Can't I dance the Charleston again, ever?"

"Well, dear. You heard what your grandmother said. She doesn't like it."

"Why not? Mummy and Daddy do it. They used to dance it ever such a lot, once. I used to hear them. They put the gramophone on down in the. shop after it shut and they charlestoned all up and down the rows of books. One night I crept downstairs and watched them. I couldn't understand what they were doing at first. I thought they looked rather silly. Then, when they saw me, they laughed and taught me to do it, too."

"Did they? Well, your Mummy and Daddy are much younger than Granny. And me, for that matter. And . . . well . . . I expect it's all a bit different in London."

May was aware that she had made an inadequate excuse. With anyone less intelligent than Emily it might have sufficed. But this was a child who thought things through. She needed sensible answers, careful handling. Even after May had got her to go to the closet and locked up the workroom for the night, she knew that Emily was still mulling over the problem as they made their way through the garden in the fading sunlight of the early April evening. As it was a Saturday, the Felt Mills had shut down at one o'clock and there was no mill hooter to mark the passing of the hours; but, away to the right May could hear, as always, the roar of the mill-race: insistent, relentless, immutable, a sound which had formed the background to her existence for as long as she could remember. She looked down at the small form beside her, clutching her doll and the remnant of blue taffeta. She wondered what, if anything, the mill-race meant to Emily. Certainly, she liked to be taken to see it, to stand holding May's hand as they watched the water flowing swiftly along and then cascading down into a bubbling white whirlpool, to feel the occasional spray that was sent up and to ask pertinent questions as to whether anyone had ever fallen into it, and to speculate about what would have happened to him or her if they had. But she supposed that Emily, quite naturally, was growing up with different memories, different values. Although the mill-race might be May's particular constant, her niece would hold other things dearer to her heart. Yet, for the life of her, May could not imagine how an only child doing the Charleston with her parents in a London bookshop could compare with the pleasure derived by a large family of brothers and sisters, holding hands of a Saturday night, as they danced round in a circle singing *Here We Go Looby-Loo*, while the mill-race played its timeless hypnotic accompaniment in the background.

How long ago that all seemed. There had been seven of them once, and now only four were still alive: Henry away in the army, Edith struggling to raise her own family up on downside, Katy in London and she herself the only one unmarried—her once-lovely cheerful face more lined of late—still living at home, supporting and caring for an increasingly irascible old lady. She prayed that this evening was not going to prove too difficult, that Sarah would not remain in one of her silent humours. It was bad enough having to wait until half past eight, the time May had arranged to be at the Snoads ready for a telephone call from Katy's husband to let them know the latest news.

As May entered the Mill House and pushed aside the tapestry

curtain which had always served as a door between the tiny hallway and the living-room, she caught sight of something else beside the usual plate of bread and butter and home-made buns laid out on the white embroidered tablecloth. "Oh, chip-patoo," she exclaimed, using that curious pet expression of hers, which invariably came out quite spontaneously whenever she was particularly pleased, and which her small niece had been quick to shorten into a nickname for her favourite aunt.

"Just look, Emily," she went on, appreciatively, feeling that there was now hope of some kind of rapprochement with Sarah, "I do believe your grandmother has bought you a Wilhampton lardy cake for tea." It was a little extravagance in which she knew her mother occasionally indulged, and May could only suppose that she must have decided on the treat when she had gone out shopping that morning.

The child's face brightened. Then, in that strangely dignified, old-fashioned way which she had noticed Emily adopt on more than one occasion, she watched her go round the table to where Sarah was sitting, lay a hand on her knee and say, quite simply, "Thank you very much, Granny."

Sarah Lodge looked down at her grandchild. For a moment, the stern grey eyes softened. Something approaching a smile seemed to wipe away the impenetrable mask which had hardened over the years.

Whatever else Emily's mother had or had not done, May said to herself as she squeezed into her usual place directly in front of the upright piano, Katy had certainly taught her daughter manners.

2

The bus came slowly over Westminster Bridge. At the back, a youngish thick-set man with dark hair and dark brown eyes stared unseeingly out of the window. He seemed quite oblivious of the scene before him: the bright bobbing lights on and around the Thames, the Houses of Parliament and Big Ben proclaiming the time—a quarter past eight. The conductor had to ask him twice where he wanted to go and waited, with ill-concealed impatience, until he eventually said, "Dover Street" and handed up a penny-halfpenny.

Half an hour ago, the Sister on the ward where he had watched his wife steadily deteriorating ever since they had cut her stomach open five days ago, had told Philip Mason that unless there was some sign of improvement within the next twenty-four hours, they would have to operate again first thing on Monday morning. With her reserved austere expression—about as unbending, Philip thought, as the stiff starched apron she was wearing—she had even produced a form for him to sign, giving his consent. He had wanted to tear it up and throw it in her face, but he knew that that would have been throwing away the only hope. Somehow he had seen it coming, had sensed, from the very first evening that he had visited Katy, still smelling of ether after she had come round from the anaesthetic in such obvious discomfort, that the operation had been bungled. When she had subsequently kept nothing down for three days, not even water, he had asked to see the surgeon, but the same Sister had looked at him askance. In any case, he had learned from her tonight that the man who had operated on his wife was now out of the country and, should another operation be necessary, it would have to be performed by his assistant, a Mr Reeves.

"Bloody man's probably gone on holiday," Philip found himself muttering out loud, so that a woman in the seat in front of him turned round in indignation.

When the bus reached Dover Street, the conductor, who had been keeping an eye on him, tapped his shoulder and, not without a certain amount of relief, reminded him that this was his destination. Wearily, Philip Mason dragged himself to his feet and stepped down into Piccadilly. As he attempted to cross it, the driver of a cab sounded his horn angrily and he was forced to step back on to the curb, watching with a kind of grim resignation the party of laughing, smartly dressed men and women inside. They would, he supposed, be off to a theatre—the place where Katy would have been a year or so ago.

He knew now, of course, only too well, that he should never have agreed to her dancing in that Musical which Kreiger had been backing. It had all been a most terrible mistake. They must have been mad, both of them. True, he had had certain reservations at the beginning, but his wife had been so keen and it was wonderful to see her completely lifted out of the depression from which she had suffered, intermittently, ever since Emily's birth. When comfortable, middle-aged Ellen from the shop had turned out to be such a splendid part-time nurse for the child, he'd given in. Besides, there was the financial aspect. It had nothing to do with anything Katy might earn—the last thing he had ever wanted or envisaged was a working wife—but Marcus Kreiger had generously offered to help him over the difficulties in which he had found himself, chiefly through rashly trying to branch out into the antiquarian book trade.

Philip Mason was well aware now that he had been just as foolish over this as he had been in letting Katy go on the stage, but rare books were something which had always appealed to him. He had also got the idea into his head that if only he could acquire some extra capital, he might be able to sit back and do something which appealed to him even more: write a book himself.

Initially, things had gone well. He was personable and gregarious and enjoyed visiting the homes of wealthy connoisseurs and patrons of the arts. That was how he first encountered his ostensible benefactor. But lacking specialized knowledge and with the world recession getting worse all the time, he soon realised he was in for trouble. Kreiger's offer couldn't have come at a more opportune moment. The man appeared so genuine, so anxious for Philip's enterprise to succeed. Having no wife or children of his own, he seemed set on taking the little Mason family under his wing. Both Katy and

Philip had come to regard him more as a father-figure than anything else. Neither had suspected that all those dinners at Boulestin's for the three of them, those trips to the country at weekends in his large Bugatti, the chauffeur to drive Katy home after the theatre, was just a way of leading up to what he was really after—and that was to get her into bed.

Philip would never forget the night she had been so late back. He had not worried at first, because she had telephoned, excitedly, to say that Kreiger wanted her to stop off for half an hour at his flat in Eaton Square, where he was entertaining an impresario whom he felt might help in furthering her career. When it got to well past midnight, Philip had become uneasy. Katy was not strong and usually wanted to get to bed as early as she could. He tried to ring Kreiger's number, but was told by the operator that it appeared to be out of order. He couldn't take himself round there because he couldn't leave Emily; for unless it was a very special occasion, Ellen did not sleep at Davies Street. By two o'clock, he was almost demented. When, eventually, he heard a cab stopping outside the shop, he had run downstairs to open the side door and Katy had flung herself into his arms, sobbing.

There had been no further communication from Marcus Kreiger since then, other than a prompt, curt, business letter requesting the repayment of five hundred pounds. Philip hadn't known what to do, where to turn. His father was now dead but, in desperation, he had travelled to Wales to see his stepmother. Belle had certainly surprised him. He knew little about her other than that she was rich in her own right and, during the few years she and Francis Mason had been married, she had appeared to make him very happy. To Philip, the only scrap of comfort in the whole situation was the fact that his father, having finally passed the shop over to him completely, had never lived to witness what a mess his son had made of things. After talking to Belle, it occurred to him that possibly she had always had a shrewder idea of what was going on in the Davies Street establishment than her husband. He remembered her sitting there during his visit: a handsome well-preserved woman, with thick black hair drawn back into a tight bun and straight penetrating blue eyes; how she had listened to his halting confession in silence and, at the end of it, remarked, "I wouldn't have thought you would have been quite such a fool, Philip. It seems to me that both you and Katy need your heads seeing to. I don't believe in lending money any more than I believe in borrowing it. You know the old adage: 'Neither a borrower nor a lender be . . .'?"

Philip had found himself breaking out into a sweat and then, quite suddenly, Belle had gone across to her desk and picked up a pen. "Here," she had said, handing him a cheque for five hundred pounds. "Take it. This is a gift. There will be no more forthcoming, mind. I advise you to go home and *work*. You must put your house in order. It seems to me that you and your pretty little wife have been burning the candle at both ends. Bright young things, eh? Poor dear Francis would turn in his grave. In a quiet way, he built up Mason and Son into one of the best small bookshops in the West End before he retired. You've let the side down. Oh, I know there's a depression on, but with all your advantages you should have been able to weather it. Incidentally, how is the child?"

"Emily? She's fine, thank God."

"Good. You have a lot to be thankful for, Philip. Next time I come to London, I'll look in. By then, I'll probably have quite a fair-sized Christmas order."

When he had tried to thank her for her generosity, she had cut him short. "I don't want *words* of gratitude. I want *actions*. The best thanks you can give me would be if, by the time I come, I find things looking up."

Philip Mason had gone back to London and taken his stepmother's advice to heart. With Katy now permanently at home and Ellen therefore able to resume her former full-time duties as a saleswoman, he had dispensed with two of his other assistants, sold off the remaining stock of rare books and spent all his own time in the shop. He knew he had been lucky, luckier than he deserved. He had been in a tight corner and Belle Mason had got him out of it. He did not intend to make the same mistakes again. Soon, his spirits rose. His natural optimism reasserted itself. With Katy by his side, he was confident that everything would come right. The country's ecnomic problems couldn't, surely, go on indefinitely. Why, in a little while he might still be able to branch out again. Meanwhile, he would pay off Kreiger and keep to rigid accounting. He would go very carefully. He would economise in every way, not take any risks. There would be no more dining out. Indeed, how could there be, now that Kreiger was no longer picking up the bills. Katy and he would definitely not have another child—although this was something they had more or less decided on some time ago.

Philip had always been rather surprised that his wife who, after all, had once been a nursery-maid to Lady Fairfax's grandson, did not seem to take more naturally to motherhood. It went without saying, of course, that they both adored Emily, but he sensed that the mental troubles which had afflicted Katy on and off since giving birth had much to do with feeling trapped by the demands of a small infant. He supposed that was why Kreiger's offer had meant so much to her. A chance of escape. Katy, when she was not overburdened by responsibilities, was so different, so vivacious, so frivolous, even. She could be such a splendid companion, such fun to be with. And such a wonderful bedmate. He had always felt, during their courtship, that that would be the case once they were married. He hadn't been disappointed. He had rejoiced in the way she had given herself to him with such abandonment on their wedding night. He felt sure that Emily had been conceived there and then. He had never ceased to marvel at that side of her. Presumably, that bloody old goat, Kreiger, had sensed it, too.

Somehow, the memory of the man's treachery kept haunting him when he left the bus that night after leaving Katy in such distress, looking so white and drawn in St Thomas's Hospital. Possibly the difference between that and the sight of the carefree glamorous party in the taxi-cab had triggered it off. Of course, Kreiger had never actually *had* his wife. Katy, bless her, had seen to that, even if she had been forced to undergo such a strenuous, ignominious struggle with the brute before getting away. But, all the same, she had never been quite her old self, since. She had never attained those periods of lighthearted gaiety which, however fleeting, had so delighted him, had never—now he came to think of it—been quite such a passionate lover. She had become altogether quieter, more preoccupied. The bouts of depression which had sometimes attacked her seemed to have turned into a more permanent, lack-lustre malaise.

It had been some time before she mentioned any physical pain. He wondered now how long she would have kept it from him, had it not been for the fact that one Saturday evening, after he had finished doing the weekly accounts and had been pleased with the result, he had come up to bed earlier than usual and attempted to make love to her. For the first time that he could ever remember, she had resisted his advances, had caught hold of the hand which had begun to caress her breasts and buried her face in his chest with a muffled, "Don't, please. Not tonight, Philip." Puzzled, he had waited a little while and then turned on the light. Nervously, she began to tell him. She had pointed to a place somewhere in the middle of her diaphragm which she said had been hurting for some time. At first, it had apparently only been an occasional niggle but, lately, it had become more constant, more acute. Tonight it was at its worst. In an effort to allay his fears, she had remarked that it was probably only indigestion—perhaps the herrings which she had bought that morning in Shepherd Market and cooked for their supper had not agreed with her.

Their doctor did not seem to take much notice when, on Philip's insistence, they had visited him the following day. He was a dour, elderly Scot, who had always made it rather obvious that he looked on Katy as a *malade imaginaire*. Some time ago, he had scribbled 'Neurasthenia' across her notes, a word which he had been apt to use, disparagingly, when confronted by overstrained or shellshock cases in the last war. It was only when, a few weeks later, Philip had found his wife doubled up with pain after bathing Emily, that Dr McGraw had made a domiciliary visit to Davies Street and agreed that perhaps some X-rays were called for.

The first results had been inconclusive; but, after a second, more thorough investigation, necessitating a twenty-four hour stay in hospital, he had informed Katy's husband that the specialist at St Thomas's had advised 'by-passing the duodenum'. Philip knew little about such jargon, but had managed to enquire, "You mean, because she has a duodenal ulcer?" Dr McGraw had then become evasive. "Possibly," he had replied, "or . . . some kind of kink." "*Kink*? What are you getting at?" In an agony of worry and suspicion, Philip became truculent. Was the doctor trying to tell him that Katy was dying from cancer, just as Flo, her eldest sister—the one he had never met—had done during the summer of 1920? It had not really helped when Dr McGraw had replied, coldly, "I am simply tyring to say, Mr Mason, that your wife has a very slight physique. She has always been thin. Lately she appears to have become thinner. Possibly some unusual exertion might have caused an . . . abnormality in the gut."

The thought had not come to Philip straight away. When it did, the sheer horror of it had made him feel sick. "Undue exertion", Dr McGraw had said. Of course, it *could* have been all that dancing . . . or the need to make some much more unnatural and frantic efforts. How about the night Kreiger had inveigled her into his flat, in which there had been no impresario—only the man himself, with his ageing execrable lust?

Philip had never mentioned such a supposition to his wife. He had discovered that 'by-passing the duodenum' was quite a commonplace operation at the time, almost fashionable, in fact. It seemed as well to let her and her family think that a gastric ulcer was the trouble. And for all he really knew, so it was.

Even tonight, as he hurried up Dover Street, down Hay Hill and into Berkeley Square, he still didn't know what was really the matter with his wife. Suddenly he realised that it was getting on for nine o'clock, and he had promised to telephone May at eight-thirty. He wondered what he should say when he got through to her. So far, he had managed to keep the seriousness of Katy's condition—especially since the operation—to himself. It was no good getting anyone else into a state, particularly his mother-in-law. The old lady might have one of her turns again, even lose her memory as she had apparently done once or twice before he had ever married her youngest daughter. Besides, she had never really liked him. She would be bound to think that Katy's illness was somehow his fault. Maybe it was, but that didn't make it any better. And once Sarah Lodge got an idea into her head, he knew from past experience that nothing would remove it. She would go on and on and then Emily would be bound to overhear her. Still, he'd have to say something about Katy's condition now—at least, to May. It seemed pretty certain that his wife would go under the knife again on Monday morning.

Once inside the shop, he went into his office at the back, sat down at his desk and stared at the instrument standing on it: tall, black and impersonal, like a candle-stick. Eventually, with reluctance, he unhooked the receiver.

3

"Hullo?" May Lodge did not like using the telephone. The long wait that evening at Mabel Snoad's had increased both her natural fear of the instrument and the dread of the news it might bring.

"I'm sorry I'm late." Despite his weariness, Philip Mason made an effort to do his best. He liked his sister-in-law. She was a good sort—devoted to Katy and, it would seem, the child.

"How are . . . things?" May asked, warily. Philip's voice sounded faint and she pushed the hand which held the receiver closer to her ear. She pictured him, eighty miles away in that strange, suspect, teeming metropolis, where she had only been once in her life—the time she had taken Katy to Upper Brook Street to begin her duties as nursery-maid to Lady Fairfax's grandson. It was not that May hadn't wanted to see London again, nor that she hadn't been asked to go there. Katy and Philip had repeatedly suggested that she and her mother should spend a holiday with them. But unfortunately Sarah had been horror-stricken at the idea; for although she had occasionally travelled the three miles to Westonbury by train, she considered any longer rail journey to be far too hazardous. Therefore, because Sarah refused to leave Wilhampton for even a few days, May was obliged to remain there also.

She did not think that she could have heard Philip aright when his next words came all the way down the line: unreal, unbelievable and, somehow, wholly shocking.

"I'm afraid . . . they're probably going to have to operate again, May."

"*Again?*"

There was silence, and then Philip's voice sounded in her ear once more, "Something's gone wrong. She can't keep anything down. A sort of complete blockage, I think."

She could sense Mabel Snoad hovering, waiting on her words in the next room. As postmistress of Wilhampton there was little she was unable to ascertain through one means or another. It was common knowledge that steaming open envelopes had at one time been her *forte*. The advent of the telephone had but given her extra scope for such detective work.

"When will you know?" May drew the mouthpiece nearer to her face.

"Monday. I'll ring again Monday night."

"Thank you, Philip."

"How's Emily?"

"She's very well."

"Good. Give her my love . . . and May?"

"Yes, Philip."

"Keep all this from her, won't you?"

"Of course, my dear."

After they had rung off, May Lodge sat for a while trying to grasp the full implications of what she had just been told. *Two* operations within a week. No nourishment of any kind in between. Dear God. How could any human being survive that? Especially Katy. She was far too delicate, as it was.

"Worse, is she?" She had not noticed Mabel come into the room until a shadow fell across the table where she was sitting and her moon-like face with the thick pebble glasses peered at her, curiously.

May stood up. "I'm afraid the news . . . isn't too good. Perhaps you wouldn't mind if I came in again to wait for another call on Monday evening, Mabel?"

"No, of course not. Anything I can do to help. Would you like a cup of tea, dearie?"

"No thanks. I must be getting back. I'm late enough as it is. Mother will be so anxious." She picked up her handbag.

"Yes . . . yes. Your poor Mother." Mabel came with her to the door, obviously disappointed that no further titbits of information were forthcoming.

It was quite dark now—and cold. Instead of the hot clamminess which May had experienced while telephoning, she began to feel shivery. As she hurried along East Street and was about to turn into River Lane, she caught sight of a tall thin figure coming towards her. When it passed beneath a gas lamp, she recognised it as none other than Maurice Fitzherbert.

"Good evening, May." He removed his dark stiff-brimmed trilby. Like the good doctor he was, his manners and appearance could never be faulted, something which May had invariably noted and appreciated. "Have you heard about Katy, today?" he went on, his keen blue eyes searching hers, anxiously.

"Yes. I've just been speaking to Philip on the telephone." She paused. She could feel the tears beginning to well up, uncontrollably. Then, without exactly meaning to, she burst out, "There might have to be another operation, Maurice." She did not often address him by his christian name only, but tonight he was not merely 'the doctor'. He was the man who had wanted to marry her youngest sister and who she had a feeling was, even now, still in love with her.

"Oh, *May*!" He seemed stunned. "Did Philip . . . say anything else?"

"Not very much. I gather . . . things didn't go right. Nothing's getting through. There's a sort of stoppage . . ."

Without replying, he began accompanying her back to the Mill House in silence. He knew that there could be post-operative strictures after any abdominal operation and presumably that was what had now happened. But from all he had heard of the case, he could not help wondering whether Katy had been opened up unnecessarily. If she had an ulcer he was of the opinion—although aware that he was very much in a minority—that it could be treated by rest and diet; whereas this diagnosis of a possible 'kink in the gut'—recently hailed with such enthusiasm by the medical profession—seemed to him a complete fallacy. The only kink as far as he was concerned was in the mind of the eminent surgeon who had first propounded it.

When they reached the gates, he waited and held out his hand. "Katy has great courage, May," he said. "She may not be strong, but she's overcome a lot of illness in the past. I remember my father telling me how she pulled through from diphtheria and meningitis as a child. Don't lose hope. Perhaps . . . I might call on you and your mother on Monday evening?"

"Oh, yes. Thank you, Maurice. We should like that very much."

We should like that *whatever happens*, she found herself thinking, as she passed through the smaller gate and locked up for the night. *Whatever happens* it would be good to have Maurice Fitzherbert around. He was such a tower of strength. If only Katy could have fallen for him as he had for her. She would be here, now, in Wilhampton, probably fit and well, the *doctor's* wife. But it wasn't to be. She'd been set on Philip. You could see that in her eyes whenever he came to the mill. She had never looked at Maurice that way, even though she liked and respected him so much. She would never have settled down at East Lodge. And, of course, while his parents had still been living in part of the house, it wouldn't have been easy. Maurice's poor crippled father would never have made trouble, but his wife—'Old Mother Mothballs', as May had always privately thought of her—would have been a trial for any daughter-in-law. It was said that there had been no love lost between her and Maurice's wife right from the start, even though the girl had come from a good family. And May was well aware that Mrs Fitzherbert senior had never thought Katy good enough for her son. In her eyes, a daughter of the late manager of the Felt Mills was not at all suitable, especially with an elder sister who had actually married one of the mill hands.

She could see Sarah standing at the open door of the Mill House before she ever reached it. On coming closer, she noticed the strain on her face and the way she was clasping and unclasping her hands in that curious 'washing' movement which she adopted whenever she was particularly distressed.

"She's worse, isn't she? Don't try to hide it from me, May. I knew, when you were gone so long."

"Yes, Mother." She realised that it was no good trying to keep it from Sarah now. She would have to know.

"What is it? What's happened?"

"They might have to do a second operation."

"Oh, my God." It was only in extreme mental agony that such an ejaculation ever escaped Sarah's lips. Now, as she went back into the living-room and sat down in her usual chair, she repeated it twice, rocking her body to and fro while covering her face with her hands.

May fetched some milk from the stone slab by the tiny window at the back of the hallway, poured some into a saucepan and set it on the range. Then she went across to the glass-fronted cabinet and extracted a small bottle of cheap cooking brandy that was kept there strictly for medicinal purposes. It was possible, she thought, that such measures might be even more necessary within the next forty-eight hours, but she hadn't liked what she had seen in Sarah's face tonight, that strange, stricken, wild-eyed look that had sometimes preceded one of her 'turns'.

"Drink this, Mother," she said, at length, handing her a glass. For a moment, she thought Sarah was going to refuse to take it, but then, suddenly, she seemed to capitulate and held out her hand.

"You've laced it, haven't you, my girl," she said, after taking a sip or two.

"Only a little, Mother. It'll help you to sleep."

"And what good is sleep to me? It can't help Katy."

"No, but we must all . . . do our best to keep calm. After all, there's Emily to consider."

At the mention of the child's name, Sarah said no more.

On Sunday morning May did not take Emily to church as she had intended, because she was fairly certain that Maurice Fitzherbert would have been in touch with the Reverend Donaldson and prayers would be said for Katy. The child would then be bound to ask questions. She therefore suggested that Sarah might go to matins and that she and Emily should stay home, cook the dinner and start to make the doll's dress.

It seemed a sensible arrangement and one with which her mother could scarcely disagree. When the bells of St Mark's began to ring out at quarter to eleven, Sarah Lodge walked slowly up River Lane, a tall, still handsome woman, proudly erect—despite her rheumatism—wearing her best black serge coat and velour hat with the pearl hat-pin, black leather gloves, and carrying her prayer-book and large black leather handbag which, like her black leather lace-up boots, had been carefully polished that morning.

Inside the Mill House, May covered Emily's Sunday dress with a make-shift apron, put some flour in a basin and broke two eggs into the well which she had made in the centre. Then, with some milk in a jug ready to be gradually poured into the mixture, she began instructing her niece into the art of making batter. She did not herself feel much like eating roast beef and Yorkshire pudding today and she doubted that Sarah would either. But they had a guest, a little thing with a good appetite who seemed to enjoy what she called the 'smoky' food cooked on her grandmother's open range. Besides, whatever the circumstances, such fare was almost a ritual observance in

Wilhampton on the Sabbath, even if, throughout the years, Sarah had been forced to buy only the cheaper cuts, such as flank or buttock, sometimes remarking, with satisfaction, after returning from her Saturday morning shopping, that she had made a "good buy" or had purchased a "pretty piece of meat".

While the meal was cooking, May set to work cutting out the dress she had promised, while Emily watched her every movement, explaining the necessity for a very pretty one so that Greta would look either like her own mother or the film star, Greta Garbo, after whom the doll had apparently been named.

"When you've finished, Aunt Chip, I'll draw a picture of her to send to Mummy. She'd like that, wouldn't she?"

"Yes, dear."

"When do you think she'll come home from the hospital?"

"I'm not . . . sure, Emily." May spoke slowly, choosing her words with care. "She may have to stay there quite a while."

"Is she ill like she was when she was a little girl?"

"Something like that."

"Did you look after her then?"

"Well, I suppose we all helped."

The child became pensive. Presently, she said, "It must have been nice having brothers and sisters. Where are they all now, Aunt Chip?"

Dear God, what a little cross-questioner she was. A veritable sea-lawyer, May felt. It wouldn't do to go into the family history, not at this moment, with Katy at death's door. In any case, how could one ever explain death to a seven-year-old? How did one tell her that her Uncle Frank was killed in the Great War? Emily didn't know what war was. That her aunt Flo had died in agony from cancer when she was only thirty-one. That Sergeant Henry Lodge hardly ever came home because he had had a shotgun marriage to a Frenchwoman who had given birth seven months after the wedding and Sarah had never forgiven him. That Neil . . . There was no way she could tell Emily her Uncle Neil had not been quite right in the head, that sex had finally destroyed him at the age of twenty-one, when, having failed to violate his sister, Katy, he had gone after young Ena Perrick at the top of River Lane and, in the process, fallen into the Willon and drowned.

May laid down the half-made doll's dress and took off her

spectacles. "Your aunt and two of your uncles are in heaven, Emily." she said quietly. "I'm sure you will come to know your Uncle Henry one of these days, and sometime soon we'll go up to downside and visit Aunt Edith and your cousins again."

"This afternoon?"

May hesitated. "Not this afternoon, I think, Emily. But we might take a short walk up through the meadows while your grandmother is resting."

Somehow, May did not want to leave Sarah alone too long. Besides, Edith and her family would not be exactly ideal company at this particular time. There would be no chance of talking to her sister and brother-in-law by themselves, not with all the children milling around. There were six of them now: noisy, out of hand, not a bit like Emily. May felt that it might be as well if Katy's child did not mix too much with them. She chided herself for disloyalty, but she felt that Emily seemed to be cast in an altogether different mould, a different class. She had already noted the wondering, almost perplexed, look in the child's eyes when Edith had brought all her brood down to the Mill House a few days ago, how Emily had failed to understand much of what they were talking about because of the broadness of their accents, how surprised and even shocked she had been at some of their table manners, and how Edith herself had been obviously embarrassed, so marked was the difference between the cousins.

It was strange, May reflected, that considering her own upbringing, Edith had let herself go so much, how her appearance, at times, though not exactly slatternly, was careless, how she seemed to lack the will-power or energy to discipline herself or her children. May was aware that her lot was not easy, that her husband's weak heart was a constant source of anxiety to her. But Edith had so many advantages which her own mother had never had: an indoor tap, for instance, a front and a back room, a wash-house and a pull-the-chain privy, both within a stone's throw of the back door.

"What are you thinking about, Aunt Chip?" Emily's voice brought May's reveries to an end.

"I'm sorry, my dear." What was she thinking about? She looked at the child, fondly. "I was wool-gathering, I expect."

"Wool-gathering?"

"Yes, bless you. Thinking about the past—and the present. Now, how about us seeing whether the potatoes have turned a nice brown. Your grandmother will soon be back from church."

4

Contrary to all fears and misgivings on the part of her family and friends—and even the medical staff who attended her—Katy Mason pulled through her second operation. For five days, while she was still on the danger list, her young husband travelled backwards and forwards to St. Thomas's Hospital in silent despair. At Wilhampton, May found it increasingly difficult to keep up a pretence of normality in front of Emily. Often, she sent the child out for a walk with Dora Parker, the undertaker's youngest daughter, whom she employed to help with the sewing. As for Sarah Lodge, she became more and more withdrawn, her face only showing signs of emotion when she stood at the door of the Mill House each evening, waiting for May to return from the Snoads with the latest news.

It was not until the following Saturday that she saw her eldest daughter actually running through the gates, waving. For a moment, Sarah hesitated: unsure, half incredulous, half fearful of she knew not what. Then she, too, began to run forward awkwardly, holding out her hands. May caught them in both her own; her eyes had tears in them, but they were not unhappy ones.

"Oh, chippatoo, Mother! Katy's sat up and eaten some fish. She's out of danger. It's early days . . . but they think . . . everything will be all right now." Suddenly, aware that even such good news was too much for Sarah, May put an arm round her and helped her back into the Mill House where, not long afterwards, there was a gentle tap on the door and they were joined by Maurice Fitzherbert. He had called on them every evening that week.

His whole being, May noticed, seemed to alter when they told him what had happened. It was impossible not to sense his cautious relief, his deep interest and concern as to the best way of caring for Katy after she came out of hospital.

"Perhaps, . . . when she is strong enough for the journey . . . she might recuperate here? With summer coming on, I can't think of a better place, nor two people who would look after her so well."

May and her mother exchanged glances. "Yes, Dr Maurice," Sarah replied, quietly. "We've hardly liked to discuss it before, but there's nowhere like home, is there, especially when you've been ill." The fact that Katy already had a husband and home of her own in London seemed to be forgotten.

"There is, of course, Emily to consider," May broke in. "It's holiday time now, but her schooling . . . I'm not sure what her parents will want to do about that." Of the three of them in the room, she seemed to be the most aware of the nuances, the uncertainties and possible complications of the situation. It was not that she wanted to prevent her sister from coming. Far from it. She knew how unsuitable London was for any convalescent. Moreover, in Davies Street who would look after both Katy and Emily? Ellen was wanted full-time in the shop and Philip could not possibly afford a nurse. Yet she was troubled. By the time Katy was allowed out of hospital her husband would have been on his own for some little while. He still seemed very much in love with his wife and, although a spell at the Mill House might be necessary and desirable, he probably would not take kindly to a further enforced parting, especially one where there was eighty miles between them. Besides, was there not someone else now sitting in this very room who, however impeccably he would always behave, was also still in love with her youngest sister? Much as May did not want to admit it to herself, she was beginning to feel, more than ever, that this was the case. Maurice Fitzherbert had never given her the impression that he was particularly happily married; and on the few occasions she had met Clare, his wife, she could understand why.

Yet from Sarah's next remark, it was obvious that she, at least, either could not or would not see that there were any problems in connection with Katy's being nursed back to health in her old home. "Emily's bright enough as it is, May," she said. "And, if need be, she could always do a few morning lessons with Ethel Sharman round in St. John's Green."

So it came about that a month later Philip Mason brought a painfully thin, fragile young wife to stay for an unspecified length of time in Wilhampton. May arranged for a car to be at the station to meet them, and at four o'clock on the appointed day, she and Emily set out across the water meadows on foot, also in order to await the London train. Summer by now seemed to have settled itself in like a long-staying guest. The field known as Lower Croft was bathed in sunlight and buttercups; the willow trees all appeared to have donned mantles of the palest green lace; a cuckoo called incessantly from somewhere over by Bulbarrow Farm. Emily, wearing a new mauve voile dress which her aunt had made specially for the occasion, skipped along with the same kind of *joie de vivre* that May remembered the child's mother had been apt to display from time to time. She hurried after her, a small trim figure—not quite as slim as she used to be—but, as always, faultlessly turned out, in a tussore navy-blue and white polka-dot two-piece, her fine fair hair now fashionably shingled, her clear blue eyes in the carefully powdered face almost as eager with anticipation as those of the little girl she was accompanying.

"Will the train blow its whistle over the Black Arch, Aunt Chip?" The railway bridge, so named because an engine had once caught fire thereon and consequently blackened the brickwork, seemed to hold a curious fascination for her niece.

"Not while your Mummy and Daddy are in it, Emily. They will be getting off before it reaches there."

"Oh." The child slowed down and kept at May's side for a while. "Wouldn't Mummy sooner come back through the meadows like you said she loved to do when she was a little girl?"

"Not today, my dear. Your Mummy won't be able to walk very far yet. You must remember, she has had an operation."

"Why did she have an operation, Aunt Chip?"

Why did Katy have an operation? Why, indeed. Philip had said that the doctors had been singularly evasive on the question; and no wonder, May felt, considering they had bungled everything so badly. From what she could gather they had merely referred to "a little trouble" in something called the duodenum, which had now been successfully by-passed and Katy would, in time, be completely restored to health. At least, thank God, it was nothing like what had happened to poor Flo.

"Your Mummy had a sore spot in her tummy. Emily. She had to have an operation to make it well again," May replied, and quickly changed the subject. "Now, mind how you get over that stile. You don't want to catch the hem of your nice new dress."

She took hold of her niece's hand as the London train, dead on time, steamed in to Wilhampton station. But as soon as Emily caught sight of her father alighting from one of the carriages, she broke away and hurled herself towards him. But when, after embracing her, Philip turned and held up his arms to lift the travesty of his once-pretty young wife down on to the platform, his small daughter looked back towards her aunt, half in puzzlement, half in fright.

We should have warned her, May said to herself. Even she had not imagined that her youngest sister would be quite so emaciated, quite so weak.

On the way back from the station in the old Buick six tourer belonging to Dora Parker's brother who had set himself up as the local taxi-driver, May rode in front while Emily sat between her parents on the back seat. Although Katy had put an arm round her daughter, May sensed that even this was an effort, that she was utterly exhausted by the journey and that the child was both shocked and bewildered by the change in her mother.

It had been arranged that Philip should stay the night at the Mill House where, perforce, he would have to sleep in the front bedroom with his sick wife in the double bed which, under ordinary circumstances, was occupied by May and, during earlier times, had been given over to poor Flo and, before her, the hapless Neil. Today, as soon as the little carload arrived at the mill, Katy was immediately tucked up in it, after which there followed a not altogether companionable evening. Philip took his daughter for a walk. Sarah, meanwhile, kept muttering to May that her son-in-law had no business to have let things come to such a "pretty pass". Katy, upstairs, mercifully slept.

It was not until Philip Mason returned to London on Sunday evening that Sarah began to relax a little, exhibiting some of the careful, sacrificial attention to the needs of her youngest daughter as she had done many years ago. Often, of a morning, when May had taken Emily round to Ethel Sharman's to join in the lessons she gave to a few local children, Sarah would start to see about Katy's toilet. She would begin by bringing up a dipper of warm soapy water from the mill, pouring it into the blue and white china basin on the stand in the corner of the bedroom, after which, while her daughter was washing, she would turn and pummel the intractable feather mattress. Then, as soon as an ethereal but steadily improving Katy came down into the living-room, she would insist on her drinking an egg flip before sending her out to lie in a long basket-work chair in the garden. The weather was glorious, that summer of 1929, and it was here where Maurice Fitzherbert invariably found her, as he stopped by for a few minutes each day after his morning surgery. From their separate vantage points in the workroom and the Mill House, May and her mother noted his visits but, because they were professional and undertaken in full view of all concerned, they did not always make it their business to be present, as they would automatically have done for any member of the family had they taken place in a bedroom or even a living-room. Besides, since Katy's arrival, they had come to treat Maurice more and more as a greatly valued, long-standing friend.

One Saturday morning in the middle of June when Katy, with Emily helping her, was sitting in the sun shelling peas, she began to wonder whether it was not now time for her to return to London. She was feeling a great deal stronger and the enforced absence from her husband was beginning to worry her. Although, so far, Philip had managed to spend every Saturday night at the mill, he had written earlier that week to tell her that his stepmother would be in London on this particular one and had asked him to dinner at her hotel followed by a visit to the theatre to see a Cochran revue. He had gone on to say that he hoped she would not mind but, as Belle had been so good to him, he hardly liked to refuse. Katy knew that it was silly, even mean of her to mind—especially as travelling cost money and times were still so hard—yet she found herself minding very much. The thought of dinner and the theatre had reawakened some of the old longing for the life she had once known. She had no intention of ever going on the stage again. It was just that it would have been nice to dress up, go out and—here, she tried, but failed, to push the thought away—have her husband make love to her afterwards, not simply share the same bed in the careful, almost afraid-to-touch way he had done during his all-too-fleeting visits to the Mill House. Now that she was so much better she had begun to chide herself for not realising how he must have been missing that side of their life together. Selfishly, she had felt too ill to care. Now, it was very much on her mind. If Philip had been coming to spend this Saturday night at Wilhampton as usual, she had been planning to surprise him, determined to make him resume their marital relations, whatever the doctors had warned him.

"You've stopped shelling, Mummy." Emily's direct piping treble broke into her thoughts. "And there's a big car drawn up at the gates," the child continued, with a small frown on her face.

Katy started, and looked up to see a chauffeur opening a car door, out of which a tall elegant woman emerged, followed by a golden-haired boy slightly older than her own daughter. Then, as the two figures came towards them, she put the colander of peas down by her side, brushed some empty pods from the skirt of her dress and rose to greet her former employer and the child whom she had once helped to care for when she had been a nursery-maid in Mayfair.

"Lady Moreton!" Katy held out her hand. "And John William," she added, turning and holding out her hand a second time. She did not say "Master John". Somehow, after all that happened to her and with her own child standing by her side, it did not seem appropriate. Whatever the circumstances, there had always been a curious sense of decorum, even dignity, about each member of the Lodge family, no doubt initiated and instilled by Sarah, but never carried out to greater perfection than by her youngest daughter.

"Katy! What a lovely surprise. My mother said that you had been home ill, but I had no idea that you would still be here. I haven't seen you since we moved to Suffolk and sold 89 Upper Brook Street. I'm afraid we've only rather a dull flat in town nowadays. And can this really be Emily?" She, too, then shook hands with Katy's daughter, before remarking, "John, take off your cap, for goodness sake. Sometimes I wonder whether you've lost all your manners since going to that horrid prep school."

Lady Fairfax's grandson removed his cap gravely and held out his hand to Emily, who took it with equal gravity. The two women, so different in their respective circumstances, nevertheless watched the little performance with the same kind of fond motherly indulgence, although Katy kept finding it hard to believe that she had once changed the nappies on both of them.

"We're staying at the Hall," Alicia Moreton went on, "because it's John William's half-term and as his school is so much nearer to Wilhampton than Bishopsdown his grandparents thought it would be such a splendid opportunity to see him. Something tells me that we shall often be this way now. And I'm afraid that I can't help being pleased about this for another purely selfish reason of my own, the one which has brought me here today." She paused and gave Katy an almost conspiratorial grin. "I was wondering whether your dear sister would be prepared to make me a . . . Oh, *good*, here she is." Alicia broke off, as May came walking towards them, her face filled with pleasure at the sight of such unexpected visitors.

There followed further exchanges of news. Katy learned that John William's sister, Phoebe, had been left behind in Suffolk because she had just had her tonsils and adenoids out; that Nanny Barlow, though not quite so active, nevertheless still tried to rule the roost over the little girl and her young governess, insisting on constant doses of Parrish's Food and Virol; that on no account was Lady Moreton going to allow Phoebe ever to go to boarding-school and that if she had been able to have her way, John would never have been sent away either. "But, as he's down for Eton, his father thought . . ." Alicia flushed, letting her remark trail away, uncertainly.

When the two older women had disappeared inside the workroom, Katy took the children over to the mill-race. For a while, they stood in silence, one on either side of her. Presently, the boy said, "What is it for?"

She looked down at him and smiled, registering the handsome intelligent face. "Well, at one time, it used to drive the big wheel that made the Felt Mills work. But nowadays electricity has taken care of all that."

"So the mill-race isn't really necessary any more," he continued, studying the swiftly-flowing water before it suddenly dropped into the frothy turbulence below him.

Katy hesitated. "Not . . . exactly, I suppose."

"Could you stop it, do you think?"

"Stop the mill-race?" This time she answered promptly, almost as if he had said something shocking. "Oh no. One couldn't stop it. Besides, I can't imagine that anyone would want to. I think it will go on . . . for ever."

She had a sudden startling feeling that she was taking part in a scene which had happened before. She was not acquainted with the expression *déjà vu*—she only knew that she was caught up in something immutable, beyond her control, as all-powerful as the race itself. She remembered how she had sat by it after her sister Flo's funeral, and how the words of the hymn they had sung at the service kept haunting her: *Time like an ever-rolling stream* . . . In spite of the heat of the day, she shivered slightly.

"I think we should go back and find your mother now, John," she said, and the two children raced ahead of her through the garden.

"You look tired, lovey," May remarked, as they stood at the mill gates, watching the huge Rolls slowly disappearing up River Lane on its way back to the Hall.

"Do I? It's nothing." Katy turned and started walking back to the house. "But I suppose . . . well . . . seeing John William and Alicia Moreton again after all these years . . . it takes one back, doesn't it?"

5

"If you went to the baker's at the Four Corners, Emily, and bought seven cakes for sixpence, how many would you get for a shilling?"

"Fourteen, Miss Sharman."

"And if you went to Miss Clutterbuck's shop in the market square and asked her for a yard of ribbon at a penny-halfpenny a yard and then decided you wanted another yard, how much would you have to spend?"

"Threepence, Miss Sharman."

"Quite right, Emily." Ethel stood up, aware that four pairs of eyes were gazing at her expectantly. "I think that will be all for this morning. You may get down now."

Ethel Sharman had been giving private lessons in Wilhampton for twenty years, ever since she had left the teachers' training college in Westonbury at the age of twenty-two. She had been a pretty young woman with a wealth of light brown hair, large blue eyes and a creamy-coloured complexion. If anything, her teeth were too prominent—the result, so it was said, of having fallen down as a child and knocked her front ones loose. An ingenious dentist had fixed them back in again, but it had unfortunately left her with a slight speech impediment so that, already possessed of a shy, retiring nature, it was not perhaps surprising that she had remained a confirmed spinster. She had found teaching any large class of children altogether too nerve-racking. Indeed, on the few occasions she had attempted it, the perspiration running down from her arm-pits had ruined several woollen dresses. Therefore, when her father had died of consumption during the war—quickly followed to the grave by his grieving widow—Ethel, an only child, had eked out her inheritance in the family home by taking in the daughters of parents in the district willing to pay for her admirable, if old-fashioned, tuition. She did not go in for teaching little boys. For one thing, she was frightened of them. For another, she felt that they would have to be segregated from her little girls, which would have meant their coming in the afternoons when at least twice a week, if the weather was fine, she liked to take her various charges on nature walks.

Today, Ethel was rather hoping to have been able to have a private word with May Lodge when she came to collect her niece. Emily was still being escorted to and from the Mill House each day, although May had intimated that she did not think it would be necessary much longer, something with which Ethel entirely agreed. Emily was more than capable of walking the short distance alone. In fact, Emily was more than capable of a lot of things. That was the trouble. She was far and away the brightest pupil Ethel had ever taught and that was what she wanted to speak to May about.

Glancing out of the window, Ethel was rather pleased to see that the child's aunt had been waylaid on the green by the garrulous Mrs Betts, who no doubt wanted yet another outfit made for her. With any luck, she would be able to see the others off before May arrived at the front door. The Lamberts, the new people at Edenbury, the village just south of Wilhampton, were already waiting for Elsie Jane in their Model T Ford. Likewise, she could see Dick Swayne, from Bulbarrow Farm, nosing his lorry along the lane towards her house to pick up his youngest child. Ethel invariably worried about taking any money at all from him for teaching Helen, because she knew what a hard time of it he was having in the present agricultural depression. But when she had once demurred, he had said, like the good father he was, "Money on education's well spent, Miss Sharman. A year or two with you will always stand Helen in good stead. I'd as soon sell another cow as see her go to the National School."

As for Ethel's fourth pupil, the Reverend Donaldson's granddaughter, there used to be a time when his gardener, old Harry Ford, would stump over the green with little Daphne Chadwick, who was being brought up at the Rectory because her parents were in India. But ever since last Christmas the child had been allowed to go to and fro by herself. Ethel was sorry to see her departing today looking a little glum, and was afraid that it was because Emily had given such an astonishingly good performance over her arithmetic. If it had not been for the fact that Ethel had a rather important cousin who worked in the Air Ministry coming to lunch and Bessie, her daily maid, had already laid the table in the dining-room, she would like to have put Emily through her paces there, leaving the others by themselves to get on with various tasks in the sitting-room. As it was, she realised that she had made Daphne jealous and, with her sensitive compassionate nature, Ethel did not like to see any of her pupils upset; even though, she had to admit to herself, it would have been nice if Emily's prowess could galvanise Elsie Jane into a little more effort.

When Ethel had eventually said goodbye to her three other charges and May was on the doorstep, she asked her if she would mind stepping inside the hall for a moment. Then, turning to Emily, she suggested that she might like to run into the garden and look for Jumbo, her tortoise. The child needed no second bidding, albeit well aware that Miss Sharman obviously wanted to 'talk secrets' with her aunt. She suspected that it must be something to do with her but, much as she would have liked to hear what it was, she would never have dreamt of not immediately acquiescing to Miss Sharman's wishes. Besides, Jumbo ws really the greater attraction. He might, Emily knew, by *anywhere*: by the cucumber frame, under the crab-apple tree, hiding in the herbaceous border. He was very old, much older than Grandmother Lodge and apparently he only moved about in the summer. Emily had never seen a tortoise before—London did not seem to have any—and Jumbo was therefore a constant source of interest and wonder. She ran off down the grassy path to the wall at the far end, on the other side of which she knew that there was a very important mysterious place: the Hall, where Lady Fairfax lived and where the golden-haired boy and his mother had been staying the time when they came to call at the mill. Emily would like to have taken a peep over the top of the wall, but it was far too high and there was such a forest of yew trees behind it that she doubted she would be able to see very much; she knew she would simply have to wait until Aunt Chip took her there one day, as she had promised to do.

Back in the house, as soon as Emily was out of earshot, Ethel Sharman said quickly, "As there might not be many more opportunities, Miss Lodge, I thought I should just like to tell you that I consider your niece to be an exceptionally clever child. Academically, I would say that she is at least a year in advance of her age."

"*A year*!" Flattered, May stored up Ethel's words verbatim, anxious to relay them to Sarah once Emily had gone to bed that night. "We always felt she was bright," she continued, "but . . . well . . . a whole year! You do surprise me, Miss Sharman."

"Yes, and it's not only over certain subjects, you understand. She is as good at sums as she is at composition. Sometimes I feel, if it were not for the unusual circumstances, she is almost wasting her time here. The others are keeping her back, although it isn't necessarily a good thing for a bright child to be brought on too quickly. Of course, it is never easy for one person, trying to deal with different ages and levels of intelligence. But I feel I am in charge of a little girl with great originality of thought and I naturally don't want to go wrong. Have you any idea what plans her parents have for her schooling?"

"No. I must ask my sister. At present she goes to a small Church of England school near where they live in London."

"And she will be resuming her classes there after this summer?"

"Yes, Miss Sharman. Her parents will both be coming down to Wilhampton in August to fetch her home again. I'm sure we're all very grateful to you for agreeing to coach Emily for the time being."

"It's been a pleasure, I assure you." Ethel's eyes strayed towards the end of the garden where Emily was still running up and down, obviously unable to locate the tortoise. "I suppose," she continued quietly, and here a certain wistfulness seemed to creep into her voice, "that it comes but once in a governess's life—indeed, sometimes never at all—to have the privilege of a gifted child in her hands. Sometimes I feel that my nature walks with Emily, the ones we have taken alone, are my best way of helping her. Living in London as she does, she seems so anxious to learn all about the flora and fauna. It is almost as if she is . . . how shall I put it? . . . starved of the countryside. Do you know what she said to me the other day? 'Miss Sharman, wouldn't it be nice if the River Willon and Grandmother's house and the mill-race were all in Hyde Park, instead of the silly old Serpentine? I don't suppose I shall ever find meadow-sweet and heart's-ease there.' Ah, look, she seems to have found Jumbo at last. I must be keeping you, Miss Lodge. Forgive me."

On the way home, Emily chattered away happily, informing her aunt that Helen Swayne had asked her and Daphne and Elsie Jane to tea on the following Saturday. With Ethel Sharman's words still very much in her mind, May could not help noticing—not for the first time—how well the child had settled down and how comparatively little she missed her parents and her London home. Although she had shed a few tears at the station on the day they had waved goodbye to Katy some weeks previously, Emily had soon begun looking for wild flowers as they walked back to the Mill House through the meadows, remarking, excitedly, that Miss Sharman had promised to take her up to Breconbury Woods on their next nature walk to look for a very special kind of orchid. "Although if we find it, I shan't be able to tell you exactly where it is, Aunt Chip," she had said. "Miss Sharman says we must keep it a secret, because if other people got to know, they might go and pick it and then there wouldn't be any more." Almost, May had felt a stab of jealousy.

It was as if Emily had somehow come to regard the whole locality as her spiritual home. Although she was a naturally healthy happy child, it seemed Ethel was right in sensing that living at the Mill House satisfied something important which she lacked in London. May wondered what would happen when she returned there. She knew that she herself would miss her niece profoundly. She had never consciously thought about it before, but she realised now that Emily, in turn, supplied her with something which she, too, needed: the fulfilment of her maternal instinct which, since her youngest sister had married and left home, had been sadly frustrated. Wrily, she reflected that in this connection she and Ethel Sharman were probably sisters in distress.

May hoped that everything was going well for Katy now. She had doubted that she had been fit enough to return to Davies Street and Sarah had been openly hostile about it. Yet they had been unable to prevent her. Katy had suddenly behaved almost as she had done on the night when she had dashed out of the Mill House after Philip, just before their marriage, desperately afraid that she was going to lose him. As for the fact that she now had a child to consider, she had obviously been only too relieved to leave Emily behind at Wilhampton. It was undoubtedly the most sensible solution and May suspected that the child's mother was well aware that she was not yet capable of caring for a home, a husband and an energetic small daughter. Moreover, the summer was so exceptionally fine, with day upon day of glorious sunshine, that it seemed virtually cruel to condemn Emily to the confines of a flat over a London shop when there was such a splendid alternative eighty miles away.

All the same, although May was overjoyed at still being able to look after Emily at the mill, she was uneasy about the situation. She noted the letters which Katy wrote regularly to her daughter—simple, sensible and cheerful—saying how much both she and her father were looking forward to seeing her again in August. Equally regularly, she supervised the child's replies in immature yet—considering her age well-formed script, illustrated by copious annotated and amazingly graphic drawings of her grandmother, her aunt, Miss Sharman, Jumbo and the other children with whom she had become friends. (There were also, May was interested to see, frequent pictures of the mill-race which, although looking more like a burst water-main than anything else, nevertheless obviously meant something in Emily's young life.)

Yet in the letters which May and Sarah received, the former noticed a curious restraint, a lack of her sister's usual spontaneity, a feeling that Katy was, perhaps, hiding something, doing her best under difficult circumstances. May hoped that her doubts and fears were groundless and that Sarah had not detected any underlying distress, but even as she hoped she knew that Sarah, with her almost uncanny perception, would have suspected something.

One evening, when the two of them were sitting on upright chairs outside the front door of the Mill House, because the heat of the day had made the interior of the living-room—with its open range for cooking—almost unbearable, Sarah said, "Katy's not happy, is she? Something's wrong."

"Wrong, Mother?" May replied, procrastinating.

"Oh, come off it, my girl. For goodness sake, you can't fool me. You must surely have read between the lines. It's my belief the trouble's more in the mind than the body this time. Illness always puts a strain on any marriage, particularly if it's the wife who's the invalid."

May noted that her mother appeared to have conveniently forgotten how much she herself had been instrumental in aiding and abetting Katy and Philip's separation and thus possibly accentuating whatever was the present problem.

6

Katy had been back in London for several weeks before suspicion became certainty. It happened one day when she was going out through the shop and the postman handed her the twelve o'clock delivery. Philip was busy at the time, talking to Ellen about the 'window' he wanted her to do after closing that evening for a new novel, *The Man Within*, by a young writer called Graham Greene. Katy took the letters back into the inner office to place on her husband's desk, glancing through them as she did so to see if there was one with a Wilhampton postmark, especially one written in Emily's large but increasingly well-formed script.

Today, however, there appeared to be nothing for her; yet there was a thickish envelope addressed to Philip in mauve flamboyant writing which had evidently been posted in New York some ten days previously. She knew that he occasionally received business communications from America, but these were always typed. This particular letter had something very personal about it and was obviously written in a female hand.

For the rest of the day her imagination took hold of her to such an extent that she went about in anguish, attempting—but failing—to come up with any satisfactory explanation for such a curious missive. Neither she nor Phillip had any personal connections overseas, unless she counted her only surviving brother's intermittent postings to Germany or Belle's trips to Monte Carlo in the winter. But she happened to know that both these individuals were at present in England and, besides, the handwriting on the envelope was completely unknown to her.

Usually, if anything of interest occurred during the day, Philip seemed only too anxious to talk to his wife about it in the evening; but on this occasion, when supper was over and he had still not referred to the letter at all, Katy could hardly contain herself any longer. When he suggested a short walk across Hyde Park she acquiesced readily, hoping against hope that this would give him the opportunity of saying something to her which would allay her fears. Yet, when they had sat by the Serpentine for at least a quarter of an hour and still he had only spoken of purely mundane matters, she suddenly turned to him and said, "I saw you had a letter from New York this morning."

"New York?" He remained staring out across the water.

"Yes. Being hand-written, I couldn't help wondering who it was from."

He was silent for so long that she knew her instinct had not let her down. Presently, with an effort at casualness, he went on, "Oh, it was just from someone I met . . . with Belle, as a matter of fact."

"With *Belle*! You mean that time she took you out?"

"Yes. It was quite accidental. She didn't plan it or anything. But some American professor she happened to know was staying at her hotel and joined us for dinner."

"Oh." For a moment relief swept over her. "I hope he wants you to send him a nice lot of books."

Again there was silence. When his reply eventually came, the words seemed to eat into her. For the first time since she had recovered from her illness, she began to feel sick. "Well, no . . . Actually, it was his daughter who wrote."

"*Daughter*?" She sat bolt upright on the green wooden bench, her hands clenching and unclenching. There was almost a look of her mother about Katy now. Two bright spots of unnatural colour appeared on either cheekbone. "Is that the reason," she continued, slowly, "that you have not made love to me since I came home, Philip?"

This time he turned to face her and held out his hand—but she did not take it.

"Yes, Katy," he replied, huskily.

She stood up then and began to run, blindly, hopelessly, in the direction of Park Lane. Quickly, he caught up with her and, slipping an arm firmly round her waist, forced her to slow down and walk beside him. "Listen, my love," he said, "you haven't given me a chance to explain."

"There isn't any need. There is nothing to explain." She tried to break away, her large grey eyes full of resentment and hostility, but he managed to pull her down beside him on to another seat.

"But there is, Katy. There is." He spoke urgently, the words tumbling out, disjointed yet forceful, willing her to accept them. "I'm never going to see Jessie McCutcheon again. I don't want to. It was . . . something which happened . . . quite by chance. It had nothing to do . . . with love. On either side. *Please* understand that. I love you, Katy. I always shall. But . . . well . . . it had been a long time since . . . I mean, the doctors warned me. Those weekends when I came to the mill were pretty good torture really, having to share the bed and not being able to . . . When I stayed in London because of Belle, it was a relief in a way. Oh, I'm *sorry*, my love. But you must see. I mean, this girl made it quite plain that she was prepared to . . . fulfil a certain need."

She was crying now and he took out a handkerchief and passed it to her.

"Where . . . did it take place? Not . . . in Davies Street?"

"Good God, no. What do you take me for? You don't think I'd be such a cad as to . . ." He broke off and looked at her miserably, unable to think of a less offensive expression than 'foul the nest'. Presently he went on more quietly, "Belle went back to Wales that Sunday and the Professor pushed off to Scotland. Jessie suddenly rang me up and said she hadn't seen enough of London. That might have been an excuse, of course, but apparently she'd never been here before, even though she'd 'done', as she put it, most of the other European capitals. She simply stayed on by herself for a few days in a private suite of rooms."

Blinking back tears, she asked him, "Was she pretty?"

This time he almost laughed with relief at her simple, typically feminine question. "No. Not at all. To me, there's never been anyone prettier than you, Katy, and you know it. Jessie was smart, certainly, and like all Americans pretty experienced. But if you really want to know, she had a rather long horse-like face. I should say she was probably quite a few years older than either of us."

"But why was she writing to you, if you're never going to see her again?"

"I think it was simply her way of saying goodbye. Tidying things up. I suppose it was silly of her. She should have guessed you might be home again. For all her sophistication, I don't think she was maybe all that bright. You can read her letter if you like."

Katy shook her head. The fact that he had offered to show it to her suddenly made it seem unnecessary, even distasteful. She knew that he was speaking the truth, that he was somehow glad that the affair was out in the open. Of course, things could never be quite the same again. Their marriage had suffered a crisis and she was not sure how their life together would take shape from now on. But Philip had told her that he still loved her and she would—indeed, she must—hang on to that. She was aware that, despite all that she had been told, she still loved him, and she sensed that he had been just as haunted during the past few weeks as she had. Thank God that at least the uncertainty and unaccustomed wariness of each other was at an end. She was still too shaken and upset to think quite clearly, but somewhere, in the back of consciousness, something told her that in future she must pay more attention to that curious sixth sense which had suddenly sent her back to London, albeit this time too late. After all, she was the seventh child of a seventh child, wasn't she? May always kept reminding her of that.

When Philip suggested that it was time to start home, she did not demur, but walked silently beside him, still pondering over the events of the past few months and how much easier it seemed to be for men to be led astray than women. No matter how ill Philip might be, she did not think she could ever be unfaithful to him. This business about Jessie 'fulfilling a need', was that only a male prerogative or necessity, the gratification of which had to be expected and accepted—or, at least, tolerated—by a wife, expecially a sick or absentee one? Certainly, if the boot had been on the other foot, she doubted that Philip would have behaved as submissively as she was now doing. She recalled how demented he had been the evening when she had returned from Kreiger's flat. She wished she knew more about men, that she was not still, at the age of twenty-seven, so hopelessly naïve. Probably being the youngest, frailest and most cosseted member of the family hadn't helped. Nor, she supposed, had marrying so young and becoming wrapped up in her husband stood her in any better stead—at least, from that point of view. If she hadn't been so shielded all her life, she would probably have become aware much earlier, firstly of her poor simple brother's designs on her and, later, that bounder, Kreiger.

Katy had never consciously given sex a great deal of thought, other than it was something which, with her husband, she wanted and enjoyed very much. After Emily's birth she had left it to Philip to take all the necessary precautions against having another child. Indeed, in the early years of their marriage she felt that there seemed little else she could do. Only back-street pharmacies sold contraceptives for women and these were not always reliable. She could not possibly have afforded to go to the strange gynaecologist who had set up in London and fitted intra-uterine rings. But she was certainly not unacquainted with the influence which Dr Marie Stopes was having in the country and had read her book *Married Love*, Philip having acquired a few copies which he kept 'under the counter'. Suddenly she found herself wondering whether she should not have taken more of the responsibility for birth control—as it was now called—upon herself. Was this what her husband had meant when he had described Jessie McCutcheon as having 'experience'?

They paused for a moment outside the shop and she waited while he checked Ellen's window display and nodded approvingly. Then, as he got out his key and opened the side door, standing back to let her enter first, he said, gently, "A penny for them, my love."

She managed a small smile. It was not natural for her to remain withdrawn or to keep any secrets from him for long. "I was thinking about men and women . . . and sex," she added, simply.

"Really?" He closed and locked the door. There was a look in his eyes which she had not seen for a very long time. Then he gathered her in his arms and carried her upstairs to bed.

7

"They won't move you up, will they, now you've been away so long?" "My mum said you'd been very ill." "We've learnt to subtract pounds, shillings and pence."

Emily Mason stood in the girls' playground of St. Nicholas's Church of England school at the start of the autumn term. She looked very brown compared to the other children surrounding her, most of whom had never been away from London in their lives. Few of her contemporaries' parents could afford a seaside holiday, especially in the present economic depression, although Patsy Milward had apparently spent a week at Clacton and Mary Gaunt had been taken to a boarding-house in Bournemouth for a whole fortnight because her father—who worked in the post office—had won a fifty-pound prize for writing a clever 'bullet' in one of *John Bull*'s weekly competitions.

Emily did not mind the various remarks directed at her. She had hitherto always been a popular child and she realised that her friends could hardly be expected to know what had happened to her. Without precocity yet with an appealing old-fashioned dignity, she now proceeded to tell them.

"I've been staying with my Granny and my Aunt Chip—well, Aunt May, really, but that's what I call her—because it was my mother who was ill. Not me. She had to have an *operation*."

There was a chorus of suitably impressed "Ohs".

"So I had private lessons. In the country."

"Private?" Her audience looked a little out of its depth. Someone said, "You mean, just you and the teacher?"

"Well, there were three others. And she wasn't a teacher. She was a governess. We went to her house for lessons every morning. She had a tortoise."

"A *tortoise*?" Several pairs of eyes regarded Emily with increased interest.

"Where did she keep it?" It was Mary Gaunt speaking. "In her back yard?"

"No. In her garden. She had a big garden, like my Granny."

"Oh." The pupils of St Nicholas's knew what gardens were

but to have had the run, so to speak, of *two* large ones all the summer was a little difficult for them to envisage.

"Was there grass, like in the parks?" asked Patsy Milward.

"Yes. Lots and lots of grass. And at my Granny's there was a river. A big river and lots of little rivers. There was a place in the big river called a mill-race, where it went extra fast and then dropped down into a kind of whirl-pool. And there were flowers. Ever so many of them. Roses and honeysuckle. My Granny's closet was covered with honeysuckle."

"Closet?"

For the first time Emily hesitated a little. "She didn't have a lavatory indoors," she explained, guardedly. She did not add, "nor a tap either," and was a little relieved when the bell sounded for morning prayers.

At the end of the day, Miss Jamieson, who had been teaching Emily for every lesson—the child having been automatically moved up on the strength of her natural intelligence and the fact that she had had private tuition—tapped on the headmistress's door and asked. if she might have a word with her about "the Mason child".

"Emily Mason, Miss Jamieson? What about her?" asked Mrs Bailey, removing her spectacles and giving all her attention to her young but, as she sometimes felt, rather too intense assistant.

"She's been brought on, Mrs Bailey. Too fast for her own good, if you ask me. Of course she always was forward, but if she stays in Lower II for another year, she'll simply be marking time."

Mrs Bailey gave a small frown. She was a good woman, in some ways not unlike Ethel Sharman, except that she possessed the confidence and capacity to accept responsibility for many children whereas Ethel could only manage a few. She had lost her young husband in the war and, with great fortitude, resumed her teachers' training, after which she had quickly risen to her present position. The study of character absorbed her, be it that of her pupils, her teachers or her friends and neighbours. The only person with whom she did not get on was Mr Corbett, her opposite number in St. Nicholas's Boys' school. There appeared to be some personal feud between them, the origin of which was something of a mystery. This afternoon, when Frances Jamieson tapped on her door, she had rather been hoping to indulge in what she sometimes jokingly referred to as her "secret vice": her second Kensitas cigarette of the day. But with Maud Bailey duty always came before pleasure. She asked Frances to sit down and picked up her fountain pen, turning it over in her hands in much the same way as she began turning the problem of Emily Mason over in her mind.

"If we move her up into Lower III, Miss Jamieson," she said, thoughtfully, "I am a little concerned about the effect it might have on her from the point of view of the friends she will leave behind. As a matter of fact Emily's parents came to see me before term started. I realise we may have scholarship material on our hands. Mr Mason feels he is now in a position to send Emily to Court House School next year and her name has been put down there. I shall be sorry to see her leave but I know it will be for the best. In the meantime, I don't want . . ." Maud Bailey searched around for a suitable way of expressing herself and then continued, "Emily to become too aware of her potential. She is at present such a friendly, natural, out-going child. It would be a pity to do anything that might change her."

"Oh, I appreciate that, Mrs Bailey. I wouldn't like to see her . . ." This time it was Frances Jamieson who was temporarily at a loss for words. "Puffed up," she eventually added.

"No." 'Conceited' was the word which Maud Bailey felt she might have used herself. She had a sudden vivid mental picture of Emily and her mother, walking across the small square at the back of the school and how impressed she had always been by the way both of them were turned out. Mrs Mason was a cut above the usual mother who escorted her child to and from St. Nicholas's. Maud knew that she had been very ill lately. She also knew that if it had not been for the hard time Mr Mason had been through, financially and emotionally, Emily would probably have been sent to Court House before now. The question of whether to make further changes in the life of a child who had already suffered considerable upheaval of one sort or another during the course of the year was something she felt she wanted a little time to think about. With that rare insight and common sense which had so swiftly secured her the post she now held, Maud Bailey said, "Miss Jamieson, I was wondering whether perhaps it might be a good idea if, tomorrow, in your composition class, you asked the pupils of Lower II to write about what they had most enjoyed last summer. I should like to see Emily Mason's effort. Then I might be better able to judge what to do for the best."

The following evening, having dealt with a complicated letter about the leasehold of St. Nicholas's, and a curt missive from Mr Corbett asking how many girl pupils would be taking part in the nativity play at Christmas, Mrs Bailey sat in the small home she had been assigned next to the school, lit a cigarette and picked up a piece of lined paper, headed in clear bold handwriting: *Last Summer* by Emily Mason. "Last summer," she read,

> I went to stay with my Grandmother and my Aunt May. (She noted that the word 'Chip' had been carefully crossed out.) They live at the Mill House, Wilhampton. Granny did not like my dancing the Charelstone. But she was kind at other times. My Aunt May looked after me most. She is nice and makes dolls dresses and says O Chippatoo when she is happy. I went to lessons with Miss Sharman. At first Aunt May took me but then I was aloud to go by myself. Miss Sharman has a tortuss. His name is Jumbo.
>
> At the mill they make felt. There are lots of black cats who sleep on the bags of wool. There is also a big river and lots of little rivers. The big river goes fast and has something called a mill-race. Sumtimes I went into the mill and watched my granny doing her washing in a big tub while she sang hyms. All round about there are meadows. They are bright green and smell riverry. They have fethery flowers in them called Meddow Sweet. They also have lots of cows who flick there tails to keep off the flys. Miss Sharman sumtimes took me to the woods on the hill to look for orkids. There was one all yellow with purpil spots. It grows in a very secret place that only Miss Sharman and me know about.
>
> I am looking forward to going back soon. The mill is a lovely place and my Granny cooks lovely dinners and sumtimes she buys lardy cakes for tea. My Mummy says the mill-race will go on for ever and ever and ever so I should like to live there for ever and ever and ever too.

Maud Bailey took off her spectacles which she was a little disconcerted to find had become misted over. Emily's simple description had brought back memories of her own youth. She also knew all about rivers and mill-races and meadows, for she had been the daughter of that special breed of agricultural worker, a drowner. Like Emily, she had been bright and, instead of ending her education at fourteen, she had won a scholarship at the age of eleven which had enabled her to go to a Grammar School. Every summer she still went back to the Somerset village where she had been brought up and listened to her elderly father, now crippled with rheumatism, recalling the days when it seemed that he and he alone controlled all the waters for miles around. When she thought about the children now under her care it saddened her that none of them knew the benefit and delight of a country upbringing. Although it had taken serious illness on the part of Emily's mother for her daughter to be sent to Wilhampton during the most glorious summer since 1921, Maud felt that the child had been given something beyond price. She decided that she would move Emily up to Lower III but keep a careful watch on her development. It would be a pity to force so promising and original a pupil. She must remember to tell Cora Peters, who would be directly in charge of her, to see that she had every opportunity to learn to spell, especially when it came to the words 'tortoise' and 'orchids'.

Emily herself took her elevated status with comparative equanimity. She was sorry not to be working alongside Patsy Milward and Mary Gaunt, but she still mixed with them in the playground. They themselves regarded her not so much with jealousy as awe. Emily Mason appeared to be 'different'. She knew things about which they were totally ignorant, like the fact that the milk which came in bottles to their parents' doorsteps each morning actually came from a cow; and that a little girl called Helen Swayne had a father who knew how to get milk out of something called a cow's 'udders'. Their curiosity was intense. Their little friend seemed a source of the most amazing and interesting information.

It was perhaps at home in Davies Street where Emily did not fare quite so well. It was not that she regretted being back with her parents again, nor that she did not delight in having one or the other of them read to her each evening—Katy had just started *The Secret Garden* which held her spellbound—but many was the time when she found herself thinking of the Mill House and its occupants, particularly Aunt Chip, and wishing that they could all go back to Wilhampton to live.

As the winter drew on, she became puzzled and alarmed by several things which she either overheard being talked about by grown-ups, or read herself on the newsvendors' placards when her mother fetched her home from school. WALL STREET CRASH was one of them, but when she asked Katy what it meant, she was told that it was nothing to worry about because Wall Street was a long way away in America and that it had not really fallen down—just a lot of people in it had lost all their money. But at the beginning of December there was something which was not quite so easy to dismiss. THAMES OVERFLOWS—HOUSES AT CHISWICK UNDER WATER, ran the headlines by Bert's stand at the corner of Berkeley Square. Emily waited silently while her mother stopped and bought an evening paper.

"What does it mean, Mummy? What's happened to the houses?" she asked, as they hurried along.

"There's been a lot of rain, darling. It's usually the way, after a fine summer. Then the floods come."

"Oh." Emily sneezed and Katy looked at her anxiously. "You haven't got another cold, have you?"

"I don't know. Mummy, will the Mill House be flooded?"

"I . . . hope not."

The child was quick to sense the hesitancy in her mother's voice. "But if the floods did get in, what would happen to Granny and Aunt Chip?" she persisted.

"Oh, I expect . . . they'd go up to Aunt Edith's on downside."

Even as she spoke, Katy knew perfectly well that the rising Willon had never yet forced Sarah to leave her own home. 'Come hell or high water' seemed more than an appropriate expression to describe her mother's stoicism in the face of floods. Besides, Edith's house was already far too small to accommodate her large unruly family. Moreover, Katy feared that there were other difficulties, an added cause for anxiety this winter. In May's last letter she had mentioned Sarah's increasing stiffness, that Maurice Fitzherbert did not seem too happy about her and that, privately, she felt her mother was 'failing'.

"Can Aunt Chip swim, Mummy?" Emily broke in on Katy's train of thought. She smiled down at her daughter affectionately, her fingers tightening on the small hand she was holding.

"No, my love. But I'm sure that won't be necessary."

Katy did her best to be reassuring, to push aside the memory of a December eleven years ago, just after the war ended, when the floods had risen, insidiously at first and then with sinister urgency, how she had been sent up to Ted Shergold, the drowner, with a note from her father—bedridden with acute bronchitis—to ask him to look to the hatches by Bulbarrow Sluice, and how Nancy Shergold—a termagant of a wife if ever there was one—had more or less shown her the door. Then, three days after Christmas, with the water slapping, gurgling and still rising in the living-room below him, Sidney Lodge had given his last agonising gasp for breath. Katy had never known another winter like that for, a few months later, she had become a nursery-maid in Mayfair and, within two years, the wife of a young bookseller in the same area. Emily, please God, would never know one. What a blessing it was that the child had only had to be sent away during the summer, that she simply knew the lighter, sweeter side of life at the Mill House, not the dark wet winter by the Willon, with its ever-present threat of destruction and disruption lurking in the background.

Yet, over this reflection, Katy discovered that she was guilty of having reckoned without her daughter's quick intelligence and vivid imagination. In the middle of the night Emily awoke, screaming. On rushing in to her room, Katy found that she had apparently had a nightmare in which "Aunt Chip was walking about with only her head above the water". Nothing her mother could say seemed to comfort the child so she eventually brought her, still trembling, back to spend the rest of the night in her and Philip's double bed.

Unfortunately, the trouble did not end there. Emily's disturbed sleep continued. Many was the time when her parents found her still wide awake when they came to bed. Katy took to leaving both doors open between their respective bedrooms and a nightlight on the landing. To satisfy herself, she would lie awake until she felt that the child had at last dropped off and then creep into her bedroom to make sure, usually finding the small body curled up in a tight ball with Greta clutched in her arms.

Quite often, Philip decided to make good use of this waiting period and one night Emily, who had not yet fallen into a deep enough sleep, awoke to hear strange sounds coming from her parents' room which she could not make out at all. It was sometimes a comfort to hear them carrying on a conversation. It made her feel less frightened. But tonight they did not appear to be talking to each other. It was almost as if they were engaged in some kind of friendly yet energetic tussle. She heard the creaking of bed-springs, a muffled laugh, her father repeating the word "Darling" at least three times, after which there was a curious, low, breathless moaning. Terrified of she knew not what, she began to shout until Katy appeared at her bedside, flushed and anxious, tugging at the shoulder straps of one of the pretty celanese nightdresses trimmed with lace, which May always made for her and which had fallen from her shoulders, partly exposing her small rounded breasts.

Emily began sobbing now and her mother did her best to persuade her to come back to her own bedroom for the rest of the night, just as she had done before. But this time the child defiantly shook her head. Distressed and confused, she felt that there had been something going on there which, in its way, was as frightening as the floods, that her parents shared some horrible secret from which they wished her to be totally excluded.

8

A week before Christmas, May Lodge closed and locked her workroom door soon after three o'clock in the afternoon. The light was fading fast and she realised that she could just as well busy herself in the warmth of the Mill House living-room. She was about to tack in the collar and cuffs on an *ensemble* that she was making for Lady Fairfax, besides trying to deal with one of the new-fangled zip fasteners which her ladyship had brought from London; as this latter task was one which May had never undertaken before, she knew it would need time and patience to get it right. Moreover, by working in the house she would be keeping Sarah company. She was aware that her mother was fretting about the rising waters and that this winter she seemed more than unusually troubled. She would either remain silent for hours on end or go about muttering and shaking her head. Once or twice, after dark, May had caught her going up through the mill, shining her big torch—which now replaced her lantern—on to the fast-flowing Willon and repeating, agitatedly, "It's just like it was before Sidney died."

May was annoyed to find George Fuller—the manager of the Felt Mills—standing at the Mill House door where he had come to collect his tea-tray. She knew that he had a perfect right to be there and that, owing to Sarah's increasing infirmity, it was good of him not to expect her mother any longer to climb the stairs to his office. But, possibly because of her long-standing antipathy towards the man, the imposition of producing tea for him five days a week—which the owners of the mill had placed upon Sarah as part of the agreement whereby she could remain in the house for her lifetime—irritated May beyond measure. George Fuller, as far as she was concerned, was a ridiculous, obsequious boor. He had a long-suffering wife and two children, but she was well aware that he 'fancied' her. He would make any excuse to stop and pass the time of day and sometimes it was all she could do to treat him civilly, especially when she thought of how she had early on christened him 'Duck and Collar', because of his long neck and weak blue eyes. Today, she saw those eyes light up at the sight of her. His opening gambit did nothing to dispel her feeling of utter distaste.

"Ah, good afternoon, Miss May. Or should I say 'Good evening'? It is uncommonly dark, is it not?"

"Yes, Mr Fuller." *Uncommonly dark*, May noted contemptuously. No one in his right mind would talk like that.

"It would seem that we are in for more rain. I fear the Willon is riding high."

"Yes."

At that moment Sarah appeared at the door with the tea-tray and May tried to end the conversation by going inside; but still the man lingered.

"I gather from Ted Shergold," he went on, "that Lord Fairfax reckons on having some extensive repairs done to the gates of Bulbarrow sluice next summer, as well as many of the hatches round about."

"Next summer's a while away, Mr Fuller," Sarah suddenly said, tartly. "The work should have been done last summer. We had a hundred and forty-six days without rain."

"Yes . . . but . . . I mean, no one was to know." It was well known that when confronted by any awkwardness, George Fuller always took to compromising. "I've told Tom Henstridge to see that the planks and sandbags are put out ready. We must just hope . . ."

"Hope's not going to keep the water out, Mr Fuller. It'll be in this house by Christmas. Or before. You mark my words."

May had seldom known her mother address anyone in such fashion other than the members of her own family. In fact, she had certainly never before heard her make the slightest derogatory remark about the Fairfaxes. For one thing, Lady Fairfax had been responsible over the years for a considerable amount of the Lodges' income and perquisites. For another, she belonged to the 'gentry' and, with few exceptions, the gentry in Sarah's eyes could do no wrong. Any bad hats which a county family might happen to spawn generally had excuses made for them. Her mother must be deeply disturbed to have spoken her mind so plainly to a man to whom, whatever she privately thought about him, she nevertheless usually accorded the respect which she considered to be his due as manager of the Felt Mills in her late husband's place.

Mr Fuller also seemed surprised by Sarah's unaccustomed

acerbity. With a hasty "We must look on the bright side, Mrs Lodge," he retreated with his tea-tray.

Inside the living-room Sarah lit the oil-lamp and sat down by the range to resume her knitting, while May placed her sewing things carefully on the horsehair sofa, the legs of which had been raised up by bricks some days ago as a precaution in case of flooding. It would be another hour or so before they themselves had tea and, to ease the tension in the atmosphere, May switched on the battery-operated valve wireless, which now replaced their old crystal set with its awkward unsociable earphones. Unfortunately, however, this only seemed to make matters worse, for she tuned straight in to *Happy Days Are Here Again* being played by Jack Payne's dance orchestra at Savoy Hill.

"Turn that thing off, May." Sarah's voice was still sharp and scolding.

"But, Mother . . ." May tried to remonstrate with her. Personally, she could think of nothing better than a little of Jack Payne's lighthearted playing. Why, the broadcast was taking place probably not more than a couple of miles away from where Katy lived, and this she tried to explain to Sarah. The wireless had given May's life an extra dimension and it saddened her to be asked to forgo so simple and, as she felt, innocent a pleasure. She could visualize well-dressed ladies and gentlemen doing the fox-trot, possibly at some West End tea dance, and how the ladies' longer skirts would be swirling gracefully about their silk-stockinged legs. (May always read the fashion news in *Britannia and Eve* and knew that 'hemlines were coming down as fast as the stock market'.) The thought that some of those far-away sophisticated beings might be dressed by Coco Chanel or Edward Molyneux gave her a vicarious kind of thrill. It seemed such a pity that, to Sarah, such goings on seemed to have the reverse effect.

"Turn it off, I say," her mother now repeated. "It's wicked for tunes like that to be played when you think of all the troubles in the country just now. Where are the happy days? You know as well as I do, my girl, there aren't any, not for the likes of you and me."

With resignation, May turned off the bakelite knob and began taking a mass of purple velvet out of the clean white linen bolster-case in which she always kept her current sewing. There was silence in the room now, save for the clicking of Sarah's steel knitting needles and the occasional noise of a cinder falling into the hearth.

Just before five-thirty Duck and Collar returned his tea-tray, after which his motor-bike could be heard chugging away from the mill. At six, the hooter sounded for the men to clock off. There was the customary heavy tramping of feet and a few raucous salutations as they filed past the house and then, once again, silence, save for the rain which had begun pattering on the windows and an occasional squally gust of wind which tore at the catches.

With difficulty, May restrained her mother from going outside to look at the river and, having placed a stone hot water-bottle in each of their beds, suggested that she should have an early night.

"Although how a body is expected to sleep," Sarah muttered as she eventually picked up her candle-stick, "I'm sure I don't know. Edith's husband's taken all the light stuff upstairs, but for goodness sake don't leave anything else lying about. We don't know what we might find come morning."

Once she was alone, May switched on the wireless again very quietly and began to listen to the news, thankful that Sarah could not hear Stuart Hibberd's voice saying, "This is London . . . The unceasing rain of the past few weeks has given cause for grave concern. Flood water all over the country is rising. The situation along the Thames embankment is crucial. Aerial photographs taken over the home counties reveal that the actual course of the rivers—particularly the Wey—is impossible to define. In the west country there is such widespread flooding that there are growing fears for the safety of both people and livestock, particularly in isolated districts. The Minister for Agriculture, Mr Noel Buxton, is to make an extensive tour of the area . . ."

There was a suitable pause and then came the words: "Speaking at a dinner in London last night, the Prime Minister said that although the figures for unemployment were still rising, living standards—outside the worst-hit regions—were creeping up. Mr Ramsay MacDonald went on to point out that . . ." But here, May switched off and pursed her lips. She had heard all she wanted to know. In Wilhampton they were in for trouble, one which was quite different from being out of work. They were in for the kind which her favourite announcer had described at the beginning of the News. They were up against the rising Willon, not the rising number of jobless in the country. Sadly, she reflected that, however much she had enjoyed the advent of wireless, although it certainly brought Jack Payne's *Happy Days* into the living-room, it also brought the bad ones right home as well. Perhaps it was a mercy that there had been none of it during the war. But that, thank God, was a war to end all wars. Had not her eldest brother, Frank, given his life to ensure that this was so?

By ten-thirty, after a small cup of soup, May herself went up to bed. As she passed through her mother's room on the way to her own she found Sarah still wide awake, with that fixed staring expression which she invariably wore in times of stress.

"Have you shut and locked the gates, May?" Although her mother's voice was still peremptory, May could not help noticing how nervously her hands plucked at the coarse sheet.

For the first time that she could ever remember, May told Sarah a direct lie.

"Yes, Mother." It seemed wrong to add to her anxiety, to explain that after the news on the wireless she had decided that, even though Tom Henstridge had the spare keys with which he let the men in every morning, it would be better just now that they should not barricade themselves so completely during the hours of darkness.

At midnight the wind rose to gale force. May had known previous storms of such magnitude. She had seen many a winter flood come and go; yet she could not recall ever having been imbued with the same kind of foreboding which she suspected she now shared with Sarah.

Just before one o'clock there was a sudden strange noise from the direction of Bulbarrow which May had never heard before. It was like a distant cracking or splintering which momentarily drowned the shrieking of the wind and the roar of the mill-race. In the next room Sarah cried out and May rushed in to find her sitting bolt upright, every muscle tensed, the expression on her face one of frozen terror.

"Mother!" May sat down and cradled the rigid body in her

arms, doing her best to stifle her own fear; for she knew that the sound which she had heard was the presage of no ordinary catastrophe, any more than Sarah's present condition was the symptom of any hitherto known affliction. Within seconds, they heard the first rush of water pounding down the mill. As it hurled itself against the side of the Mill House, Sarah's eyes seemed to roll upwards and then glaze over. A minute later she fell back, lifeless, against the pillows.

At first, May was too stunned to do other than stay beside Sarah's body, her left arm more or less pinioned beneath it. She was dimly aware of water heaving and gurgling in the living-room below, while an icy draught of air came straight up the staircase. When she was at last able to move, the fingers of her right hand searched in vain for her mother's pulse, even though she knew that she would not find it. May had seen death before: her father, Neil and Flo. After ten more minutes, very gently, she drew the sheet over Sarah's face. Then, picking up a torch, she went to the window and watched its faint gleam shining down on to a wilderness of water which seemed to be pouring out of the downstairs windows into some turbulent black lake.

May had no idea of the depth of the flood, but she knew that it was impossible to get help. There was no one near enough at hand to whom she could call out. She was desperately conscious that Sarah needed the last offices but that she lacked the skill to perform them herself. It was this, rather than any danger she might be in, which was uppermost in her mind. Her mother, so proud, so impeccably clean and neat throughout her life, must be decently laid out as soon as possible. With every hour that went by the task would become more difficult.

Just before dawn, May heard the sound of a voice calling her. She went again to the window and leaned out, shining her torch as before on to the water below. From the direction of River Lane she could see a boat approaching in which there were two figures. As they drew nearer the house, she recognised them as none other than Maurice Fitzherbert and his gardener, Fred Musselwhite.

"May, are you all right?" Maurice, his voice quick and anxious, put out a hand and grasped the top of the porch. Then, steadying both himself and the boat, he stood up, his head little more than six inches below her own. "May, if I help, do you think you and your mother could get out of this window?"

"Mother is dead, Maurice," she replied, quietly.

"*Dead?*" He looked at her incredulously, his face white and drawn in the flickering torchlight.

"Yes. She had a stroke when the first rush of water from Bulbarrow hit the house."

"Oh, my God. May, my dear. I am so very sorry. Look, I'm coming up."

With extraordinary dexterity, he swung himself out of the boat and, within seconds, had squeezed through the window and was standing beside her in the room. A quick examination of Sarah's body confirmed May's words and he turned to look at her, imploringly.

"May, you must come away. Now."

Although she had the greatest respect for him, she looked at Maurice Fitzherbert askance.

"I cannot leave Sarah *alone*, Maurice . . . not properly laid out, uncoffined . . . But thank you for coming," she added, hastily, feeling that perhaps she was being ungrateful.

"But May . . ." He hesitated for a moment. He had guessed what her reply might be, but he felt that there was something else which had to be said. "May . . . there's a nasty gap in the side of the house. I'm afraid . . . of the foundations . . . There could be some subsidence."

She looked at him levelly. "I understand, Maurice. But, all the same, I could not leave."

He did not argue. He knew the Lodges. They were like some of the men he had fought with in the war. They did not quit. They might be highly strung and nervous, but in times of trouble they stood their ground, closed ranks and went on with some kind of innate courage and a sense of what was right and proper. He realised that May Lodge would sooner die than cease her vigil. Out of one of his inner pockets, he produced a small flask of brandy which he pressed into her hands with the words, "I'll send help as soon as I can." Then he let himself out of the window and down into the boat.

As Fred Musselwhite picked up the oars and drew away into River Lane, there came into Maurice's mind some words which he remembered the Reverend Donaldson having used many years ago as a text for one of his sermons. It had been when he was hoping to marry Katy Lodge and he had never forgotten them: *Many waters cannot quench love, neither can the floods drown it*. The love which Sarah Lodge had given to the members of her family must sometimes have seemed of a curious kind: harsh, protective, tyrannical and demanding. Yet in times of real crisis she would never fail them any more than her eldest living daughter would fail her now.

Back at the wreck of the Mill House, calm with the dignity of love and grief, May Lodge waited for morning.

9

One Saturday morning towards the end of January, a small neatly-dressed woman and a pretty, though serious-eyed, little girl wearing a scarlet coat and smart, leather, buttoned-up gaiters, could be seen feeding the pigeons in Grosvenor Square. When the bag of stale crusts which they had brought with them was empty, Emily Mason turned to May Lodge and said, "Why must you go away tomorrow, Aunt Chip? Why can't you stay and live with us in London?"

May looked down at her niece, fondly. "Because I have work to do, Emily, back in the country."

"But Mummy said you wouldn't be able to work at the mill any more."

"No, dear. But I'm very lucky. I'm going to have this new little home I told you about, where I shall be able to do all my sewing."

"But why can't you do it up here? I heard Mummy telling Daddy that there were lots of people in Mayfair who could give . . ." The child hesitated a little, before adding "their ears for one of your creations."

"*Did* you, then?" May smiled. "Well, there a lot of people in Wilhampton who also seem to need my creations, as you call them. And somehow I must hurry up and see about making them, as well as putting to right all the things that got damaged by the floods."

There. She hadn't wanted to mention the word but it had somehow slipped out. Emily became silent and May felt that, one way or another, the child had probably heard more than was good for her about the recent disaster, however much she and Katy and Philip had tried to keep it from her. May sensed that a change had come over her niece since she had last seen her. She was no longer the happy, carefree, eager young thing she had been back in the summer, rushing home to the Mill House from Miss Sharman's, breathlessly reporting on some latest piece of learning or the stealthy movements of Jumbo. She seemed to have become suddenly older, altogether quieter; and May did not think it was entirely to do with the fact that her grandmother had died and the Mill House was to be pulled down, much as she knew that the news had saddened her.

For a while, May's mind was jolted back to that terrible night before Christmas and the following morning when Sarah's body, wrapped in a sheet, had had to be lowered from the bedroom window into a boat, this time under the direction of Arnold Parker, the undertaker, after which, a little later on, he had returned for May. She recalled how, before clambering out herself into the strong waiting arms of Arnold's son, she had managed to hand him down a few of her possessions, such as her rosewood treasure chest, some necessary items of personal clothing and two bolster cases containing half-made orders, including Lady Fairfax's purple velvet *ensemble*. And then, as she was rowed to safety, she had turned to look at the full devastation of the scene behind her: the huge gaping hole where one side of the living-room had been, the upended horsehair sofa, her mother's favourite picture of *The Last Supper* hanging incongruously in space and the old tapestry door curtain floating like some magic carpet by the partially submerged piano.

Up until then, May had remained steadfast and composed. Now, the full shock of all that had taken place began to sink in. She could not remember very much about the subsequent sequence of events, except how kind people had been and that, although Edith had wanted her to go up to downside, Maurice Fitzherbert had insisted that she must stay at East Lodge—even though May later suspected that his wife had been far from pleased, especially when Katy appeared. She was vaguely aware that her youngest sister seemed to come and go and then return again with Philip for Sarah's funeral, to which both Henry and Marianne had come. She thought it must have been the evening before that, when she had been sitting quietly by herself in one of Maurice's spare bedrooms—still in a state of semi-shock—Lady Fairfax called to see her. There had been a light tap on her door and she recalled Maurice taking her down to the drawing-room, where he left them alone. She had an impression of being embraced, but that Lady Fairfax's manner was somehow different—there appeared to be a certain nervousness about her, even an air of contrition. When she spoke, her sentences were disjointed, a little difficult to follow.

"May, my *dear* . . ." There had been a long pause and then she had continued, all in a rush, "What can I say? Words seem so useless . . . As I told Jimmy last night . . . there must be actions—*now*. I . . . that is, we . . . would like you to have old Mrs Hardiman's cottage. You know, Number Three, Cob Lane."

For a moment May had been too taken aback to speak. Then, with the realisation of all that she was being offered, she murmured gratefully, "It's so very kind . . ." Yet there was something bothering her, a thought which seemed to jostle for attention among the many others in her still confused mind. "But your ladyship," she at last managed to say, "isn't Number Three earmarked for Percy Hooper when he marries the Roper girl next April?"

There had then been such a long pause that May began to worry that she had said something offensive. It was with obvious effort that her visitor eventually started to tell her that, sadly, Sarah had not been the only casualty in the floods. Percy Hooper had attempted to carry his aunt, Mabel Snoad, to safety on his shoulders but had slipped; although Mabel had survived, Percy had been knocked out and carried away by the current.

May remembered that it had seemed very quiet in the Fitzherbert drawing-room then. She knew Percy well. She had watched him grow up. She could see him as a lad on his red bicycle and how, in the war, he had brought the telegram with the news of her eldest brother's death on the Somme; and then, early in 1919, a second one telling of Henry's marriage to Marianne. He had always been polite and willing and, if still alive, would have taken charge of the post office when Mabel retired. That poor girl he was to have married. Why, May had promised to make her wedding-dress. It did not seem right that Dolly Roper's loss should be her gain and she said as much to her visitor. But her remark was gently but firmly dismissed.

May had then raised another point which was troubling her. There was the question of rent. She and Sarah had accumulated a few savings between them and she knew that, as the only unmarried child, her mother's share would now come to her. But it would be very little. She would no longer be able to afford much help with her sewing. She would have to work hard, very hard. But she would not, could not, accept charity. It was finally agreed that Luke Ridley, the Fairfaxes' agent, would come to see May about this and at last her visitor rose, the word 'peppercorn' coming from her lips more than once before she left the room. It was not until much later, when May had had time to mull over the conversation, that she kept thinking about Lady Fairfax's curious unease, how she had never looked her straight in the eye during her entire visit and that perhaps Sarah—as so often before—had been right when she had told George Fuller that the repair work in the meadows should have been done the previous summer.

May had been staying with Katy in London for quite a while before a semblance of her old self became apparent. It was possibly the company of her niece rather than that of her sister and brother-in-law which helped to restore her natural outgoing responsiveness to the world around her. Gradually, May became increasingly aware that the child needed her in some way which was hard to define. This was confirmed more than ever on the morning when they were walking back to Davies Street after feeding the pigeons.

"You'll have me to stay in your new home, won't you, Aunt Chip, often?" Emily said, slipping a small hand in hers.

"Why yes, my dear. As often as Mummy and Daddy can spare you in the holidays." Sensing that perhaps they were getting on to a delicate subject, May continued, "Now, let's think. We've still got a little time before we're expected home. Suppose you take me along to Bond Street so that I can look in the windows and see what all the fashionable ladies are wearing. Then I'll be able to make the same sort of things when I get back to Wilhampton."

How long ago it seemed, May thought, as they made their way, since the day when she had brought a timorous Katy up to London to begin her duties as nursery-maid in the Moreton establishment and, before going home, had walked the length of Bond Street because she had once cherished a dream that she and Flo could have set up shop there. And now, here was Katy's child, living within a stone's throw of the place, leading her towards it with a hop and a skip and the words, "Oh, *yes*, Aunt Chip. We'll go to Asprey's first and then Madame de Rosa's. Mummy says she has the best ready-made coats and skirts in London, but that we must never call them *costumes*." May smiled again at the subtle niceties of speech with which Katy was evidently imbuing her daughter. She was glad to think that, if only for a few moments, she had been able to bring back the Emily of last summer before she had become subdued and hurt by May knew not what.

Once she had returned to her home town, the mass of work which awaited her, combined with the support of countless friends and neighbours, all helped to ensure that the benefit which she had derived from her stay in London was by no means wasted. To her astonishment and gratitude, she found that her new home had been scrubbed out from top to bottom by two of the girls who worked at the mill; that Edith, despite the constant demands of her family, had managed to fit and hang curtains in every window; that a brand-new carpet—a present from Edwina and Ernest Fielding, the owners of the mill—had been laid in her sitting-room and that as much furniture as could be salvaged from the Mill House had been installed, albeit somewhat incongruously, in her tiny rooms. To her great joy she also found that Arnold Parker's son had rescued, stripped and reassembled her treadle sewing-machine so that it gleamed as new. Only one little gesture of goodwill seemed to jar. On the sitting-room table there was a large box to which was attached a label reading: "To a brave little lady". She knew the writing. With a mixture of dismay yet—to her mortification—growing excitement, she opened it to find that Duck and Collar had sent her a brand new wireless set.

It was not until the end of March that May was able to bring herself to go anywhere near the mill again. She had written George Fuller what she hoped was a suitably appreciative letter of thanks, while praying that they would not actually meet—at least for some time. She therefore chose a Saturday afternoon for her visit when, with luck, she hoped that there would be no one about. She was relieved to find that the gates were unlocked and that there was no need to ask Tom Henstridge for the keys. But once inside she was brought up short, unable to orientate herself, so great was the shock she received.

Where the Mill House had stood there was now only a pile of rubble. It was as if, suddenly, her bearings had been swept from under her, her roots cut off, the whole of her past life but an illusion. She found herself clenching and unclenching her fingers rather as Sarah had done in times of great distress. For a while she even wondered if she were dreaming. She had known no other home for nearly forty years, save the tiny one to which she was now endeavouring to become accustomed. The Mill House had been a stronghold, a refuge, a ship which had seemed incapable of capsizing. It had been commanded by a woman, hard yet vulnerable, fearful yet courageous. With no indoor sanitation of any kind, one living-room, desperately inadequate sleeping space and little money, she had reared seven children to know love and anger, gaiety and sadness. In a word, she had given and maintained *life*—good life. And now there was no life. There was not even death. There was—desolation. Only a few daffodils tossing bravely in the breeze by the garden gate seemed to give any indication that here was once vital human habitation. Even her workroom, May noticed, was being transformed into a red-brick eyesore, for whose edification a willow-tree had been slain and slaughtered.

Then she heard it. She supposed that she would have done so before had she not been so grieved and distracted by the scene around her. Slowly, May walked towards the mill-race. She did not know how long she stood beside it. She only knew that it seemed to be giving her back something she had lost. It was just the same. The floods had not altered it one whit. It was the guarantor of the past, the present and the future. She waited while the shadows lengthened, watching the water flowing, falling and bubbling up again before it swirled around and then drifted away quite calmly, even serenely, towards the sea. It would go on like this for ever. She must remember to tell Emily that in her next letter.

May Lodge opened her handbag, took out a clean white linen handkerchief and quietly blew her nose.

10

"I want to see *Anna Christie* at the Empire," ran Belle Mason's letter at the beginning of April, "and I've been sent these two tickets for the Private View at the Royal Academy on Friday, May 2nd, so I've decided to come up to town for that weekend. I thought perhaps both of you would like to see Garbo's first talking picture and Katy might care to accompany me to the R.A."

"*Accompany Belle to the Private View*?" Katy stared at her husband in astonishment, as he read the letter out loud at the breakfast table. "But . . . how . . . I mean, I didn't know Belle ever went to things like *that*. Who would have sent her the tickets?"

"Search me. But I think, in a quiet way, old Belle has quite a few influential friends through her first husband. She's always been interested in the arts. I'm delighted she's asked you. I'll write back and say you'd love to come, shall I?"

"No. Please don't. I can't possibly accept."

This time it was Philip who looked at his wife in disbelief, as he asked, quickly, "Why on earth not?"

"I . . . It would mean a new outfit. I could make a dress, of course, but it's not just that. It's everything—shoes, hat, bag . . . even gloves. We can't possibly afford it."

Philip Mason was silent for a while. Then he said, quietly, "It's time you had a new outfit, my love. We're going to afford it. You can't say we've been exactly extravagant the last few years. We've lived pretty quietly since . . ." he hesitated a little, hardly wanting to refer to the event, before continuing, "since Belle helped me out of that hole I was in. Besides," he went on, more cheerfully, "look how much you've done for me behind the scenes since you got better. I know things are still pretty tight, but the business seems to be holding its own, in spite of the recession. Between you and me, I think Belle's been quite favourably impressed. Otherwise, she'd never have made the suggestion. You'd better start doing some window-shopping straight away."

To Emily's acute embarrassment, she watched her mother

suddenly get up, throw her arms round her husband and give him a long affectionate kiss. Since that night during the last winter when the child had overheard their secret, puzzling, yet obviously pleasurable activities, any overt demonstration of love between her parents seemed somehow unacceptable. Many was the time—however guilty it made her feel—when she could not help wishing that her mother was more like dear dependable Aunt Chip.

Katy herself was not unaware of her small daughter's changed attitude towards her nor, greatly to her chagrin, the reason for it. Nowadays, she made a conscious effort to appear correct—even rather prudish—in her presence. She was resolved that never again would Emily hear any sounds of physical imtimacy taking place between herself and Philip, however much she longed to give in to his far from infrequent desires, the delaying of which often proved frustrating and inhibiting to them both. Today's spontaneous loving response to his magnanimous suggestion was, she felt, an unfortunate lapse on her part. With a "Hurry up and get ready for school, darling," she chivvied the child out of the room.

But on the way back from escorting Emily by bus to Court House, Katy's mind reverted swiftly to the exciting prospect ahead. It had, as Philip said, been a long time since they had indulged in anything but the most prudent expenditure. Now, suddenly, that mercurial temperament which occasionally transported her from a dutiful, conscientious wife and mother into a carefree young girl again took hold to such an extent that Katy told the conductor she wished to be put down at Queen's Road. After all, there was no time like the present. She was so near Whiteleys and she would only be *looking*, giving their materials a little pinch between finger and thumb—just as she had been taught to do—to make sure of their quality.

Something in black and white, she wondered, as she made her way along the pavement. One could never go wrong with that. It was always smart. Of course, the Private View took place at an unpredictable time of the year. Printed chiffon would be nice, but the beginning of next month could still be cold. She could not possibly run to a dress *and* a coat, whatever Philip said and however many gorgeous revolutionary proofed materials were now appearing in the shops. Perhaps a simple lightweight silk or wool suit would be best, worn with a little pillbox or a broad-brimmed deep-crowned Garbo hat? She fancied the latter, although would that be right with a *suit*? She wished that her bobbed hair had had time to grow a little longer and that she could have a permanent wave, in keeping with the current trend. What a pity May was not with her. Dear May. Even if she did not live in London, she always seemed to know best. Her youngest sister supposed that being responsible over the years for making so many of Lady Fairfax's clothes probably had a great deal to do with it—that, and her assiduous study of the latest fashion news.

Katy was almost at the main doors of Whiteleys when she saw in their window something which caused her to stop and stand quite still for several minutes. Cunningly draped over a garden seat was a quantity of black and white printed chiffon at three and elevenpence halfpenny a yard. Laid nonchalantly beside it, almost as if its owner had forgotten to pick it up, was a large—unpriced—black straw hat, trimmed with the same material.

Katy did some mental arithmetic. She knew that the hat would be out of the question. It could be anything from three guineas upwards—and she still had to get shoes, bag and gloves. But surely, with a bit of ingenuity, she could buy a straw crown and trim it herself? Of course, there was still the problem of the weather, but it wasn't as if the Academy was out of doors. She'd always heard that the glass in the roof at Burlington House tended to attract the heat and, after all, she only had to get there and back. She hesitated for only a fraction longer and then went inside to make her purchase.

Katy was well aware that, if she asked, her eldest sister would have been only too willing and eager to make the dress for her; but she desisted for several reasons. For one thing, she knew that May—fortunately, as usual—had more than enough work on her hands. (In her last letter she had mentioned that she was already starting on Lady Fairfax's Ascot clothes.) For another, May would never allow any of her family to pay her. But apart from these considerations, Katy was anxious to see what she could create on her own. It would be, as she wrote to May that night, a challenge; and as the time went by she became increasingly absorbed in her efforts. When the date of the Private View drew nearer, she began—much to Philip's amusement—listening carefully to the weather forecasts on the wireless, even though she knew they were mostly unreliable and, as little as twelve hours beforehand, could be totally wrong.

Three days before the actual event, a large box arrived at Davies Street bearing a Wilhampton postmark. Mystified, Katy opened it to discover, meticulously packed between layer upon layer of clean tissue paper, a black garment which, on lifting it out, proved to be a lightweight proofed cloak made from just the kind of material she might have bought if she could have afforded it. In May's immaculate script there was a short letter which read: "You said you had taken a gamble on it being fine for the 2nd, but I thought the enclosed wouldn't come amiss if it isn't. Anyway, whatever happens, this sort of thing never dates and will last a lifetime. I've made it on the long side and only tacked the hem in case it needs adjusting."

Almost in tears, Katy put down the note and tried the cloak on. How *did* May do it? What must the material have cost? Even allowing for some small dividends from her savings in the Co-operative Society, her income was probably not much more than four pounds a week. Katy was well aware that she invariably undercharged her customers—even Lady Fairfax. It seemed so sad to think that her eldest sister rarely went to any of the occasions for which she so assiduously decked out others. Yet she never seemed to mind. She was nearly always cheerful. Presumably, in doing her work behind the scenes, she reaped her own particular reward.

Belle Mason was certainly unprepared for the vision which arrived in the foyer of Brown's hotel three days later. She had always known that her stepson's wife was attractive and had flair, but this extremely chic young woman, with almost a Parisian look about her, seemed scarcely recognisable. With her large black hat, classic black accessories, and what appeared to be a black and white swirling chiffon dress beneath a smart black cloak, Belle noticed several heads turn as Katy walked towards her.

"My dear! How . . . charming you look." The older woman rose, wondering for a moment whether Philip's wife had taken up acting again. Where on earth had she acquired her *ensemble*? It must have cost a pretty penny. She hoped that the young couple were not heading for further financial difficulties.

As if reading her thoughts, Katy said quickly, "I'm glad you think so. I made the dress and hat and my sister, May, made the cloak."

"*Really*?" Never having been exactly good with her needle, Belle Mason could not refrain from staring at her guest in silent admiration.

"Well, yes. Perhaps you forget. All my sisters and I learnt sewing."

Having decided—albeit a little sadly—to leave the cloak at the hotel owing to the day's increasing warmth and brightness, Belle was not surprised to find even more heads turned in their direction when they arrived at Burlington House. She felt that her young protegée could easily have been an artist's model. At one point, while they were studying Laura Knight's *Ballet Girl and Dressmaker*, a voice behind them said, "Why, Katy, how lovely to see you. It *is* you, isn't it, hiding under that gorgeous hat?" On turning round, rather to her surprise, Belle found herself being shyly introduced to someone called Lady Moreton. On the way back to Brown's for lunch, Katy explained that she had once worked for the Moretons when they had lived in Upper Brook Street, adding quietly, "That's how I came to meet Philip."

"I *see*." Belle glanced at her curiously. Katy had certainly come on a lot since the diffident little thing she remembered marrying her stepson nine years previously. "I know so little about you, my dear," she continued. "I shall try to make amends."

During the rest of her visit, Belle Mason's interest in the members of the small family she had so surprisingly acquired through re-marriage in later life increased with each time she saw them. She was particularly impressed by the solemn, well-mannered little girl. Having never had any children of her own, she had hitherto considered them a drawback. Now, she was not so sure. There was something to be said, as one grew older, for taking an interest in the younger generation, or generations. Emily Mason seemed an unusual child. With those long-lashed, enormous brown eyes and expressive face, she could be a beauty in ten years' time. With guidance, Belle felt that she might well be able to revolutionize Emily's life. Her mother was pretty and she definitely had a certain something about her; but she was obviously a mercurial type, delicate and on the nervy side. The daughter would appear to be made of more sober, sterner stuff—so long as she was brought up aright. Emily Mason was the young girl she herself might have been had she not been born with rather too large a nose and thickish ankles so that, only in her late twenties—aided by a natural vitality and enquiring mind—had she managed to achieve an assurance and poise which overcame such handicaps.

Now, at the age of fifty-five, it suddenly came to Belle Mason that, through her step-grand-daughter she might live again. When Emily was a little older she would have her to stay. She could even take her travelling. It would be nice to have a healthy young companion, even if, later on, it was necessary to watch out for and ward off undesirable suitors. She was pleased that the child was going to a better school. She was glad that she had come to her stepson's rescue when he had been in difficulties some years ago. He was not the first person to whom she had given money in times of trouble and so far her generosity had never been misplaced. It was obvious that Philip had buckled to and taken her advice, which could have hardly been easy with a seriously ill wife on his hands. She felt that she would like to do more for him now, possibly take steps to ensure that his little daughter soon received even better tuition. Emily was clever, apparently, and there was talk of a scholarship but, if this did not come to pass, there were other ways of seeing that she received a first-class education, especially when it came to finishing schools.

Belle Mason found herself looking forward to many things as the train taking her home steamed out of Paddington station. She might be once again alone in life, but she knew that she had a lot to be thankful for, not the least, financial security—that is, so far as anyone could have that in such uncertain times. She decided that she would definitely buy the new Austin car she was constantly seeing advertised and take up driving. It would be as well to start in the summer months and she would see about it as soon as she got back.

Well content, Belle Mason settled herself into the corner of a first-class carriage and, turning her mind to more immediate pleasures, opened a small attaché case at her side. Here, she took out *The Good Companions*, one of the half a dozen new books which she had purchased from her stepson. There was nothing like a good read and she did not think she would be disappointed in the latest J. B. Priestley. She knew that it was a mutual love of books which had brought about her surprising but—except for its shortness—extremely satisfying second marriage.

What Belle Mason did not know was that it was exactly the same thing which had started Philip's and Katy's romance when, in the spring of 1920, he had sold her a copy of *Wuthering Heights* and why, nine months after their wedding, they christened their baby daughter Emily, after its author.

11

Since May Lodge had moved into Cob Lane, she and Ethel Sharman had become more and more friendly, for they found they had much in common. They now lived but a minute's walk away from each other, both were spinsters of about the same age, both had above-average intelligence and both were of a sensitive, caring disposition. But the main bond between them was undoubtedly their mutual interest in Emily Mason who, during the summer holidays, had spent a whole fortnight with her aunt in her new home.

Far from any longer harbouring feelings of jealousy over Ethel's fondness for Emily, May was now only too glad to have her niece taken for nature walks once again by her neighbour, as it enabled her to get on with her sewing. Besides, she realised that her small back yard was no substitute for the old-fashioned spacious garden at the mill and that it was wrong to have such a young thing cooped up with her for too long at a stretch. Neither did she feel that it was suitable to let Emily spend too much time in her sister Edith's overcrowded and distressingly disordered household. Sad as it seemed, the difference between Katy's only child and Edith's six unruly ones became increasingly apparent whenever the cousins met.

Although May remained loyal to a degree and would never breathe a word of such innermost thoughts to anyone, many was the time that she silently shook her head over Edith's lack of discipline, both in connection with the way she brought up her family and the way she had let herself go so much in recent years. May did her best to make excuses for Edith, knowing that tiredness, depression after losing all her teeth, shortage of money and a none-too-strong husband had much to do with such a sorry state of affairs. She was constantly trying to help out, running up a pair of small boy's trousers on her machine or a pinafore frock for a little girl. Nevertheless, it was impossible not to deplore the fact that Edith's children seemed so coarse, that they all spoke with such broad west-country accents, that the eldest, Donald, had become an agricultural labourer and the twin girls, Della and Debbie, were apparently hoping to get jobs as usherettes at the picture-house in Westonbury. Yet May had to admit to herself that Katy, whom she had once more or less forced into becoming a mere nursery-maid in order to get her away from the attentions of a simpleton brother, had actually this year gone to the Private View at the Royal Academy. One could never tell what might transpire in life. It was such a lottery.

Once Emily had returned home at the end of August and the nights began drawing in, Ethel Sharman and May Lodge often spent the evening together. Mostly, this took place in May's little sitting-room, where they could talk while she carried on with her sewing. Although much of their conversation inevitably turned on Emily or local matters, they also took a lively interest in current affairs, Ethel providing the more serious background knowledge, May, with her increasing penchant for the wireless, often making pertinent and humorous remarks about the foibles of public figures or her disagreement with the Labour Government.

Sometimes, May felt quite guilty about the pleasure she derived from George Fuller's present to her and once, when she had accidentally met him in the street, she had asked him if he would like to bring his wife and children to tea. But this half-innocent, half-clever suggestion had had the effect which, in previous years, she would have given anything to bring about. Duck and Collar had backed away as if thunderstruck. With a "It's most kind of you, Miss Lodge, but . . . I fear . . . my wife being delicate . . ." he had disappeared in the direction of the mill and May realised that, whereas George Fuller would have been more than happy to visit Cob Lane by himself, nothing would induce him to bring his family with him.

So May remained in her little home, listening to George's wireless set and hoping that he was not now regretting his generosity. Sometimes, as she cut, tacked, machined or stitched some garment, she reflected on how much her job—or profession, as Sarah would have called it—brought her into the stream of things, giving her experience of so many aspects of life and the hopes and fears of such a cross section of the community. When she was asked to make a wedding-dress, May thought about love—even if sometimes she suspected the bride was pregnant and the bridegroom marrying under a certain duress, or what the local inhabitants called "force put". Later on, when she was asked to make maternity clothes, she thought about the strange miracle of birth. Usually young mothers made their own layettes, but May was often requested by those of better means to make little girls' party frocks or bridesmaids' dresses, for which she did the most intricate smocking. On these occasions she thought about Emily and the pain and joy of growing up. Then there were the purely social events: the parties and receptions for which all women wanted to look their best. "A tuck here, perhaps, Miss Lodge, do you think?" someone might say during a fitting, or, "Possibly a little deeper armhole . . . Unfortunately . . . perspiration, although I have bought the latest brassière with the rubber *shields* . . ." And if May knew her client well, she might reply, "I believe the new Odorono is quite effective," which remark was sometimes countered with, "Oh, I *know*, Miss Lodge, but I believe it is apt to rot the material and my mother feels it is dangerous to use . . . against nature . . . one does not know what one might be damming up."

Lastly, of course, there was the mourning, and that was always a sad task. Just now, at the beginning of October, May was making mourning for the niece, by marriage, of Miss Fortescue, who had died quite peacefully in her sleep at the Moat House.

"Such a nice woman," Ethel Sharman said, when she called one Sunday evening and noticed the half-made black coat hanging up behind the sitting-room door. (May never worked for remuneration on the Sabbath, although she was busy making Edith a new woollen skirt.) "I was so sorry when I heard she'd passed on. She was so fond of Wilhampton. In a way, she put us on the map with all those books she wrote about the west country. She'll be greatly missed. I wonder who will take the Moat."

"Yes. I hope it will be someone she would have approved of. I've always thought it such a pleasant home. A good atmosphere. One can always tell. Poor dear Mother used to say that personality got into the woodwork. Would you like me to turn on the wireless, Ethel?" Although May would never dream of admitting it, she always found herself keener to indulge in her favourite pastime on a Sunday, possibly because, however moral and high-minded the programmes, none of them started—apart from the religious ones—until three o'clock in the afternoon.

But, whatever the day, one thing May never liked missing was the news. By no means a vain woman, it always gave her a kind of personal satisfaction—even thrill—to hear the chimes of Big Ben and the words: "This is London", and to know that her youngest sister was living there, right in the heart of things. It was almost as if Katy was alongside the announcer. Although the latter never actually divulged his name, May had come to know them all through their photographs in the *Radio Times* and putting two and two together, and tonight, even before John Snagge had uttered the word "disaster", she knew from the gravity of his voice that some terrible calamity had occurred. Silently, the two women sat staring at each other as, sentence by sentence, the full horror of the R 101's crash in Northern France was gradually revealed to them. When, finally, the words "It is not yet known whether there are any survivors from the fifty-four people on board" May leaned forward and switched off the set. She felt, rather as she had done during another disaster nearer home the previous winter that, just for the moment, she had heard enough.

There was now complete silence for a while in the little sitting-room. Presently Ethel said, "My cousin, Edwin, the one at the Air Ministry, told me a bit about that airship. He said it was known to be too heavy compared to the R 100, but there was too much pressure from the politicians to go ahead with the maiden flight. He said it hadn't had enough proper trials. I believe someone at the top wanted to prove that State enterprise was best. There's been a lot of bad feeling. He never thought personally that it would reach India."

"Oh." May was still stunned and Ethel's inside information was a little difficult for her to follow. She was thinking of the fire and all the poor souls who couldn't get out. "Recrimination's not going to bring them back," she said slowly, almost to herself.

"Oh, I know, May. Nothing can do that." Again there was silence before Ethel continued, quietly, "Although you can't help wondering, can you, about air travel? I've never been too sure. I suppose it's the thing of the future. It stands to reason, but I wouldn't want to leave *terra firma* myself. Last August, when Emily and I were walking along the top of the old Barbury turnpike, I remember there was a tiny aeroplane flying across the valley and at one point it looked as if it was dead level and coming straight at us. I don't mind telling you, May, I was scared, but I tried not to let Emily notice. When it was only a little distance away, it rose and just hopped over us, so to speak, and we could see the pilot waving. I daresay she told you all about it."

"Yes. She said that if it hadn't been for you she would have run away. She had one of her nightmares afterwards. But perhaps it was just as well she felt like that. After all, we don't want another Amy Johnson on our hands in a few years' time."

"No, although by then . . ." Ethel broke off, uncertainly, before going on, "Edwin seems to think that anything could happen. Now that there's this man called Hitler getting more and more power in Germany, he says there might be another war and if there is, as like as not, most of it will be fought in the air."

May looked at her visitor incredulously. "Oh no, Ethel. You must have got it wrong. There won't be another war. The last one made quite sure of that."

"Please God, you're right, my dear." Ethel stood up. "I must be going. I've some letters to write and I want to see the books are all set out ready for tomorrow's lessons. Perhaps I could call in again during the evening. We shall have further news by then."

After May had wished her visitor goodnight, she sat quite still for a while staring into the fire. Today's tragedy and Ethel's words had brought back memories of the last war, many of which she would have preferred to forget. Her brother Frank's death, for instance, and her own and Flo's disillusionment with two particular men who had danced attendance on them before leaving for the front. She recalled the terrible Sunday when, due to her naïveté, believing the major with whom she was in love was ill and needed help, she had been tricked into going to his suite where, despite a struggle, she had been forced to fulfil quite a different kind of need from any she had had in mind. She remembered how she and Flo had agonised together for eighteen days afterwards, until she knew she was not pregnant and then how, the following year, she had had to act as helpmate and comforter to her eldest sister. Poor Flo. The whole family had thought it was a foregone conclusion that she would marry Captain Guy Armitage and then he had been suddenly snapped up by Grace Sinca, the strange newcomer at the Warren, a woman whom the whole of Wilhampton considered "no better than she should be". The first intimation that Flo had of Guy's faithlessness was when she had read the announcement of his marriage in the *Westonbury Journal*. She had rushed off and shut herself in the closet where May, managing to get in and sit beside her on the wide wooden seat, had done her best to reassure her that she was "well out of it". When, not long afterwards, Guy Armitage had returned from Passchendaele with both his legs blown off, she had kept quiet. She was not a vindictive woman. Whatever hurt the man had done to her sister, she did not think in terms of retribution. It was only Sarah who, one night when the two of them happened to be alone, mentioned the word "come-uppance".

It seemed such a very long time ago. Katy had been but a child. She hardly knew what war was about. She and Flo had made her a kilt and May could see the little thing now, gaily swinging along the pavement in it, keeping time with the troops as they marched through Wilhampton singing *Colonel Bogey* and *Pack Up Your Troubles*. It was silly of Ethel to talk about anything like that happening again, even if she felt that it would never be *quite* like that. The trouble with Ethel was that she was a little too full of theories, apt to pay too much attention to that cousin of hers in the Air Ministry.

The cat, Tommy, which May had acquired since coming to Cob Lane, suddenly jumped up into her lap, purring. She stroked him absently, still lost in reverie, thinking that although she had never moved very far away from her home ground, she had experienced quite a bit of life, one way or another. She would be forty next birthday. She was aware that she no longer possessed the slim waistline for which she had once had such a reputation. She was middle-aged now and she was alone; but if the good Lord granted her health and strength she hoped she would be able to carry on working for many years to come. Her greatest fear was the thought of becoming dependent on anyone.

Her dearest wish was that she would live to see Emily grow up. She would so like to be able to make her wedding dress. However much she herself might be disillusioned by men, she was still an incurable romantic at heart. Emily would look lovely in cream satin with a veil of Brussels lace . . .

12

"Mrs Mason was in no way to blame for the accident, you understand, Mr Mason. She had taken to driving very well. This man in the Lagonda simply came round the corner on the wrong side. She didn't stand a chance."

"I see." Philip sat in the offices of a firm of solicitors in Monmouth and stared at its senior partner, a Mr Thomas Morgan. He had travelled to Wales from London after receiving a letter from the latter informing him of his stepmother's death and the date of her funeral.

Philip had still been unable to believe it, even as he had watched Belle's coffin lowered into the grave that morning. It was impossible to think he would never see her again. She had seemed so very much alive, so vital, so altogether charming on her last visit, back in May, when she had taken Katy to the Private View. He had felt it quite easy to understand her attraction for men, even though he had never ceased to be surprised that, being such a woman of the world, she had fallen for his quiet unassuming father. But perhaps their very differences—apart from the interest in books which they had in common—had all helped to account for what had seemed to him to be a strange union. He wished now that he had taken the trouble to get to know his stepmother better. She had certainly been kind to him, much kinder than he deserved. But it had never occurred to him that her magnanimity would stretch beyond the grave. He had always supposed that she had many other relatives and commitments.

"Mrs Mason made certain specific bequests," he heard Mr Morgan continue, in a high sing-song Welsh accent, "such as to her housekeeper, Mrs Williams, for instance, and to one or two friends, but her residual estate is to be divided: half outright to yourself and half in trust for your daughter."

"I see," Philip said again. He wondered vaguely what this would amount to: one thousand, two? He had no idea. Mr Morgan did not seem in any particular hurry to enlighten him and he naturally did not like to ask.

"Mrs Mason remade her will, Mr Mason, just after returning

from London last summer. I helped her to draw it up. She happened to mention how pleased she was with the way you were now managing your late father's business. She was particularly taken with your little daughter—Emily, as I believe she is called. I shall always remember . . ." He broke off before continuing with a smile, "I'm sure you won't mind my telling you this, but when she got up from the chair where you are now sitting, she said, 'My stepson has come on quite a bit, Mr Morgan, during the last few years. I think he would have a better idea of knowing how to handle an inheritance . . . well, that is to say, in a few years' time. Naturally I hope it won't be coming to him just yet'. She looked so bonny as she went out. We were all so sorry when we heard about the accident. It seems, indeed, quite tragic."

"Yes. Yes, it does." Philip felt his responses to be totally inadequate, but Mr Morgan appeared not to notice.

"I was wondering whether you would like to visit the house, Mr Mason? Mrs Williams is still living there. A valuation for probate was done yesterday. As I mentioned before, my wife and I would be happy to put you up for the night if you should wish."

"I . . . well, it's very kind of you but . . ." Philip hesitated, unsure, confused. He had brought no overnight bag and had told Katy he would be returning that evening.

As if reading his thoughts, Mr Morgan continued. "There is a late train which would get you back to London about eleven thirty, if that would suit you better. We could take a quick look at the Hollies and then you might wish to bring your wife another time?"

"I . . . yes." Would Katy want to see it? Was Mr Morgan expecting them to live in it? Surely not.

Once again, the man before him seemed to know what was going through his mind. "I was thinking perhaps, that there might be certain things belonging to Mrs Mason which you would like to have in your London home. I believe you have a flat above the bookshop?" Then, quite suddenly, as if his next statement was a mere formality and would come as no surprise, Mr Morgan went on, "If the house and its contents are to be sold, I should say that after the very generous provision which Mrs Mason has made for Mrs Williams and the other small bequests, something in the region of ten thousand pounds would be coming to you outright and ten thousand to your daughter in trust, as I said, to be administered by myself and one of my colleagues. I believe that Mrs Mason was extremely anxious that Emily should have the benefit of a first-class education and it was something she was meaning to discuss with you on her next visit to London, possibly making some provision for this during her lifetime."

Philip was silent. Twenty thousand between himself and Emily. It seemed a fortune. "I had no idea," he said, at length, "that my stepmother was so wealthy."

"No? Her first husband . . ." Mr Morgan hesitated and then went on, "Well, I don't suppose I would be betraying any confidences if I say he made quite a bit of money towards the end of his life dealing in art. He was very knowledgeable. Mrs Mason had some fine pictures."

Philip tried to think back to the few occasions when he had visited the Hollies. He had always been vaguely aware that it was a pleasant, well-appointed, comfortable home, but he had never been there for very long and mostly such times had been taken up with other considerations: his father's funeral, for instance, and the day when he had gone to ask his stepmother for help and had been too agitated to retain anything other than a mental picture of Belle herself, immaculate, poised, sitting at her desk as she wrote him a cheque.

On the way back to London that night, after Mr Morgan had shown him round the house, he still hadn't been able to recall many details other than, as the solicitor had said, his stepmother had one or two fine pictures and he had been surprised by the sumptuousness of her bedroom which, presumably, his father had once shared. He had found himself staring at the large mahogany four-poster and wondering about the sexual side of their marriage. He had always imagined that, after his mother's death, his father had ceased to be interested in that kind of thing. He had seemed so wrapped up in the shop, too old for such activities. Yet he had only been fifty-five when he died—much younger, in fact, than that brute, Kreiger, who had tried to seduce Katy. He would certainly have to bring her down to see the Hollies soon. He wondered what she would say to the news. He wondered what they would do.

The idea did not really take hold of him until the train was well past Reading, although he was aware that it had been there: flitting in and out of consciousness throughout most of the journey. He was fairly sure that Katy would not want to live in Wales. On the other hand, there would be no need to remain in their small flat above the shop, would there? Why not get a manager to live in it? There was somewhere else where he and Katy and Emily could go which might suit them all very much better. Should he suggest it at once, or perhaps wait a little while? Perhaps the latter course would be more prudent, although plans for the future of the Mason family were presenting themselves thick and fast. Belle's legacy would perhaps enable him to do something which he had not thought possible since his marriage. Yet had he not told Katy during their courtship that he had an ambition other than bookselling? Somehow, the advent of Emily, the decline in his fortunes, his unwise foray into the antiquarian trade and then Katy's illness had pushed it into the background.

As the train neared Paddington, it slowed down to a crawl. A thick pea-souper lay over the capital. It was almost one o'clock before he alighted on to the platform and realised that the quickest way of getting to Davies Street was on foot. Hunching his shoulders and tucking up the collar of his overcoat, he set off, ignoring more than one entreaty from some shivering, ghostly, female figure as it loomed up at him out of the fog with such words as, "Wouldn't you like a bit of home comfort on a night like this, dearie?"

He hurried on, longing for the home comfort which he knew would be awaiting him a little further away. He guessed that Katy would be waiting up and was afraid that she would be worried which, indeed, she was. Clad in a warm pink woollen dressing-gown, she was half way down the stairs before he had time to close the side door to the street. Her eyes, as always on such occasions, seemed enormous, the blue shadows beneath them which had never wholly disappeared since her illness, very much darker than usual.

"Darling!" She wound her arms round him, tightly. Suddenly, he realised that she had never before been left alone so late at night. She seemed all at once a child again, in desperate need of protection, in desperate need of love.

"There." He held her closely and kissed her several times. "There, my love, I'm sorry I'm so late. The fog's terrible."

"Yes, I know. I couldn't help thinking of . . . well, accidents," she added, softly, smiling now, as she started back ahead of him up the stairs. "I've been keeping your supper warm in the oven. I hope it's not ruined."

He began to tell her whilst he ate it and she sat opposite, staring at him intently, her elbows resting on the table, her small face cupped in her hands. When he got to the actual figure which would be coming their way, her eyes widened and she looked almost fearful.

"But . . . darling . . . I mean, what will you *do*?"

"I've been thinking, love, all the way home. I've got one or two ideas up my sleeve, but perhaps now isn't the time to talk about them. You're tired. So am I. Let's go to bed."

They tiptoed quietly past Emily's room. Although the child was sleeping better, there were still nights when she awoke and needed comforting. When he at last had Katy in his arms, Philip hoped that this would not be one of them. In spite of having talked about tiredness, he found himself making love to his wife who, to his joy, responded with something akin to her former ardour. Afterwards, as they lay intertwined, he murmured, softly, "Katy, love, d'you remember that afternoon on Putney Heath, way back the year we first met?"

"Yes, Philip, of course," she replied, equally softly.

"And I said there was something else I might do besides selling books?"

"Yes."

"Well, I've never got around to it, have I?"

"No."

"Well, I was wondering whether now mightn't be the time to try, once we've moved."

"Moved? But where . . .?"

"Katy, don't you remember that other day, a bit later on at the end of the summer, when I'd come to see you at your home and we went up on Breconbury Down?"

"I remember it very well." Indeed, she thought, it was etched on memory, bitter-sweet, the afternoon when she might so easily have lost her virginity.

"Well, I've never forgotten either. You were so lovely, Katy.

I just didn't know how to . . ."

She tightened her arms around him. "And there was something else you said was lovely that day, too, Philip."

"Yes. I think I said that it was a lovely place where you lived and that I wouldn't mind living there myself one day."

13

"So how much do you think the Moat House might fetch, Cyril?" May Lodge had led up to the question cautiously, doing her best to bring it into the conversation simply as a matter for general discussion. The last thing she wanted was for it to get around Wilhampton that Katy and her husband were interested in buying the place. But after her youngest sister's last letter, May had been hoping that she might come across Cyril Butt, the retired auctioneer—quite by accident, of course—as he went out for his daily constitutional.

She had been lucky. On her way to Miss Clutterbuck's to purchase a few yards of dimity for re-covering her old feather mattress, she had caught sight of Cyril coming down East Street towards Mulberry Cottage, his home in a corner of the market place. He was always easily recognisable for, with his fawn whipcord breeches, shiny brown leather gaiters, check coat and cap and long stout thumb-stick, he was a typical John Bull figure, invariably accompanied by Lion, his aged golden retriever. As casually as she could, May slackened pace and slightly altered her course so that, by the time she reached the war memorial in the centre of the square, Cyril was courteously raising his cap and wishing her good morning.

Ever since Flo's last illness, May had never felt altogether kindly disposed towards Cyril because, for many years prior to that, it was obvious that he was 'sweet' on her eldest sister—not that Flo had given him the slightest encouragement. All the same, many people thought that, as the dutiful only son of a tyrannical mother, when the latter died Cyril would be sure to 'pop the question'. Yet, after Mrs Butt eventually passed on round about the time when it became public knowledge that Flo had cancer, Cyril's attentions had been noticeable only for their absence. "You'd think," Sarah had remarked on more than one occasion, "that he'd send word or call to enquire now and then," to which sentiment May had been forced to agree, albeit sometimes adding, "I suppose he's one of those who are scared of the disease, always being so healthy himself."

Now, on this particular morning, Cyril did, indeed, still look amazingly robust. Puffing out his red cheeks against the cold, he had observed cheerfully that it looked as if they might be in for a hard winter. "Never seen so many berries as there are along the Barbury turnpike, May. Incidentally, talking of that, would you care to come in and have a glass of sloe gin? Just the thing on a day like this."

May had been torn between desire to do so but fear of what people would think. For a comely middle-aged spinster to be seen going into the home of an elderly bachelor was something which some busybody would be sure to notice, even though Cyril had a living-in housekeeper. But over the latter state of affairs there had never been any gossip, simply because, May supposed, prim Phyllis Hopkins was a good few years older than Cyril and had been housekeeper at Mulberry Cottage throughout his mother's day.

Possibly because he had sensed May's hesitation and the reason for it, Cyril had suddenly and somewhat ostentatiously pulled out his watch on its gold chain—even though he could perfectly well have glanced up at the town hall clock—and continued pleasantly, "Edgar Swanton said he'd probably call in round about now after he's been to see Dick Swayne up at Bulbarrow. Did you know that Dick's decided to grass down the whole of his farm and go in for this new method of open-air machine milking? Wise fellow. Farmers can't make money out of arable land these days, not with the government importing so much cheap wheat."

The information that Cyril was expecting another caller helped May to accept his invitation. To have the chance of chatting with *two* knowledgeable auctioneers—even if one of them *was* more interested in land than houses—was too good to miss. She had therefore found herself crossing the threshold of Mulberry Cottage for the first time for over ten years and that sipping sloe gin in Cyril's sitting-room in front of his open log fire was a very welcome change from her usual hard-working routine.

After Edgar Swanton had joined them, she had been quite happy to remain the least talkative of the three, surreptitiously appraising Cyril's antiques—she felt she had to hand it to Phyllis Hopkins for the shine on them—while listening to the men's remarks concerning the agricultural depression and their admiration for the way Dick Swayne was attempting to help himself out of it. Somehow it had then seemed entirely natural for the conversation to progress from land to houses and this was where May had been able to ask their opinion about the Moat.

"Twelve? Maybe fifteen hundred, wouldn't you say, Edgar," Cyril remarked, re-lighting his pipe.

"Yes. Thereabouts, I suppose. Depends if there's anyone who particularly wants it. I believe it's been let go a bit lately since Maggie started failing. But it's a sound buy. A compact little property. I should say that that's the kind of reserve Maggie's heirs are intending to put on the place when it comes up for auction next month."

May found herself colouring slightly. Edgar's reference to "anyone particular" had made her wonder whether he could possibly have heard about Katy; but she decided that that would have been impossible. She had told no one, not even Ethel Sharman, about the correspondence she had been having with her youngest sister.

When May had first realised why Katy was so interested in the Moat House, her reaction had been one of total confusion. The possibility that the girl—as she still thought of her—might be mistress of such an establishment was too astonishing to envisage. It went without saying that it would be wonderful to have her favourite sister and niece living in Wilhampton. But would Katy be able to adjust to what would be a very different way of life from that which she had hitherto known in her home town? And could Philip really afford to leave the bookshop to a manager? Or would it mean him travelling up and down to London each week? And Emily's schooling? Might it not be difficult to get her into Wickfield House without her name having been put down years ago? It was a fine public school on the outskirts of Westonbury, taking boarders and day girls, but May believed that there was a long waiting list for both. There seemed so many imponderables about the whole scheme. It was such a big step to take. She felt scared and excited. She wished the young couple had some older man to advise them, someone perhaps a little more worldly-wise than either of the two before her, who had now got on to the subject of Ramsay MacDonald and whether his government could last much longer.

Moreover, there was another vague niggle of doubt in the back of May's mind which simply would not go away. She knew that it was one which Katy and Philip, in their love for each other, would probably never stop to consider. Yet, as she made he way back to Cob Lane that morning and saw Maurice Fitzherbert driving out of the Hall gates, she found herself worrying about it more than ever. She was convinced that, for all the outwardly calm and pleasant manner which he showed to the world, he was, at heart, a deeply unhappy man. It would have helped, she felt, if he had had children, but he and his wife had been married for several years now and still there was no sign of a family. Many was the time she had noticed the fond way he had looked at Emily when the child had been staying with her, and how he never seemed to miss an opportunity of enquiring after Katy.

On entering her front door, May found yet another letter from her youngest sister which had arrived by the second post. It was, perhaps, not quite so enthusiastic as the others and she sensed that Katy herself had now begun to have certain misgivings, even if none of them included the close proximity of a long-standing admirer. Nevertheless, it appeared that she and Philip were planning to leave Emily in the care of Ellen and come down to Wilhampton for a day the following week in order to look over the Moat House—after which visit, May thought grimly, it will be all over the town. She wondered whether it would be possible to have a word with her youngest sister in private when the time came.

On the day before the proposed visit, May prepared a dish which she knew to be Katy and Philip's favourite: jugged hare. Fortunately, Ted Pretty, the new head keeper on the Fairfax estate, had been asked to leave a hare with her a few days previously and this she now skinned and cut up, frying the pieces until brown before putting them in a stew jar with a little salt, an onion stuck with cloves, lemon juice, peppercorns, parsley, thyme and a small glass of port from the bottle which Ethel Sharman—somewhat surprisingly—had given her on her last birthday. Then, covering all the ingredients with stock from the stock-pot she invariably kept going throughout the winter, she stood the jar in a saucepan of water to simmer for several hours on her small gas stove. During this time, she set about making forcemeat—which she shaped into small quenelles ready for frying—and peeled some potatoes and carrots. She felt it was important not to be overburdened by too many tasks the following morning, even though there would be no need to go to the station to welcome her visitors, as they were apparently stopping off at Westonbury and being driven out to the Moat by one of Edgar Swanton's colleagues in the firm in which Cyril's name still took precedence, Butt and Swanton.

As on previous occasions of late, May was once again struck by her youngest sister's appearance when Katy and Philip eventually arrived at Cob Lane. There was, May felt, a stamp of the big city about the fine-drawn young lady who came through the door. Katy could well have been a model. The fur-trimmed coat she was wearing—made, so she afterwards explained, by herself—fitted her slim figure to perfection. The little fur hat to match was perched at just the right angle on the soft brown hair which—much to Sarah's disapproval—had been bobbed a few years ago but recently allowed to grow again so that it could be marcel waved. Katy's complexion—always flawless—was, even so, now definitely enhanced by the most skilful use of make-up. She looked fragile, almost ethereally beautiful. Would she, May wondered, take to country life again if she and Philip really did buy the Moat? It would, admittedly, be a vastly more comfortable home than the one in which she now lived. But, all the same, May could not help feeling that, as the three of them settled down to eat, it was her brother-in-law who was the most enthusiastic about the whole idea.

"It would be marvellous for Emily," Philip was now saying. "Of course, we haven't liked to say too much in front of her. But I mean, just think, May, if she went to Wickfield House. That's what Belle would have wanted, I'm sure. And the child seems to have an almost uncanny affinity with Wilhampton. You've mentioned it yourself."

"Yes. There's no doubt that she's uncommonly at home here, Philip." And she would be but a stone's throw away, May thought, just as Katy would have been if she'd married Maurice Fitzherbert. Almost, it would be like a dream come true . . . Surely, she could not, would not, raise any nebulous fears in the face of so much youthful optimism. She was a silly old spinster who was now, quite fortuitously, being offered a second chance in life: that of living for and through her youngest sister and niece. Even so, Philip's next suggestion was one she had never, for one moment, contemplated.

"We were wondering, May, just supposing we did get the Moat, whether you'd come and live with us. You know the house. There would be plenty of room."

"Oh, *Philip.*" She was caught off guard, completely flabbergasted.

"Just think, though," her brother-in-law went on. "You could have the big west bedroom all to yourself, which I believe Maggie Fortescue's companion used to have."

"I . . ." May was still at a loss. To have been asked was so very gratifying and yet . . .

"We'd so love you to come," Katy broke in, her eyes bright and entreating. "And it's not entirely disinterested, mind. Philip might have to be away quite a bit. I'd want some company then."

May looked across at her youngest sister, registering, despite the optimism and genuine warmth of feeling, a certain nervousness, almost helplessness in her manner, as if she were in need of much more support than her husband could possibly give her. Even so, May held back. A sixth sense or, perhaps, simply a basic common sense, told her that the proposition would not work. However much she might wish to be involved in the young people's lives, her own was—and always would be—altogether different. She had her independence now. True, she paid but a peppercorn rent for it, but Number Three, Cob Lane, was hers for as long as she wanted to live there. She was a dressmaker—a much respected one—of Wilhampton. For as long as she could, she intended to go on being one. How could she possibly carry on with such an occupation if she lived with Katy and Philip at the Moat House? How would her brother-in-law like clients such as Arnold Parker's wife walking up the drive to be fitted? Or did they imagine that she would merely become a lady of leisure living off their charity? But, whichever way she looked at it, she knew that it was not—as her mother used to say—feasible. Levelly, she met the gaze of the two eager faces across the table as she laid down her knife and fork.

"Thank you, my dears, for asking me," she said, simply. "I

appreciate it more than I can say, but . . . I believe it would be best for me to remain where I am. Although," and here May smiled slightly before adding, "if ever you needed me, well, I shouldn't be far away, should I?"

14

"Just a shade longer, I think, May, don't you? Skirts really do seem to have come down a lot lately, thank goodness. I always thought the short style a few years ago was quite abominable, even for women with pretty legs."

"Yes. I couldn't agree more, your ladyship." May knelt on the floor in front of the coal fire in Lady Fairfax's boudoir and adjusted some pins on the hem of a wool romaine afternoon frock. "There." She stood up and took a few steps backwards, while her client surveyed herself in a long gilt mirror and nodded, approvingly.

"Excellent, May. Quite excellent. I really don't know how you do it. And you must have had so many demands on your time lately, with Katy moving into the Moat."

May helped Lady Fairfax out of the partially made garment before replying, quietly, "Yes, it's been a busy few months, but I've tried not to let it interfere too much with my work. And Katy is quite capable, even though I sometimes think she looks as though a puff of wind might blow her away."

"Dear thing. Do give her my love. I shall call on her later on, when she's had more time to settle in. You must let me know when it would be convenient. How's Emily, by the way? I'm sure she must be thrilled to be living in Wilhampton, isn't she?"

"Oh yes, your ladyship." May fastened some hooks and eyes on the placket of the tweed skirt which Lady Fairfax had now put on again and continued, "We're just a little concerned about her schooling, though. My brother-in-law hoped to have got her into Wickfield House next September term, but unfortunately she may have to wait at least another year or more."

"What's happening to her meanwhile?"

May could not but appreciate the directness, the quickness of mind which had always been able to grasp the essence of a difficult situation and which had made Lady Fairfax, if not exactly loved, certainly greatly revered throughout the neighbourhood.

"Ethel Sharman is teaching her again for the moment," May replied, "as she did the summer before last when my sister was so ill. But I fear that Emily is really too far advanced now for the kind of tuition Ethel is able to offer."

There was a pause. May carefully folded up the dress and placed it, along with her other bits and pieces, in the small suitcase which she had brought with her.

Presently, Lady Fairfax said, "I can't promise anything, mind, but you do know I'm on the governing board of Wickfield, don't you, May? We've got a meeting coming up next week. I'll see if I can have a word or two afterwards with Miss Lawrence, the headmistress."

"Oh." May coloured. "I . . ." She did, indeed, know that Lady Fairfax was on the board of governors because Philip had shown her the school's brochure, but the last thing she would have dreamt of doing was to try to take advantage of the situation. "I do hope you did not think that I . . ." she continued, hesitantly.

Lady Fairfax cut her short. "Of course not, May. I know you better than that. But in certain instances I see no harm in seeing whether I can do anything to help. I understand Emily is a very bright little girl. Let's hope that whatever happens she will do well at Wickfield when she gets there."

On her way back to Cob Lane, May called in at the Moat. Although it was mid-March there had been freak snowstorms throughout the country and, as she crossed over the small bridge leading up to the front door, she found Emily, Helen Swayne and Daphne Chadwick attempting to make a snowman in the garden. Immediately, her niece disengaged herself from the others and came running towards her.

"Aunt Chip! Aunt Chip! Have you come to tea?" Emily threw her arms round May and looked up at her, expectantly.

"No, dear. I've just called to see Mummy for a few minutes. Is she in?"

"Yes. She and Rose are making curtains. Daddy's in London, but he'll be back tonight. Do stop to tea. We've got indigestibles."

"*What*, my dear?"

Emily went off into peals of laughter. "That's what Daddy calls them. You know, the baker's seven cakes for sixpence that Miss Sharman is always making us do sums about."

May smiled. "I think I'd better leave those to you and your

friends, Emily. Besides, I have to think of my figure these days."

"Well, you could still have a biscuit or something. Perhaps Mummy will make you change your mind."

Katy did, in fact, persuade May to stop for an early cup of tea with her alone. "I'll be glad of a break," she said, a little wearily. "Making all the upstairs curtains is more of a job than I bargained for. I suppose I should have got Burt and Burt to do them like the downstairs ones, but it seemed such a wicked extravagance."

It was the first time May had heard Katy refer directly to the cost of moving house. She hoped that her sister and brother-in-law had not underestimated their total commitment. Belle's legacy had seemed almost beyond belief, yet, nevertheless, May kept thinking of all the outgoings there must be just now: two young living-in maids, Rose and Miriam, for instance—not that either of them was getting more than five shilling a week. But then there was the Morris Cowley Philip had bought and all the furniture that was needed. True, the Moat was a comparatively small country residence and Katy had managed to pick up some excellent bargains at the local auctions. Philip had given her a book on antiques which she had put to good use, so much so that Mr Motcombe, the auctioneer's clerk in the furniture department of Butt and Swanton, had complimented her on the acquisition of a particularly fine Queen Anne walnut bureau bookcase. Even so, May thought, as she sat drinking tea in the small sitting-room overlooking the lawn where the three children were still playing, there was the garden to keep up and once Abel Firman, Maggie Fortescue's ancient gardener, could no longer manage it, some new man might want more than the thirty-two and sixpence which she believed old Abel to be getting.

"You look worried, May." Katy held out her hand for her sister's cup and refilled it. "Is anything wrong?"

"Oh no, my dear," May replied quickly, embarrassed at having to dissemble a little. "In fact, I may have some good news. Mind you, don't let on to anyone but Philip, but Lady Fairfax says that after the next governors' meeting she's going to have a word with Miss Lawrence about the possibility of getting Emily into Wickfield House a little earlier."

"*What?*"

"Yes. I happened to mention the difficulty, quite by chance after she'd asked about the child. She simply volunteered to see what she could do."

"Oh, *May*! It would be wonderful if Emily could start there this September. Helen and Daphne are both going then. Of course, they've had their names down for ages. God knows how Dick Swayne's going to afford the fees, but apparently he's determined to do it somehow. Emily's bound to feel so left out if she can't start with them. And Ethel, naturally, will be taking on some younger pupils this autumn, so the poor kid will be worse off than ever. Philip and I have been racking our brains to know what to do for the best."

"Well, don't get too excited, my dear. Perhaps I shouldn't have said anything to you yet, but I've just come from the Hall and I couldn't help wanting to let you know. It's almost like history repeating itself, isn't it? Lady Fairfax seems to be taking as much interest in Emily as she did in you when you were a little girl. Incidentally, she wants to call on you when you're straight."

"Oh." Katy flushed and turned away for a moment. When at last she spoke, her eyes had lost their temporary look of hopefulness which had been so apparent while May had been talking about Wickfield House. "It's complicated, isn't it?" she said, slowly.

"Complicated?"

"Well, yes. I mean, me, here, mistress of the Moat, a daughter down for Wickfield . . . You know. There's people in Wilhampton who give me a funny look sometimes. Even Edith, the other day . . . I'm sure she was trying to avoid me."

"Oh no, my dear. You must be mistaken. Edie loves you."

"Yes, I *know*. But she feels awkward. We both do. And her kids. They and Emily have nothing in common. I don't suppose I thought about all that sufficiently when Philip first proposed the idea. I felt I'd had enough of London and it would be lovely to come back here again. It's only really now that we've arrived that it's becoming so difficult. And this business about Lady Fairfax calling. Strictly speaking, I'm meant to call back—anyway, on people I don't know. Leave cards. All that sort of thing. Philip's made me get some. But May, I can't see myself doing that, can you?" Quite suddenly, Katy covered her face with her hands and burst into tears.

May went back to Cob lane more troubled than she cared to admit. Her little sister was up against problems far more demanding and confusing than the making of new curtains. She was a stranger on her home ground. She was out of her depth: neither mill manager's daughter nor wife of a local inhabitant, as she would have been had she married Maurice Fitzherbert. May was well aware that becoming wife and mistress of East Lodge would have necessitated plenty of adjustment; but with Maurice beside her, she felt, Katy would have found it so much easier. He was thought the world of in the district, just as his father had been. With his support and gentle encouragement, he would have helped his young wife over many a hurdle. He knew what to do; he had the right touch with all and sundry. He was unfailingly reliable and full of common sense unless, perhaps, one counted falling in love with Katy as a deviation from his customary conventional way of life. But surely he couldn't be blamed for that? She had been so lovely and appealing that summer of 1920, when she had come home to help nurse Flo and Maurice had had to make regular visits to the Mill House. She was just as lovely today—more so, perhaps. But though her appearance might now be that of a desirable woman, she was still very much a child at heart. That wilful mercurial temperament needed some kind of sheet anchor. Suddenly, there crept into May's mind an old adage of her mother's which she had not thought about in ten years: 'The ivy needs the oak'.

Once inside her front door, she was pleased to find that her carefully-guarded fire was still glowing. She was also rather relieved to feel that Ethel would not be calling that evening, as she was going to a concert in the Assembly Rooms in Westonbury. May had declined to accompany her because, besides having so much work to do, she knew that a string quartet would not play the kind of music which appealed to her. She much preferred what she called a 'proper tune', one to which she could dance, or hum, or—at least nowadays—simply listen to on the wireless.

With her customary efficiency, May swiftly lit the gas mantle, made up the fire, washed her hands in her tiny scullery and went back into the sitting-room, where she switched on Duck and Collar's present, delighted to find that she was still in time for the *Thé Dansant* immediately preceding Children's Hour, which had been advertised in the *Radio Times*.

There was nothing better to take one's mind off one's troubles, May reflected, as she settled down to work on Lady Fairfax's dress, than a little light dance music, especially when it was Henry Hall and his orchestra playing *A Room with a View* and *My Blue Heaven*.

15

Philip Mason sat in his small study at the Moat—the one which Maggie Fortescue had always used—and tore up twelve sheets of foolscap. It was the middle of July and he had written four chapters of a novel. The fifth was now in the waste-paper basket.

Out of the window he could see Katy talking to Abel. They seemed to be in earnest consultation about something or other. He knew that they got on well together and he was pleased. Abel was not one of those people about whom Katy sometimes complained, the ones who looked at her 'sideways'. Abel called her "Ma'am" and was obviously impressed by her knowledge of gardening. Philip also sometimes expressed surprise at her aptitude in this connection; then she would remind him, gaily, that he had forgotten she was the daughter of a man who had regularly won first prize at the annual Westonbury Show, for growing roses as well as onions.

Yet it was not often that her light-heartedness broke through these days. He sensed that she was finding their new way of life far more trying than she cared to let him know. He was annoyed that he seemed to be able to do so little about it. Surely there was nothing wrong in a local girl coming back with a comparatively affluent husband to live in the place where she was born? He found himself becoming angry at the small-mindedness, the illogical and, as he felt, totally unreasonable attitudes adopted by so many Wilhampton residents and all the petty gossip that went on. He only heard about it, of course, from Katy; and half the time he felt—and, indeed, hoped—that, with her vivid imagination, she was probably fantasising. On the other hand, he supposed that there must be a few grains of truth in what she said. Otherwise, he would not catch her looking so strained when she was off guard.

Philip had never lived in a community before—especially a country one. His early upbringing in Putney could scarcely be counted because, even then, the Masons had kept themselves very much to themselves: his father seemingly content to devote his life to his books, his mother delicate and increasingly withdrawn. When they had moved to the West End and his mother's health began to fail, they seemed to have fewer friends, their old ones dropping away when it became no longer possible to visit or entertain. He had never realised until now how lonely his father must have been and what the advent of Belle must have meant to him. He supposed that, in a way, meeting Katy had had something of the same sort of effect on him.

If only he could make her see now that she had nothing to worry about, that they had taken a big step forward together and that everything would come right. Perhaps if the book which he had set himself to write proved to be a winner, she would be able to laugh away the feeling that people thought she was giving herself airs. In any case, she would have enough to give herself airs about. If money did not mean all that much to the people of Wilhampton, surely being the wife of a successful author did? The trouble was that he was finding writing so much more difficult than he had anticipated. When he had shown Katy his initial chapters, although she had obviously been very interested, he had been a shade disappointed that she had not been more enthusiastic about them. She was a voracious reader and he valued her opinion. He decided that he would not show her any more of his work until someone else had seen it. That was why he was going up to London the following day to see an agent. He was also due for a visit to the shop and was intending to combine the two engagements, spending a night in their old flat, the use of this being one of the conditions laid down when he had installed Jack Lumley, his manager, in it.

Presently, he got up to join Katy in the garden. There seemed no point in starting to rewrite Chapter Five until he had had a personal talk with someone from A. J. Smythe's and received a report on the first four. Meanwhile, he would try to forget about his fictional *Sun in the Morning* and try to enjoy some of the real stuff which happened to be all too rare that summer.

Katy was bending over one of the borders, weeding, by the time he reached her. Abel was nowhere to be seen. He caught her by the waist and attempted to kiss the nape of her neck, but she straightened up quickly and disengaged herself from his embrace.

"Philip, please. Abel's somewhere around."

"So what?"

"Well, I mean . . ." She backed a few steps away from him. There was a small smudge of earth on one of her cheeks. Her eyes had that discouraging look in them that he had come to resent.

"We're married, aren't we. It's not as if I was trying to play fast and loose with your local adulteress, as I gather Grace Armitage up at the Warren is, or was, called."

"No. Don't be silly. But I think this sort of thing ought to be reserved for when we're quite alone. Besides, Emily will soon be coming back from Bulbarrow and probably bringing Helen with her. I expect she'll have been up on the Swaynes' old pony again. Apparently, she's longing to learn to ride."

"So I gather. Well, that's all right by me if you can arrange it."

Katy was silent. "I suppose she could go to Joan Cory's riding school," she said after a while, "although I must say I'm not all that keen."

"Why on earth not?"

Again she was silent before eventually replying, "I daresay I'm just nervous about it all. And when little girls first get bitten with riding, as I believe Emily will, then there's no stopping them. She'll want a pony of her own and goodness knows what."

It was Philip who now did not answer immediately. Then, as they began walking over to the summer-house together, he said, "Hadn't we better meet that one when the time comes, darling? Besides, now that Emily's going to Wickfield House this autumn, there won't be all that opportunity for riding. I must say your sister did a damn good job over that."

"Oh, *Philip*." She wished he would not talk in this way. It seemed crass, insensitive. "You *know* May acted quite unconsciously."

"Of course I do, silly. All the same, I believe your eldest sister's *unconscious* often works a great deal better than most people's conscious."

They went inside the summer-house. She could not help smiling at his last remark and he took her hand. This time she did not remove it.

Katy knew that Philip was right about May. There was a

curious artlessness about her which somehow achieved the most amazing results. Totally without guile, she went on her way, free from almost all the adverse emotions which destroyed, or at least hampered, the rest of mankind. True, she worried, but her worries were all for others and even these she tried not to show. She was not a particularly religious woman but she seemed to have a blind faith that by doing her best, the best would automatically follow. Everyone liked her and—with the possible exception of George Fuller, Cyril Butt and Grace Armitage—she liked everyone. What was more, May adored Wilhampton. To her there was no place on earth to compare with it, not that she really knew any other place to compare it with. All the same, as she grew older, she was often apt to remark that certain things in her home town were infinitely superior to those to be found in Westonbury: the Wilhampton vegetables, for instance, which mostly came from the Hall nurseries; the water in the reservoir half way up Breconbury Down, which was pumped by Ikey Shepherd in his shining immaculately-kept pumping house; the doctor, who was the kindest and cleverest on earth. Even the unpredictability of the Willon, which had, in turn, carried away her father, her youngest brother, her mother and, in the end, the family home, was somehow put down to 'the way of the river'—albeit now mercifully under stricter control, since the completion of the work which the Fairfaxes had put in hand on Bulbarrow Sluice and the surrounding hatches after the catastrophic floods in the winter of 1929.

One could say, Katy reflected wrily, that May was altogether too good, too trusting. And yet, she was no fool when it came to the question of human relationships. She was acutely aware of atmosphere, of problems which had not even been voiced. Katy knew that her sister completely understood, far more than her husband, the sense of insecurity from which she now suffered.

There was the sound of children's voices on the bridge over the front driveway and presently Emily and Helen came into view, Emily with a bandaged arm. Katy stood up and went towards her daughter quickly.

"Darling! Whatever's happened to you?"

It was Helen Swayne who answered. "I'm so sorry, Mrs Mason, but she had a fall. Beauty slipped on the cobble stones in the yard. My mother bathed Emily's arm at once and put on iodine. She says that she doesn't think there's anything to worry about."

"But . . . how deep are the cuts?" Katy did not want to doubt the efficacy of her neighbour's first aid treatment, especially in the presence of Dorothy's daughter yet, all the same, she had a particular fear of such mishaps, remembering how her own grandfather had died from lockjaw. If Emily had fallen in the yard, there would bound to have been horse manure about.

"It's only a graze, Mummy, I promise you. It really doesn't hurt at all now," Emily said, quickly.

Katy let the matter drop, but with misgiving. As soon as Helen had gone home after tea, she decided to undo the bandage and take a look. Certainly, the area above Emily's elbow looked clean but definitely red and swollen.

"I think," she said, thoughtfully, "perhaps we'll just let the doctor see it." Ignoring Emily's protests, she went downstairs and telephoned Maurice Fitzherbert.

Fortunately, she found him in. "If you bring her round straight away, Katy," he informed her, "I can see her before evening surgery." Chivvying a still-protesting daughter they set off for East Lodge.

The days had passed when Katy would have automatically gone to the surgery entrance at the doctor's house, along with the majority of local inhabitants who were 'on the panel'. She and Philip had become paying patients—not that as yet they had had to bother Maurice much; but nevertheless they were now entitled to knock on his front door through which, this evening, they were ushered into the hall and along to the drawing-room by a rather scared young woman whom Katy did not know, but could only assume to be one of the innumerable domestics who seemed to come and go in rapid succession at East Lodge, ever since Maurice's wife had been in charge of it.

It was the same room into which Katy had first gone eleven years ago when, shaking with apprehension, she had come to a buffet party before being escorted by Maurice to her very first dance. Now, during the few moments she and Emily waited there, she thought how little it had changed. There was the same heavy Victorian furniture which she remembered in his parents' day, the enormous ebony-framed pictures of highland cattle; even the antimacassars on the chairbacks looked as if, apart from possibly one or two washings, they might have been placed there by 'Old Mother Mothballs', as she happened to know May had called Maurice's mother. She wondered why the present mistress of East Lodge had done so little to the room and found herself thinking about how she would set about improving it: pale walls, flowers, a little chintz, she felt, would have worked wonders.

And then Maurice was with them. Gravely and courteously, he took them along to his small consulting room in between the surgery and the rest of the house. With infinite care and gentleness, he examined Emily's wound and re-dressed it. Then he sent her back to the drawing-room so that he might have a few words with Katy alone.

"You're thinking about lockjaw, aren't you?" he said, closing the door and coming straight to the point.

"Yes, Maurice."

"Look, Katy. There have been certain adverse reactions to the anti-tetanus serum. The treatment is still in its infancy. Dorothy Swayne did a good job and what is more she did it immediately. I don't think you need worry. I see plenty of worse injuries daily—and there must be even more I never see. Just keep an eye on it. There shouldn't be any problems." He smiled and changed the subject. "How's the Moat coming along?"

"Oh, fine, Maurice. I . . . we . . . were hoping perhaps you and Clare would come to a meal with us sometime, perhaps Sunday lunch?"

For a fleeting moment a look of distress, almost hopelessness, seemed to cross his face and then it was quickly masked. His normal pleasant manner reasserted itself and he said, quietly, "It's very kind of you, Katy. Perhaps a little later on. Clare . . . hasn't been feeling too good lately."

She knew that it was an excuse and that he knew that she knew. She stood up. "I mustn't keep you, Maurice. Thank you so very much for seeing Emily."

He stood also. She noticed how grey his hair had become at the temples, how he stooped much more these days, how incredibly like his father he was becoming. She had made no attempt at dressing up to see the doctor, as many people in her position were apt to do. She was still wearing what she thought of as her gardening clothes: a simple but well-fitting brown linen dress and old brogue shoes. Her hair was slightly tousled. Although she had made up her face carefully that morning, this was no longer so apparent, for that teatime she had simply rubbed the smudge of earth from her cheek and dabbed some powder on a rather shiny nose.

Yet, after Maurice Fitzherbert had shown Katy Mason and her daughter out, he had gone back to his consulting room and sat quite still for several minutes, lost in thought. He supposed that Katy must have been about ten years old when she had first seemed to need his help, coming down the steep wooden steps of St. Mark's steeple when the Reverend Donaldson had taken them up to see his bells. She would have been about eleven when, forgetting her shyness for once, she had warned him that he might catch diphtheria if he put the gobstopper he had been sucking back into his mouth after it had rolled in the gutter. He could remember quite clearly trying to allay her fears by telling her that Abie Grant, his father's dispenser, would be certain to have something to save him from that. Then there had been a gap when they had not met for some time. Apart from brief visits, his medical training and army service had kept him away from Wilhampton. She must have been eighteen, that evening when he had surprised her in the meadows while she was taking a rest from the heart-breaking task of helping to nurse her dying sister. He could visualize her quite distinctly, as if it were yesterday: the way she had put up her hair, the slimness of her waist, the simple blue cotton frock she was wearing and how its bodice strained a little over her small rounded breasts, her large eyes which seemed unconsciously to be asking for love and protection and the way her colour seemed to come and go. And then—Philip Mason, damn him, had stepped in and shattered all his hopes and dreams.

Gradually, the murmuring from the other side of his consulting-room wall grew louder. He pulled out his watch. It was two minutes past six. He had never, unless he had been called out in an emergency, been late for surgery before. Wearily, he stood up and opened a door. The hum of conversation ceased abruptly and Maurice Fitzherbert called for his first patient.

16

"I'll do my best to let you have a report on these as quickly as possible, Mr Mason."

The young woman sitting behind the desk at A. J. Smythe's held up the four chapters of *Sun in the Morning* and flashed Philip a brilliant smile. In fact, she seemed to have been smiling at him most of the time since he had first entered her office, which had been encouraging. She had glanced briefly at the synopsis which he had attached to his slim folder and said, "Hmm, sounds interesting, almost like a love affair between town and country. And I approve your title."

Philip had felt even more hopeful. It was good to have found someone so positive and optimistic. He had been expecting to consult a Mr Burgess and had been initially rather annoyed at being told that Miss Woodley would see him as Mr Burgess had been unexpectedly called away. But he had soon come round to thinking that possibly a female agent was exactly what he wanted. After all, he knew enough about the book trade to know that it was mostly ladies who bought books, ladies who liked novels, ladies for whom he was presumably trying to write. He found himself wondering why Miss Woodley was not married and how she had come to be doing her present job. He could not say that she was exactly pretty. Her features were too bold, her figure too flat and her whole appearance really rather mannish. She seemed to be still adhering to the fashions of a few years ago: her dark hair was eton cropped and she wore a curiously shapeless black sleeveless dress that contrasted sharply with her bare white arms, which she waved about rather dramatically—especially the one holding a long cigarette holder. Yet she definitely exuded some kind of sex appeal which Philip could not quite define. He felt that she bore a slight resemblance to a cross between Belle and Grace Armitage.

"When do you go back to the country, Mr Mason?" she continued. "Incidentally, may I call you Philip? I'm Barbara. I always like to get on christian name terms with my authors as soon as I can. It's so much easier when it comes to discussing their books."

"Of course." Philip found her friendliness disarming. And she had actually called him an author. All the same, he did not think he could quite bring himself to say Barbara just yet. "I shall be leaving London tomorrow at midday," he informed her, "after I have seen to some business at the shop."

"Ah." She looked at him thoughtfully, the elbow of one white arm now resting on her desk as it held up a well-manicured hand to support her chin. "You don't know how lucky you are, Philip," she said, at length, "to have such *intimate* knowledge of the book world. I really can't wait to start reading this." She glanced down momentarily at his manuscript and then raised her greeny-grey eyes once more to his. "If I can," she went on, "I'll see what I can do tonight and give you a ring first thing in the morning."

"Really?" It was more than he had dared to hope for.

"Where will you be staying?"

"At my flat. I mean, at my former home. Above Masons. I let my manager have it on the understanding that there would be a bed for me there whenever I wanted it."

"Ah, I *see*." Barbara Woodley had a low husky voice which often laid great emphasis on certain words, somehow making them seem extremely meaningful—if only to her. It occurred to him that perhaps she had a sore throat and was smoking so much today in order to soothe it, as the cigarette advertisements were constantly advocating.

Philip rose to go and she stood also, coming round the desk to accompany him to the door. He was aware of her heavy musky scent—not the pleasant summery kind that Katy used—which he did not care for at all. In fact, on the way back to Davies Street, he thought how much more attractive Barbara Woodley could have made herself if she had wanted to; although perhaps she did not really care for men, except as business propositions. For all he knew, she might be one of those incomprehensible women like those in Radclyffe Hall's *Well of Loneliness*. He remembered all the fuss there had been about the book three years before, how the judge had condemned it outright at the obscenity trial. Philip had managed to get hold of copy, but he had not let Katy read it. Still, there was no point in making conjectures about Barbara Woodley's private life. It had nothing to do with him. The great thing was that she seemed interested in his work and that was all that mattered.

For the rest of the day Philip was kept busy going through certain accounts and discussing various problems with Jack Lumley, so much so that when, at eight o'clock, Jack's wife suggested sending them both down some cold supper on a tray, it seemed the most sensible thing to accept her kind offer. Philip had not been up to town for a fortnight and was surprised at what a lot of tricky questions had arisen in his absence to which only he could provide an answer.

He was also surprised next morning when, before the shop opened, Jack came to tell him that he was wanted on the telephone. Surely . . . no . . . it wasn't possible that Barbara Woodley would be ringing him so soon. It must be Katy. He hoped there was nothing wrong and that she was telephoning, as she was sometimes apt to do, merely to ask him to bring back something or other which she was unable to buy in Westonbury.

"Philip?" The voice seemed even more husky than it had yesterday. "I thought those chapters quite fascinating."

He found himself swallowing hard. His heart began to thump as if he had been running.

"I'm glad," he managed to say at last.

"Look, we *must* talk about them. There's certain things I'd like to suggest. I mean, I don't want to interfere in any way, but . . . you know, just one or two tiny points. I think it would be helpful to meet again before you go and bury yourself in all that cow parsley or whatever it is you do down in Wilhampton. I was wondering . . . You couldn't have lunch with me today, could you?"

"I . . ." He had told Katy he would catch the midday train. She and Emily were going to the Westonbury Show and he had promised to look for them in the tea tent at four o'clock and drive them home. "I could," he went on, quickly. "I shall just have to alter some arrangements in the country." Katy would surely understand. This was so much more important.

"Oh, *good*. It *does* seem such an opportunity, Philip. Can you meet me at one o'clock at the Casa Mara?" She gave him the address and rang off immediately.

Katy was actually none too pleased when he got through to her a few minutes later, but on hearing how impressed A. J.

Smythe's appeared to be with what he had shown them, she gave in with a good grace. As he put down the receiver, he realised that he had omitted to mention that it was a lady who was taking him out to lunch; but then he reflected that it would be much easier to explain about all that when he got back to Wilhampton.

During the morning Philip found his thoughts straying more and more to his forthcoming engagement with Barbara Woodley. For one thing, apart from his stepmother, he had never been taken out to lunch by a female before. Even if this was a business affair, surely he should pay? Would Barbara want to go over his manuscript with him at the table? Or were her 'one or two points' simply something she wished to discuss in more general terms? Then he was surprised at her choice of restaurant, for the Casa Mara was nowhere near A. J. Smythe's. It was in Kensington—a long way from the Strand. But he supposed that there was probably some very good explanation and he would soon find out.

He arrived a little before one and waited in the small foyer which, after the glare outside, seemed incredibly dark. At one point he began to wonder whether Barbara might also be lurking in one of the dim alcoves and took the precaution of wandering round to make sure. Then, to his relief, he saw her coming through the door. With the light behind her she made rather a striking silhouette. It could almost have been that of a young boy, except that she was wearing a straight, thin, yet rather revealing dress—a kind which he believed Katy would describe as 'button-through'—long pear-shaped earrings and, on the hand which she raised in greeting, he noticed several bangles around the wrist. To his dismay, he also noticed that she did not appear to be carrying his manuscript. He had a copy, of course, but could she possibly have left it in a taxi? Surely she wasn't intending to *keep* his initial chapters?

"Hullo, there!" At least Barbara did not seem to be worried about anything.

"Hullo."

"Would you like a drink here or shall we go straight through and have one while we're ordering? I've booked a table right at the end where we shall be least disturbed. There's so much to-ing and fro-ing here."

He was annoyed with himself for not asking her first about a drink. Feeling that it was expected of him to comply with her latter suggestion, he answered, "Yes, perhaps it would be best to have drinks at the table, you must let me . . ."

With a quick, "This is on the firm, Philip," she brushed his remark aside and they followed a waiter down a dark passageway between separate little cubicles resembling, he felt, horses' loose-boxes, each seemingly lit by scarcely more than a night-light. When they had eventually squeezed themselves side by side behind their table, he became uncomfortably aware of two things: the overpowering musky scent she had worn yesterday and the fact that it was more or less impossible for their thighs not to touch.

"You'd like a martini, wouldn't you? They make rather good ones here." She had turned to face him and her lips, when she spoke, seemed less than two or three inches from his.

"Thank you. A martini sounds . . . fine."

Then, when the waiter placed the drinks in front of them, she raised her own and, looking him once again full in the face, said solemnly, "To *Sun in the Morning*," before giving a low little laugh.

Philip glowed. His amazing luck at having been taken on by Barbara Woodley instead of Mr Burgess, her obvious admiration for his work, the exceptionally strong martini to which he was not accustomed—especially at midday—were all combining to make him feel on top of the world. His book was going to be a winner. He'd had an expert's opinion about that. It had been silly of Katy not to have recognised the quality of his first four chapters at once, silly of him to have ever let her lack of enthusiasm depress him. After all, his wife was still very much a provincial little thing at heart. She did not *know* what went to make a best-seller. This woman beside him did. Barbara was reading manuscripts every day. But, incredibly, it would seem that she had not read anything as good as *Sun in the Morning* for a long time.

"It's so . . . refreshing, Philip," she was now saying. "Of course, you'll be *expanding* the characters all the time."

"Expanding?"

"Yes, well, developing. I mean, so far we've only got Elspeth in her . . . how shall I put it . . . *unawakened* days."

Again he noticed, just as he had done yesterday, the slightly mysterious allusive way in which she spoke. She had somehow managed to make the word 'unawakened' sound infinitely exciting.

"Is that one of the points you mentioned that you wanted to talk to me about?" he asked, becoming more at ease with her.

"Did I?" She laughed again. "Maybe. But as a matter of fact, Philip, I've really no criticism. I *long* to read more. I'm *dying* to know when Howard . . ." She stopped, suddenly.

"When Howard what?"

This time she gave him a look of mock disapproval. "Oh, come now, Philip. You know perfectly well what I'm waiting for. I'm always interested to know how my authors deal with the subject. Personally, I should think you'd do it rather well."

All his growing confidence deserted him. He found himself becoming hot all over. Fortunately, their food arrived at that point and Barbara appeared not to notice his discomfiture as she began to eat.

It was not until the end of the meal, after they had talked—mostly about himself and his life in Wilhampton—that he began to wonder what the time was. He had told Katy he would catch either the three-thirty or the five-thirty train. He was sure that the first one was now out of the question. Even so, he felt that some sort of move should be made. For one thing, surely Barbara would have to get back to A. J. Smythe's. Surreptitiously, he looked at his watch.

She was quick to notice. Dropping a hand lightly on his, she said, "Philip, I'm so sorry. You must have been wondering what on earth I've done with your manuscript. It's quite safe, but it's at my flat. I left it there when I went to the office this morning meaning to pick it up on my way here, but I got held up by an incredibly dull man who's writing a book about the Andes. So I came straight on as I didn't want to be too late. But I only live a few steps away. Would you care to come along and get it with me?"

"Yes. Yes, of course." He felt tremendously relieved.

After reassuring him about lunch being on the firm, she signed the bill and then, allowing him to leave the tip, they made their way outside.

It was very hot on the pavement and he was glad when she led him down a side street into a small shady square. At a tall Victorian dilapidated-looking house in one corner, she stopped and got out her keys. "It's rather a sad façade, don't you think," she said, half apologetically, "I believe it belonged to some American who came to grief in the Wall Street crash. Then some entrepreneur snapped it up for a song. He was meant to be converting it into separate flats but so far nothing much has happened. I've just got a bed-sitting-room on the first floor and the use of a bathroom. But at least my room's large. When I'm feeling depressed I like to imagine all the receptions that must once have taken place in it. Although sometimes, I must admit, that makes me feel even more sorry for myself."

He had not thought of Barbara Woodley as ever feeling sorry for herself. She did not appear to be that kind of person, although he was still uncertain as to what kind of person she really was. He could have kicked himself for not asking more about her at lunch.

As soon as he followed her into her room, Philip could see what she meant about it. It was certainly large and the ceiling was high and ornate; yet the paintwork was peeling and there was an overall look of neglect about the place. Heavy worn curtains, assisted by the plane trees now in full leaf in the square, shut out much of the light. For a while, the green murkiness prevented him from seeing into the corners, but presently he became aware of a screen in one of them, round which he could just discern a small gas ring and a wash bowl; in another, to his astonishment, there was a bed made up on the floor. There appeared to be little other furniture, but a vast quantity of books and pile upon pile of papers and manuscripts. He wondered where his own was.

"It's not quite what you were expecting, is it, Philip?" Barbara had made no move to look for *Sun in the Morning*, but was standing watching him, almost defiantly.

"I . . . well, I don't know what I was expecting, exactly." He smiled, but he felt uneasy and wished to goodness that he had not been obliged to visit the place where she lived.

"No?" This time she gave another of her low little laughs. He saw that she seemed to be deliberately fiddling with one of the buttons at the top of her dress. He watched her silently as she undid it and her fingers dropped to the one below. It was very quiet in the room now, except for the occasional distant muffled sound of traffic from the Kensington Road. He tried to tell himself that he did not know what she was about, that all he wanted was to find his manuscript and get out. Yet somehow he could only stand and stare at her as she revealed more and more of her slim boyish body.

"You asked me at the beginning of lunch, Philip," Barbara went on slowly, in that strange hypnotic husky voice, "about those one or two little points I mentioned. Well, as I said, I've really no criticisms—only that at this stage of the book I honestly believe I could help you *expand* Elspeth, if only you would stop looking so frightened and come here."

17

"Emily dear, stand still, do. I can't possibly fit you for your school overalls if you keep jigging that silly yo-yo up and down."

"Sorry, Aunt Chip."

It was the end of August and Katy was ill in bed with summer 'flu. May had volunteered to finish making the remainder of the uniform which the pupils of Wickfield House were requested to wear. Personally, she thought much of it quite unnecessary, especially the items listed for a day-girl. How could Emily possibly need three long-sleeved red tobralco overalls? Or five long-sleeved wincyette navy and white striped blouses with ten detachable white piqué collars?

Katy had bought most of the basic requirements from Burt and Burt in Westonbury: her daughter's navy West of England overcoat, for instance; a smart navy serge skirt and pleated gym tunic; and such necessities as Emily's 'board', the straw boater with the navy ribbon and red badge on the front, which all the Wickfield young ladies took a pride in wearing as long, so Emily informed May, as it did not look too new. "No one wants to look like a *new* girl, Aunt Chip. Helen and Daphne and I are determined to make our boards look positively ancient as soon as possible."

All the same, Emily looked very much like a new girl, May thought, as she accompanied her and her mother to Wickfield House on the first day of the September term in 1931. Her face had that apprehensive vulnerable look of which May had been so aware when she had stayed in Davies Street getting on for two years ago now. Since Emily had come to live in Wilhampton May thought that the child had seemed to recover her usual *joie de vivre*; but just lately there had been times when she was not so sure. She wondered if it had something to do with Katy, whether perhaps Emily over-reacted to her mother's recent unaccountable fits of depression, however much May knew that her sister tried to disguise them.

There was no doubt that both Katy and Emily had, understandably, been disappointed that Philip had had to be in

London on this particular day, even though Katy had learned to drive the family car and delivering a daughter to school on such an occasion was not exactly a father's responsibility. Indeed, it was an exclusively female gathering, May noted, which milled about in the hall of Wickfield's junior house, as more and more small girls arrived with their escorts, incuding Helen Swayne and her mother. There appeared to be no sign of Daphne Chadwick, but May supposed that the little thing must have already been taken care of as, owing to her grandfather's imminent retirement and the fact that her parents were still in India, Daphne had been obliged to become a boarder and, consequently, taken to the school the previous evening.

Always interested in whatever was going on around her—especially in a situation such as today's which she had not hitherto experienced—May was delighted to see that Emily's uniform fitted a great deal better than most of the other children's; also that her niece was one of the prettiest amongst them. Presently, there was a call for silence and then, one by one, each new girl was put in the charge of a companion: a child who had already been at the school for at least two terms. In the case of Emily, a diminutive ginger-haired little boarder called Charlotte Blakeley suddenly whisked her away through an inner door and Katy and May were left, rather sadly, to make their way outside and back to the car.

"It was good of you to come, May. I must say I felt in need of a bit of support. Wickfield's so vast. I didn't like seeing Emily swallowed up like that, did you?" Katy opened the near side door of the Morris for her sister and then went round and slid into the driving seat.

"No. But it isn't as if she's a boarder like Daphne Chadwick and that other poor mite who led her away. You'll be fetching her home again at half past three."

"Yes. Silly of me to mind," Katy replied, drawing away from the kerb. "But with Philip having to go to London so much these days, Emily's a good little companion."

May was silent for a while. She knew what Katy meant. She had been aware of Philip's increasing absences from home for some time and wondered whether all was well with the shop. She did not like to probe but occasionally, as now, it seemed as if her sister might almost welcome some kind of friendly enquiry.

"How's Philip getting on with his book?" May asked at length. "I suppose having to be in town rather holds him up."

"Yes, in a way, although . . ." Katy waited for a policeman to wave them over a cross roads and then went on, "It's really often the book which takes him to London."

"How do you mean?"

"Well, he's got these agents. Apparently there's someone there who's advising him as he goes along. A mannish young woman, as he calls her, who is very enthusiastic about it."

"Oh." May had not come across any mannish young women. In Wilhampton, even if a girl was as 'plain as a yard of pump water', as her mother was apt to put it, she was never described as mannish. She felt her brother-in-law's statement to be rather odd.

"I hope she knows what she's talking about," Katy continued, expertly double-declutching as she negotiated some of Westonbury's narrow old streets. May was surprised at what a good careful driver her youngest sister had become—an even better one, she felt, than Philip, who was apt to jerk the gears and get annoyed when he was overtaken.

"I suppose she wouldn't be in her job if she didn't, would she?" May answered, trying to be comforting in a conversation which was somewhat beyond her. She found it hard to imagine how anyone wrote a book and had been astonished when she had heard that her brother-in-law was attempting it.

"No. All the same, I should have thought it would have been far better for Philip to get on and finish it now. I know I wouldn't want anybody breathing down my neck if I were trying to create something or other."

May could not help noticing the tone of exasperation which had crept into Katy's voice and she kept thinking about their conversation long after her sister had dropped her in Cob Lane. Often that day she laid down her sewing and sat staring into the fire, allowing the cat to jump up into her lap. Katy wasn't happy. She had not really been happy since coming back to Wilhampton. Apart from all the other difficulties her sister was up against, May felt that it was possible she had been away too long. Katy had severed—or almost severed—that strange hold which May always vowed her home ground seemed to exercise over its inhabitants; although, when she came to think about it, she had to admit that it was not necessarily those who were born and bred there who seemed to come under its spell. Had not Philip himself been the prime motivator in moving his wife and child back to the place? Ever since he had spent his holiday working on the Swaynes' farm during the summer when he was courting Katy, May knew that he had hankered after living in the district. Nevertheless, what, ostensibly, had seemed a good idea did not now appear to be working out. May wondered whether it would ever do so. She was still convinced that she had been right to maintain her own independence and decline to live at the Moat as she had been asked, but, all the same, she wished that she was able to give her youngest sister more positive support. It had been good to have been needed this morning, even if it was not for very long. She was looking forward to hearing how Emily had got on when the child paid her a promised visit at the weekend.

May was by no means the only one waiting on such news. That evening, Ethel Sharman called in soon after tea. She, too, had just started out on a new term's lessons. It was often a difficult time for her and this September she had felt particularly bereft. For several years she had known and taught the same three little girls—Emily, perhaps, not so long as the others, yet Ethel felt that she knew her better. Emily had certainly been her favourite, although she had done her best not to show it. She wondered so much what would happen to them all now that they had left her care. It was hard having to adjust to new faces, different levels of intelligence. She was therefore all the more grateful for the unexpected compensation that had just come her way and about which, after listening to May's description of all that had taken place that morning, she proceeded to give her neighbour the details.

"I've got another new pupil arriving next week, May. You'll never guess who. Not in a month of Sundays."

"Then tell me, Ethel, do." May looked up from the buttonhole she was working on a blouse for the mayoress elect: Arnold Parker's daughter-in-law.

"Phoebe Moreton," replied Ethel, watching intently to see the effect the name would have on her listener.

"*Phoebe Moreton*? Oh, chippatoo! You don't mean it, Ethel."

"Yes I do. Lady Fairfax asked me to go round to the Hall this afternoon and it's all fixed up. Apparently her daughter and her husband are off to the States for a couple of months. The boy, John William, is at boarding-school, as you know. But Lady Moreton is insistent that the girl must always be taught privately. It seems, however, that she finds it difficult to keep a governess." Though not given to gossip, Ethel's voice now dropped to a confidential whisper. She was obviously excited. "It seems to me," she went on, "Phoebe's a bit wild. But there's another drawback. The governesses don't like old Nanny Barlow forever interfering and telling them how to care for the child. Lady Fairfax didn't *say* that exactly . . . I mean, not in so many words. But one could sense that there's a difficult situation going on in Suffolk. Anyway, the long and the short of it is that while Sir Charles and Lady Moreton are abroad, Phoebe and Nanny Barlow and some young helper called Daisy from their local village are all coming to Wilhampton, and Phoebe will be brought to me each day for lessons."

"Well I never did. But you'll like that, won't you, Ethel?" May resumed her sewing, conscious that she had let herself get behindhand with it that day.

"Yes, I suppose so. It's a challenge, so to speak. But mind you, I don't want a subversive influence disrupting my classes. I don't quite know *how* wild Phoebe is. I've still got Elsie Jane, remember, until her parents move after Christmas, and she's so easily led astray."

"I'm sure you'll manage, Ethel. And besides, I shouldn't think Lady Fairfax would stand any nonsense from her granddaughter. It will probably do the child a power of good to have a spell at the Hall."

Ethel's news certainly took May's mind off her more personal concerns and, later on when she was in bed that night, she found herself speculating as to which side of the family Phoebe's wildness came from. She would never have described dear Miss Alicia—as she always thought of her—as *wild*. On the other hand, she was obviously highly strung. There was that bad breakdown she had had the year after John William had been born. There had been a lot of speculation about that, although no one in Wilhampton had really heard much. The Fairfaxes had hushed it up pretty effectively, simply letting it be known that their daughter had been overdoing things and ordered to have a complete rest. But May had been well aware of the rumours which had gone round, how some people hinted that it was a case of delayed puerperal depression. Personally, she had never thought that. She had felt it probably had much more to do with husband trouble. Besides, the word *divorce* had actually crept into certain conversations, as well as the name of Grace Armitage. May, like Ethel Sharman, did not hold with gossip but, all the same, she had not been able to help *wondering*. The Moretons had not spent a great deal of time in Wilhampton that year, but it was well known that Grace, according to the Fairfaxes' housekeeper, was forever "waltzing off to London". May supposed that it was just possible that Charles Moreton had fallen victim to whatever strange alchemy Grace seemed to have for the opposite sex. Men were so fickle, as she knew to her cost. They could so easily be led astray.

Was that, she hazarded, as her mind reverted to her own kith and kin, what had happened to Philip? Why Katy was so on edge these days? Unable to settle down? That derisory reference she had made this morning to some "mannish young woman . . ." The more May thought about it, the more she came to realise that Grace Armitage could hardly be called the fluffy feminine type.

18

"There's my bus, Aunt Chip."

Emily's rendering of *Over the Waves* came to an abrupt halt. The lid of May's piano suddenly shut with a bang, after which she heard her niece dash out of the front door and across the green into Wilhampton market square.

From her bedroom window in Cob Lane, May stood watching the flying figure, waited for several minutes until it was joined by Helen Swayne and an older Wickfield pupil and then, after seeing all three board the Westonbury bus, she went back to making her bed.

It had been like that for several weeks now. Ever since their respective mothers had mutually agreed that, at least in the mornings, Emily and Helen could be trusted to take this form of transport to school as long as Hazel Betts could escort them, May had become accustomed to the front door of her cottage opening unceremoniously, often as early as seven forty-five, and straight away finding herself listening to some of her niece's latest musical accomplishments.

Although she was pleased to have this fleeting daily contact with the child, May was becoming increasingly perturbed by Emily's almost obsessional fear of being late for school through missing her bus. However much she pointed out that the driver always waited at least ten minutes in the market square and, if the worst came to the worst, there was always a second bus which followed on in a quarter of an hour, Emily was invariably out of the door as soon as the big red double-decker came into sight before it slowly turned round and halted in its customary place, while the driver and conductor sauntered off to the local café for a cup of coffee.

May had actually brought up the subject of the child's unnatural agitation with Katy, only to receive the rather despairing reply, "Oh, I *know*. I've even mentioned it to Maurice because Emily won't sit still long enough to eat a proper breakfast, but all he says is that she'll probably come out of it and meanwhile I'd better give her a piece of toast to eat as she runs down the drive." To which May had said, "Or let her have breakfast with me rather than playing the piano."

Emily was completely oblivious of the fact that her mother and aunt were so concerned about her behaviour. For the moment, Wickfield House was the most important thing in her life, that is, apart from some incomprehensible incidents at home which made her wonder whether other day girls ever suffered from the same tribulations. Surely Helen Swayne's mother never lay on the bed in the daytime with the curtains drawn? Or started weeping for no apparent reason? In any case, grown-ups were not meant to weep. Only people of her own age were allowed that privilege, such as yesterday when it had been quite understandable for Helen to cry in the cloakroom after gym.

Emily had done her best to console her friend by calling Miss Burrows "preposterous" and "a monster", but she knew that Helen was still desperately hurt and embarrassed by what had happened that morning when her mother arrived to drive them both home in the afternoon. For after Helen had climbed right to the top of one of the ropes in the junior section of the gym, Miss Burrows had told her to stay there. Then she had asked the rest of the class to look up and say what was wrong with the small figure, miserably clutching on several feet above them. There had been a few feeble sniggers and then Janie Crossman, a pert sharp-featured girl, had piped up, "She's got smiles, Miss Burrows." And Miss Burrows had said, "Quite right, Janie. You may come down now, Helen, but please ask your mother to buy you some longer black stockings."

Much as Emily adored being at Wickfield, she had been appalled at Miss Burrows's mean behaviour. Although she knew that no one was meant to show gaps of flesh between the tops of her stockings and the bottoms of her knickers and that sometimes culprits were teased for having so-called 'smiles', it seemed quite unjustifiable for poor Helen to have been singled out by a mistress in such a shockingly unkind way.

Today, as they sat together on top of the bus, Emily noticed that Helen was still very subdued. Only when Hazel Betts had disappeared into the senior school and they themselves were alone together in the junior cloakroom did Helen suddenly pull Emily into the corner behind the hot water tank, lift her skirt and say, "Look, Mummy sewed some black stuff round the tops. You see, these stockings are new ones. She couldn't afford to buy me any more just now."

"Oh, I see." Emily did not know what else to say, even though she did not really see why Helen's mother could not buy her another pair of stockings. She was vaguely aware that her own parents occasionally talked about something called a depression and referred to the Swaynes as being badly hit by it and very hard up; yet to Emily they always seemed to have so much: a large rambling farmhouse, countless buildings and outhouses, acres and acres of green fields, cows and chickens galore and a *pony*. True, Black Beauty somewhat belied her name. No one could describe her as exactly beautiful today. For many years past she had patiently borne Helen's two older brothers on her broad back. Now she was old and fat and lazy, not a bit like the smart shining pony which Emily had seen Phoebe Moreton riding in the company of the Fairfaxes' groom. All the same, Helen had something she longed for and it distressed Emily that her mother kept procrastinating about letting her have proper riding lessons with Miss Cory.

When half-term came and there was a meet of the local hounds at the Hall, Emily inveigled Katy into taking her to it. Almost at once, she caught sight of Phoebe Moreton astride the same pony, both of them looking even more dashing than ever. Then suddenly, she saw Phoebe's brother, the golden-haired boy whom she remembered meeting at the mill. Incredibly, he seemed to notice her just at the same moment and came sauntering over to where she and her mother were standing.

"Good morning," he said, raising his cap and smiling first at one and then the other of them. He wore long fawn corduroy trousers and a smart check sports jacket which exactly matched his cap. She wondered why he was not mounted like his sister. She smiled, shyly, relieved that her mother was able to do the talking for them both.

"How nice to see you, John. It must be your half-term, too."

"Yes. I'm here until Monday night."

"You're not riding then, like Phoebe?"

He frowned slightly. "No," he said and then, after a slight hesitation, added, "as a matter of fact, I don't much care for it. Ridiculous animals, horses."

Emily found herself staring at him in astonishment. It

seemed an extraordinary attitude to adopt. Here was a boy with every opportunity at his command, who could have ridden whenever he came home to his parents or grandparents—and yet he spurned the idea. She felt that there must be something very odd about him. Almost, as if he sensed her silent disapproval, he suddenly continued, defensively, "Phoebe and I are going to see Charlie Chaplin at the picture house in Westonbury on Monday afternoon. Would you like to come?"

Again her mother came to the rescue. "I expect your grandmother has arranged the treat just for the two of you, John. I don't think . . ." But at that point, Lady Fairfax came up to them all and her grandson wasted no time in asking if Emily could accompany them.

"But, of course." Was there, Katy wondered, a faint flicker of irritation in the ageing blue eyes, a slight forcedness in her usual spontaneity? "I will get Johnson to drive us all round to the Moat so that we can pick Emily up and drop her again when we come back. I would have suggested her coming to the Hall for tea, but I'm afraid that will have to be rather a rushed affair, as we have to get John William back to school by seven p.m."

"Yes, I quite understand. But it will be lovely for Emily to see the film. Thank you so much."

Lady Fairfax's attention was claimed elsewhere and in that seemingly vague yet skilful way which Katy remembered so well, she watched her drift away towards a top-hatted, pink-coated gentleman, who leaned down from his mount and began saying something to her about the new national government. But soon their conversation was drowned by the sound of a hunting horn and the hounds moving off in the charge of Colonel Egremont, the master, Tim Cutler, his huntsman, and an amateur whipper-in called Major Freddie Waring. Emily stood spellbound as the field came after them, Phoebe Moreton, although at the back and on a leading rein, looking extremely self-confident and disdainful and obviously not taking kindly to the admonishment from Tom Bartlett, the Fairfaxes' groom, to "Hold back there, Miss. There's no hurry. They're only going to draw Home Farm cover first."

With a sudden surge of uncustomary hatred and jealousy, Emily watched her pass, noted the black velvet peaked cap, the beautifully-fitting jacket and jodhpurs, the yellow string gloves and the way she kept tossing her head, a little in keeping with the pony she was riding.

Although Emily had never been taken to the pictures, she said to her mother on the way home, "I don't want to go to that Charlie Chaplin film with John William and his sister on Monday. I think he's soppy and Phoebe's quite *preposterous*." The last newly-acquired adjective was one which Emily was apt to use these days as often as she could, particularly in connection with the Wickfield gym mistress.

Katy Mason looked at her daughter in some concern. "I don't think we can refuse now, darling. You'll probably enjoy it when you get there. Besides, you heard what Lady Fairfax said. You don't have to go back to the Hall for tea with them."

"No, I suppose not."

Nevertheless, when Monday afternoon arrived, Emily felt very much in the same frame of mind as, just before two o'clock, she waited for her escorts by a downstairs window, wearing a pretty blue tweed dress and coat, made by her aunt—a blue velour hat, brown hand-knitted gloves and stockings—made by her mother—and smart brown leather shoes with a bar and buckle. As soon as the Fairfaxes' car could be seen approaching, Katy opened the front door, watched while the chauffeur stopped, got out and carefully helped Emily into the back seat, where Lady Fairfax was just visible giving a small wave as the little party drove off again.

"And I wonder," said Philip, suddenly coming out of his study at that moment, "what our young daughter will have to tell us about *that* little outing when she gets back."

Katy shrugged and began to walk away. It had been like that between them for some time now whenever they had been alone.

"Katy." He called after her as she began to mount the stairs. "I think you should know something." She halted, but still remained with her back towards him, one hand on the banisters. "I no longer have an agent," he continued, quietly.

This time she turned and stared at him. "Have you finished *Sun in the Morning* then?"

"No."

"But . . . I don't understand."

"I decided that . . . I might be better off alone . . . I mean, an agent seemed to interfere . . ."

"In more ways than one," she answered, bitterly.

"If you put it like that."

There was silence in the hall then. A wintry sunlight filtered through the window on the stairs. Her small figure seemed fragile and defenceless as it waited motionless, caught in its rays. He took a step towards her, conscious of how perfectly dressed she was, as always, of the way she now wore her hair so that it fell in soft brown waves round her pale face, of the wary look in her large grey eyes. He had been a fool. He felt he could have killed himself for the hurt he had caused her.

Instead, he held out his arms.

19

"And then he carried her upstairs."

"Why? Was she took bad?"

"No, silly. He just carried her on into their bedroom and *locked the door.*"

"But . . . whatever for?"

Rose put down her iron and burst out laughing. It was the following day. Emily was back at school. Philip and Katy had gone to London together and May was due at the Moat at four o'clock in order to take charge during their absence. It was the first time that Rose had had an opportunity of telling Miriam what she had witnessed the previous afternoon from behind a crack in the baize door, while her friend had been allowed out to visit her sick mother. She now looked at Miriam with a mixture of knowing indulgence, suddenly aware of the gap in their ages—Rose was just seventeen and Miriam two years younger—and wondering how best to enlighten her on such matters.

"Well," she said, at length, picking up the iron and holding it to her face to test the heat before banging it down again on a pillow case, "it isn't as if they're not married, is it? I expect he just wanted to . . ." Rose dropped her voice, even though they were alone in the house, "well, *you know*," she whispered.

Miriam did not know. She sat on one of the wooden kitchen chairs and stared at Rose in bewilderment. She was a short, thickset girl with a pale moon-like face, straight dark hair and round, steel-framed spectacles. She was not one of a family, for her mother had been widowed at the end of the war while she was still a baby. She had no idea what Rose was talking about, nor could she appreciate the significance of her next remark which did not seem to bear much relation to the earlier ones.

"They didn't come downstairs until just before Miss Emily come back from the pictures, about five o'clock."

"Oh."

"I suppose they could have 'ad a bit of a sleep afterwards."

"After what?"

This time Rose frowned a little in exasperation. Miriam was being singularly stupid. Was she really unable to grasp what was being said to her? Of course, with looks like hers it was perhaps natural for her not to have much interest in the opposite sex, nor they in her. She did not have a young man like Rose's Archie Carter, who would keep putting his hands where he shouldn't while they said goodnight in the shrubbery, when he brought her back to the Moat at nine thirty after her half-day off. Still, it was time Miriam was acquainted with the facts of life. Perhaps she could jolt her slow intelligence by a perfectly simple straightforward statement, something which she could not fail to understand.

"She might have another baby because of what they did yesterday."

Miriam's eyes behind her spectacles seemed to grow twice their size.

"You don't mean they . . .?" Her words trailed off, uncertainly. She was vaguely aware that a baby could not be produced except through some kind of secret and shameful goings-on between a man and a woman; but exactly what form such goings-on took she had no idea, other than that she believed they happened at night.

"Of course I do," Rose answered, smugly.

"But in the *afternoon*?"

Suddenly, the memory of her last half-day off came vividly into Rose's mind. She knew that it wasn't going to be easy fending off Archie Carter much longer, especially if they were still walking out next spring when the lighter evenings came and they went up to Breconbury Woods. "There's no set time for that sort of thing, Miriam," she now replied, as one with experience.

"Oh."

"Anyway, I can tell you that whatever happened made Mrs Mason ever so pleased. Madam's been such a down-in-the-mouth lately, but yesterday evening, when I was clearing away the tea things, she was all smiles. She and Mr Mason were laughing away while Miss Emily was pretending to be Charlie Chaplin and then, this morning, when she came to tell me they was going to London, she asked me if I'd iron that pretty new nightdress Miss Lodge made her a little while ago so's she could take it with her."

May, too, had certainly noticed a dramatic change in her

youngest sister when Katy had suddenly burst in on her early that morning, asking if she would spend the night at the Moat because she and Philip wanted to go to London unexpectedly. "He's taking me to Noel Coward's *Cavalcade*, May. It's a miracle he got tickets. It's only been on a few weeks, but he rang up and there were two cancellations, so then he asked Jack Lumley to send someone straight down to Drury Lane to buy them." She seemed all at once a girl again, the one May remembered just before her marriage: elated, flushed, her whole being excited as a child's at the thought of a promised treat. It was difficult to credit that she was the mother of a little one who would be ten years old in a few weeks' time.

In fact, May reflected, as she locked up Number Three Cob Lane that afternoon and started to walk towards the Moat, the child in Katy was never far from the surface, for all her seeming air of sophistication which she did her best to show to the world. Only perhaps those close to her knew the fearful, immature, despondent side of her nature and even they did not always understand it. May had had a shrewd idea of the present trouble, but she had never been directly confided in. However, thank goodness whatever it was had presumably now been resolved; yet she wondered for how long. All the old reservations she had had about Philip before Katy had married him kept coming back, but to a greater degree. He wasn't stable enough, he was too impulsive, too full of impractical ideas. This business of writing a book, for instance . . . Not for the first time did six little words keep repeating themselves in her mind: *Katy should have married Maurice Fitzherbert.*

May had not been long at the Moat before she saw the Swaynes' car coming up the drive. She knew that when it was their turn to collect Emily and Helen from Wickfield it usually just stopped at the gate. But today it turned in and from where she was standing at the drawing-room window she watched Dick Swayne get out and accompany her niece up the steps. She went to the front door anxiously, wondering whether something was wrong with the child and was relieved when Emily simply threw her arms around her as usual and skipped into the house. All the same, she thought that Dick looked unnaturally grave, as he took off his cap.

"I wondered if you'd heard the news, May."

"News . . .?" She stared at him, blankly.

"About Lord Fairfax. He died today."

"*No!*"

"Yes. I had to call at the estate office on my way into Westonbury and they told me there. Apparently he had a stroke this morning."

"Oh, *Dick* . . ." May was well aware that James Fairfax had never been an exactly strong character, he had never had the same force of personality as his wife, nor commanded the same respect. Many people in Wilhampton still held him and his *laisser faire* attitude responsible for the floods in 1929; but all the same, he had been lord of the manor for as long as May could remember. Within his limits, he was kind and meant well. It was just that his nature was too easy-going, too lackadaisical for the duties demanded of it. But his wife seemed to have more than compensated for such defects. In fact, when May came to think about it, they had always gone well in double-harness, as Sarah would have put it. She could not imagine what the Hall would be like without them. For Lady Fairfax would almost certainly move out and their eldest son, Edmund, and his wife, take over; and Edmund, so it was rumoured—the owner of a small estate in the next county—was hardly ever at home. At least Lord Fairfax had usually been around somewhere, even if it was mostly with a gun under his arm during the winter and a fishing-rod in his hand in the summer.

After May had said goodbye to Dick Swayne, she found it hard to concentrate on Emily's excited chatter throughout the rest of the evening. She realised that it was only to be expected that the death of Lord Fairfax meant little to the child, even if she had gone to the pictures with his grandson and granddaughter the day before. She knew well that grandparents were often shadowy figures to the younger generation, becoming more and more so as the latter grew up. She herself had extremely dim memories of her own. But now, in middle age, it made her feel sad to think how the old, who were coming to the end of their days, had so much more interest in the young who, with hardly a backward glance, imagined life would go on for ever. For May, although the passing of Lord Fairfax evoked no personal grief, nevertheless it emphasised the end of an era, rather as her mother's death had done two years previously; but then, with her habitual way of trying to make the best of things, she reminded herself that at least he and Sarah had had a reasonable innings.

She was not altogether surprised when, after seeing Emily on to the school bus the following morning, she returned home to find an envelope addressed to her in Lady Fairfax's handwriting lying on the front mat. She had already wondered about mourning, for although she knew that the wardrobe of her most distinguished client invariably contained plenty of black, the death of her *husband* would almost certainly necessitate more. Therefore later that day, a little before the requested hour of three p.m., May set off, discreetly, for the Hall.

When she arrived and was shown up to Lady Fairfax's boudoir, she found her, as she had anticipated, perfectly calm and composed. Her face was pale and there were deep lines beneath the eyes which showed signs of having recently shed tears, yet tears which May felt certain would have been shed in private. Her voice, when she spoke, was quieter than usual, yet it still had the same clear authoritarian ring about it.

"The funeral won't be for well over a week, May," she said, after the latter had proffered some simple condolences. "I've had a cable from Alicia. She and her husband are sailing from New York on the Mauretania tomorrow, but one has to allow for the weather in the Atlantic at this time of the year. It could take up to eight days, so as there's time, I thought perhaps you could possibly make me a two-piece with this length of black bouclé I bought in London only last month." She went over to a chaise longue and picked up the material. "You know the style I like, May," she continued, handing it to her, "and you've got all my measurements. I don't think my figure's altered since last time, except that I would like you now to make the skirt a good three inches longer."

There was a knock on the door and a parlourmaid appeared to tell her that she was wanted by her son on the telephone. With a hasty, "Perhaps you'd have a word with Nanny before you go, my dear. I'm afraid the news has been a terrible shock to her," she hurried away.

Although May had heard from Ethel Sharman how much Nanny Barlow had aged, she was unprepared for such a pathetic sight when the same young parlourmaid showed her along several passages and into a small room near the nursery quarters. The old lady sat hunched in a wicker chair by the fire, her face blotched, her eyes puffed and swollen. She wore a black knitted shawl over her shoulders and her whole body seemed to have shrunk to half its former size. It seemed impossible to believe that this was the upright, well-preserved woman under whose jurisdiction and care May had once put Katy over twelve years ago. For a moment, she did not appear to recognise her visitor and then, when she did, she said, querulously. "Ah, it's May, isn't it? May Lodge. Come about the mourning, have you?"

"Yes, Nanny."

"A bad business. A very bad business. And Miss Alicia on the other side of the world. She'd no call to go waltzing off like that and leaving Phoebe with this silly girl, Daisy."

"But Phoebe's had you, Nanny. And Lady Fairfax, and even Ethel Sharman in the mornings to keep an eye on her." May did her best to be placatory. "And it's probably been good for her coming to . . ." May almost said grandparents, but corrected herself in time. "The Hall," she added, quickly.

Nanny Barlow seemed not to pay the slightest attention to her words. "Her mother ought to be here," she said, "especially at a time like this." The voice had become fiercer now. "Phoebe's headstrong," she went on. "With my arthritis, I can't be with her every minute of the day and she needs a firm hand. What do you think happened this afternoon? She was gallivanting down the back stairs all dressed up for her daily ride. I was only just in time to stop her. The Lord knows where Daisy was. Of course, Tom Bartlett would never have taken her once she'd got to the stables, but just think of the child running across the forecourt in her riding clothes with her grandfather hardly cold. Why, when Miss Alicia and her brother were small and Lady Fairfax's mother died, I had black armbands on 'em within the hour *and* I never took them into Wilhampton for three months afterwards."

May was silent. From the direction of the day nursery she could hear a few faltering notes being played on the piano and then a child's voice raised in argument. She remembered her own mother's attitude to death. But time had gone on since then. Things had changed; although obviously Nanny Barlow had not changed with them. Suddenly, the piano-playing started up again, louder than before. Despite all her infirmities, May realised that the old lady before her was not exactly deaf. Nanny Barlow rose, with difficulty, and walked towards the door shaking her head. "*Little Brown Jug*," May heard her mutter, as she left the room. "I ask you. Playing *Little Brown Jug* with death in the house."

Almost it could have been Sarah speaking, in the spring of 1919, after Katy had won a prize for doing an impromptu turn at the fair: "And how do you think I shall look? It will be all over Wilhampton tomorrow. My youngest daughter singing *Our Lodger's Such A Nice Young Man* and her father not dead three months."

20

The telephone rang on an afternoon when Katy had gone into Westonbury to do some shopping and fetch Emily and Helen home from school. Philip got up and went into the hall to answer it, not without a certain amount of relief. He felt that he could do with a respite. He had been working on another chapter of *Sun in the Morning* but, although Barbara Woodley was no longer interfering with the plot, he was finding it heavy going.

"Philip." He had forgotten just how deep and husky her voice was.

He found himself staring at the tall black mouthpiece clutched in his right hand as if it had turned into something venomous, an instrument of torture. Fear and fury welled up inside him. The woman had no business to be ringing. Thank God Katy was out of the house.

"I have nothing else to say, Barbara."

"Perhaps *you* haven't, my sweet. But I'm afraid *I* have. Are you alone?"

"For the moment." He dropped his voice, suddenly conscious that Rose or Miriam might be listening from behind the baize door. Rose, particularly, had been altogether too full of herself lately and he had not liked the way she had sometimes glanced at him. He wished he had not spoken Barbara's name. "I have to go now," he added, curtly.

"Just a minute, darling. I don't think you quite understand. It isn't as easy as all that. You must realise. I wouldn't have rung otherwise. I have to see you. It's very important."

"That's impossible." He was careful not to mention her name again. He found he was actually shaking now. "Goodbye," he said, flatly, and was about to hook up the receiver when her next words made him pause.

"Philip, wait. Please. I'm desperate. I'm . . . pregnant."

He could feel a tightness in his chest. He was sweating profusely although it was freezing in the hall. Out of the corner of his eye he suddenly noticed the Morris turning in at the gate.

"I'll write," he replied, quickly. "Someone is coming. Don't ring again."

He was still standing by the telephone when Katy and Emily came through the front door, their arms full of parcels. He watched them from what seemed like a great distance, as if his wife and child were on the other side of some thick glass barrier, one which he could not and, indeed, had no right to break through. He knew that he had to get away for a while.

"I want to take the car to the garage for some more oil," he mumbled, and almost bolted from the house.

It was getting quite dark as he drove up to Breconbury Woods, turned round and switched off both the lights and the engine. There were high scudding clouds in the sky from behind which, every so often, a moon shone down on the scene before him. He was bitterly cold now, for he had come out without an overcoat, but it did not seem to matter. Nothing mattered. He had failed the two people who meant more to him than anything else in the world. He lit a cigarette with hands that still shook and remained staring down into the valley below, while the lights of Wilhampton appeared one by one. God, what a mess. He had allowed Barbara Woodley to trick him as if he were some kind of greenhorn. He had believed what he supposed he had wanted to believe. With what had appeared to be the most touching sincerity she had told him, on that first afternoon when she had inveigled him into her home and her bed, that much as she adored children she would never be able to have any because a doctor had diagnosed a twisted fallopian tube. How *could* he have been so gullible? Anyway what exactly was a fallopian tube and how, when and why had it been diagnosed? But just then, as far as he was concerned, Barbara's handicap had seemed highly convenient. He had made love to her almost savagely; in fact, there had always been a curious element of reckless animosity in their relationship, as if it were an unwelcome necessity. As the weeks went by he came to suspect she was a nymphomaniac. It angered him that he never wholly seemed able to satisfy her. At the end of their sessions together, when he was about to leave her room which, for all its size, was beginning to give him claustrophobia, she would sit up in her bed on the floor, looking like some Lorelei in the greeny half light, her naked torso with its small flat breasts somehow half appealing, half repellent, as she held out her arms and whispered, huskily, "Please, Philip. Please." And he would find himself becoming ensnared once more by her strange magnetism and fall back into bed with her, while hating himself for so doing.

She had become almost hysterical when, with all the determination he could muster, he had called to tell her that their affair must cease and their business association as well. She had accused him of every felony she could think of, including a final taunt of being bourgeois. "All writers have mistresses, Philip," she had said. "That's what gives inspiration to their writing. I'm not harming your cosy country domestic set-up. I'm helping it. That precious little wife of yours will have only me to thank, if she did but know it, when *Sun in the Morning* hits the headlines. *She'll* be the one who will bask in all the reflected glory. Not me. But I'm prepared for that . . . just as long as you . . ." And here she had burst into wild, uncontrollable sobs.

It was the disparaging reference to Katy which had made him fighting mad and helped to strengthen his resolve; for even while Barbara had been hurling abuse at him he could feel his sensuality being aroused, knew that he had only to take a step or two towards her and he would be able to quieten her tirade in a way which would have been pleasurable to them both. When he had managed to make it quite clear that he meant what he said, that he was not going to make love to her that day or any other day and, apart from anything else, it was he who was writing *Sun in the Morning* and he did not want an agent continually imposing her own ideas on it, she had given him a cold hard look and thrown the offending manuscript across the floor. He could recall her standing, clad only in a black silk kimono—the garb she usually received him in—as he gathered it up and hurried out of the door, how she had shrieked after him, regardless of any other tenants in the house, "You'll pay for this, Philip Mason, in more ways than one."

Well, she had been right on that score. His whole life was in ruins now. He had failed as a husband, a father, a writer and even an antiquarian bookseller. The only thing he had ever been any good at—and even that was merely in a mediocre way—was taking on Mason & Son; and he was not at all sure that he was not now falling down over this. Jack Lumley was a nice enough, conscientious man, but his management left a lot to be desired. Even the possession of something which Philip knew that he did not deserve—Katy's love—was now in jeopardy. How could she possibly go on loving him if she knew the truth? He could never bring himself to tell her, but she would be bound to find out sooner or later. It would be better if he were dead.

He realised that she would already have started to worry about him now, wondering what had kept him. She always worried when he was late, bless her. He remembered the night he had come back from Wales in the fog and how she had thrown her arms around him with relief when he had finally walked through the door, how he made love to her a little later on after telling her about Belle's legacy. Under the circumstances, it probably hadn't been an exactly fitting thing to do, but somehow he hadn't been able to help it. He had been so full of plans for their future. And she had been just as excited, too. He had thought, by bringing her back to Wilhampton into such a much better home, that everything would be just about perfect. But it hadn't worked out like that. People said money didn't bring happiness and they were right. Although it wasn't the money, really, that was the trouble. It was he who was to blame. If only he'd had the sense not to fool around, Katy would have come to make the necessary adjustments and enjoy her role as mistress of the Moat House. In fact, on the evening of that fatal day when he had first gone to Barbara's home and let his wife and child down over the Westonbury Show, Katy had been so taken up with the roses she intended to grow and exhibit the following year that she appeared not to have noticed his own preoccupation. Why on earth, when he had had so much, had he gone and fouled it all up? They could have had a good life, watching Emily grow into a young woman, giving her the education of which Belle would have approved. How could he ever have thought that Barbara Woodley had anything which his wife did not? Why, Katy was a princess compared to her.

He knew now what he had to do and the sooner the better. So great was his anguish, it never occurred to him that Barbara Woodley might have had other lovers, that he was not necessarily the father of her child. In the moonlight he noticed, lying in the pocket of the car's dashboard, a small notepad on which Katy sometimes made a shopping list. He pulled it towards him and took out his fountain pen. Tearing off the first scribbled-on sheet, he wrote "May" at the top of the next blank one. He scrawled a few more words and put it on the front passenger seat. Then he got out of the car and began to walk.

It took him about three quarters of an hour. At one point he knew he must be passing within a few feet of the spot where he and Katy had lain together on that never-to-be-forgotten evening during their courting days when, but for the grace of God, he might have taken her virginity. A little lower down he recognised the place where they had met Grace Armitage on their homeward journey and he had been given some inkling of the nature of the woman—undoubtedly another Barbara Woodley, he now thought, bitterly. Then he came in sight of Bulbarrow Farmhouse and buildings, remembering how Dorothy Swayne had given them a cheerful greeting as she crossed over to the barn carrying something for the harvest supper to be held later on. She could well have been pregnant with Helen at the time, he supposed, knowing that Emily's little friend was the elder by several months. His walk tonight seemed to bring the past back in painfully sharp relief, as if he were now engaged on its inevitable sequence or conclusion, as though he were being called to account, his actions predetermined, foredoomed. The only deviation he made in the route was when he turned off at the outskirts of the town, for he knew that the mill gates would be shut and locked at this hour and in order to reach his destination he would have to go by the meadow path.

He heard it now, becoming louder with every step he took. It was about a mile away, then half, then a quarter. He crossed over the stile by the place which Katy always called Nomansland and here it sounded very close. Not much longer now. His mind was made up. And once he had done what he had to do, he would be close to Katy for ever. She would understand why he had chosen the mill-race. She had great perception.

He walked on, something telling him that this was the way, the only way, the way of the river.

21

May was listening to some dance music on the wireless when the knock came on her door, loud and insistent. Slightly annoyed at having to switch off Roy Fox's rendering of *Whispering*, she got up to answer it, wondering who her caller could possibly be at this hour, for Ethel had long since come and gone.

She was confronted by the small dumpy figure of Miriam, her face anxious and whiter than usual, her eyes blinking rapidly behind her steel spectacles, as she burst out, breathlessly, "Please Miss Lodge, Mrs Mason says can you come at once. It's something about Mr Mason."

"What about him?" May's voice was sharp, alarm sweeping away all its usual warmth and sweetness.

"Well, ma'am, it seems as how he went out in the car at tea-time and . . ." The girl before her took another deep breath before adding, "He's not come home."

"All right, Miriam. You run straight back and tell Mrs Mason I'll be on my way. I expect Mr Mason's car has broken down or he's just had a puncture," May replied quickly, doing her best to allay what seemed like rising hysteria. She knew well what any drama of this sort could do to young girls like Miriam, how they tended to exaggerate and work themselves up, while deep down revelling in the importance of being the harbinger of disaster. All the same, she thought it unlikely that a breakdown or a simple puncture would have prevented Philip from sending word by now. It was getting on for nine o'clock. She wished that Katy had asked for her sooner. Where could her brother-in-law possibly have gone? Whatever he might or might not do in London, he had behaved most circumspectly in Wilhampton. It was uncharacteristic of him to leave his wife guessing as to his whereabouts. As May went back into her sitting-room and hastily began damping down the fire, something warned her to put a few overnight things into a bag.

She was just locking her front door when she heard the sound of heavy male footsteps at the end of Cob Lane. She looked up and, in the light of one of the street lamps, saw George Burbage, the Wilhampton policeman, coming towards her.

"Miss Lodge . . . ?"

"Yes, George." This time she knew real fear: all-consuming, paralysing, the kind she had experienced on a few other occasions in her life, but always hoped she would never experience again. She remained motionless, the key still in her hand.

"You'll be going to the Moat, ma'am, I daresay." He was plainly distressed. "I have bad news, I'm afraid. Could we go back inside your house for a while?"

She led him in and relit the gas mantle. Awkwardly, he removed his helmet and then pulled a piece of paper from one of his pockets. "This'll be for you, Miss Lodge, I reckon," he said, handing it to her.

May took the note and stared at it in bewilderment, although it was short and painfully explicit. The words seemed to bounce back at her, clear, challenging, yet somehow curiously simple and trusting: "May. Tell Katy I'm sorry. I love her and Emily so much. Please take care of them for me. Philip."

There was silence in the little room. She put out a hand and steadied herself on the back of a chair, but she did not sit down.

"Have you . . . found him yet?" she asked, at length.

"No ma'am. We didn't know anything was amiss until a little while ago when Mrs Mason telephoned. And then, just after, this note was brought in to the station."

"Who by?"

"Ted Pretty, the Fairfaxes' new keeper. He happened to be out after poachers up at Breconbury Woods and came on Mr Mason's car parked with no lights on. So he took a look inside."

"Then . . . there's still hope . . . ?"

George Burbage hesitated. "I suppose so, ma'am. We wondered . . . if you might have any idea where . . ." He coughed, unable to go on.

It came into her mind with curious inevitability. She looked straight into George's troubled eyes. "The race," she said, quietly. "Have you tried the mill-race?"

"I think the keeper's down there now," he answered gruffly, "although being night-time and the moon gone . . ."

She nodded. "I see. Thank you for coming, George."

He asked for the note, explaining that she would be given a typed copy. She handed it back to him and, as soon as he had left her, she set out once again for the Moat. Of all the things which she had had to face in her life, May knew that this would be the worst. Until there was definite news, she would have to keep up some form of pretence—and May Lodge was not good at any kind of subterfuge.

As soon as she turned into the driveway, she saw Katy's figure silhouetted in one of the lighted hall windows; then, quickly, it moved away. Almost immediately, the front door opened and her sister came flying down the steps.

"Oh, May, I thought you were never coming. What can have happened? He said he was going to Parker's for some oil for the car, but that was hours ago. It's so unlike him. And it isn't as if . . ." she continued, and then broke off as they went into the house.

"As if what, my dear?" May put down her small case and took off her coat, feeling that it might be as well to keep Katy talking, especially as by so doing she might glean some useful information.

"Well, I mean . . . you must have guessed. We've had a bad patch, but it was all over. We've been so happy these last few weeks . . . ever since we went to *Cavalcade*, you remember? It's been like another honeymoon lately, May."

"I'm glad, Katy," She *was* glad, too. Whatever happened, whatever the future held in store for her sister, at least Katy would have that to remember and hold on to. She had always had such great capacity for happiness, however short-lived it might sometimes have been. When May managed to persuade her to come away from the hall window and into the warmth of the drawing-room, she asked her whether she had eaten anything that evening, and was hardly surprised to receive the swift reply, "Of course not. How could I?"

"What about Emily?"

"She's had her supper and is in bed asleep, thank God. If it hadn't been for her, I suppose I might have raised the alarm earlier, but I tried not to show I was worried. I managed to pass off Philip's absence by saying he'd probably called in for a chat with Dick Swayne or someone. But I didn't think it was very likely. As soon as she was upstairs, I telephoned Dorothy . . . and when she said they hadn't seen him, I rang the police."

May was silent. She watched her sister light a cigarette, her hands making several attempts at striking a match. She knew that Katy was drawing on all the resources at her command in order to remain calm, yet with every moment that passed she was finding it more difficult. Presently, she got up and went into the hall where May heard her telephoning the police station again, after which she returned with two stiff brandies and sodas. May took one with misgiving, remembering their mother's 'medicinal' bottle which she used to keep for emergencies. The amount of alcohol which Katy had poured out tonight would just about have filled poor Sarah's flask to the top. She also felt that the effect on her sister's empty stomach might be disastrous, yet she noticed that after taking a few sips, Katy certainly seemed to brighten a little. "They say at the station there's no further news, May, but Philip *could* just walk in," she said, with a pathetic attempt at optimism. "You don't know," she went on, "there might be an explanation. Funny things happen. I mean, he could have lost his memory, like Mother did, remember?"

"Yes, dear," May replied, while hating herself for lying. She felt fairly certain that, distraught and confused as her brother-in-law might have been, he had not actually suffered any loss of memory. There must be a deeper, more complicated reason for the situation although, after Katy's patently honest revelation of their recent happiness, she could not, for the life of her, think what it was.

Neither sister went to bed that night. Each remained, fully clothed, sitting one on either side of the fireplace waiting for news, mostly in silence. Once or twice May tried to get Katy to lie down on the sofa, but any such suggestion was met with fierce resistance. When, around midnight, May made a tentative suggestion that she could ring Maurice Fitzherbert, this also received a negative response. "There's nothing he could do," Katy replied, and May knew that, for the moment, she was right. As the night wore on, one or the other of them threw another log on the fire; occasionally May went into the kitchen to make some tea, glad that Katy had shown no attempt to replenish their glasses.

When morning approached, they mutually agreed that, if possible, it would be best to get Emily off to school as usual, that they would simply tell her that her father was unwell and, if it became necessary, that he had had to go to hospital—which wouldn't be far wrong, May thought grimly. For whatever happened, that was where, in all probability, Philip would be taken, just as Neil had been taken all those years ago, after he had accidentally fallen into the Willon.

Rather to her relief and astonishment, her niece accepted the situation without too many awkward questions and, as May hurried her down to the market square at a quarter to eight, she was more than thankful to be able to say, "Why, I do believe that for once Helen is ahead of you," and to see Emily's flying figure running to catch up with her friend.

May had taken the precaution of telephoning the Swaynes half an hour earlier. They had already heard the news that Philip was missing, but Dorothy assured her that nothing had been said in front of their small daughter. The possibility that someone else could make an unfortunate remark which Emily might overhear that day was a chance which May felt simply had to be taken. It was preferable to having the child hanging about at the Moat where she might possibly be subjected to something far worse.

The sight of Maurice Fitzherbert's car on the gravel outside the house as she returned to it made May send up a small prayer of thanks that she had got Emily away in time. Although she knew that Maurice was more than likely to make a courtesy call if he heard any patient of his was in trouble, she somehow had a feeling that he had now called to see Katy for a very specific purpose. She was not proved wrong. She found him standing by the fireplace in the drawing-room while her sister sat staring straight in front of her, in the same chair in which she had kept her vigil throughout the night. She did not look up as May came in. She did not seem to be aware of either of them. Her eyes were quite blank, her mind obviously far away.

Then, quite suddenly, the sound of the eight o'clock mill hooter seemed to galvanize her into action. With a swift movement, she stood up and rushed towards Maurice. He put out one of his hands, but she shook it away angrily. "You must take me to him," she said. "Where is he? What have you done with him?" She seemed to be beside herself now, flailing at him with her fists, forcing him to catch hold of both her arms tightly.

"Steady, Katy, my dear. Steady. Not now. It wouldn't be . . . right."

"Right?" May heard her voice rise. "Right?" she repeated. "It's my right, isn't it? Someone's got to identify him. I'm his wife, aren't I? Besides, just because he's dead doesn't mean he wouldn't want me to be with him now."

All at once she seemed to crumple, so that he had to hold her up. "Please," she whispered. "Please, Maurice." Her eyes were luminous, pleading. May knew that he could not refuse.

He helped her gently from the room and across the hall. Then, with a quiet, "Her coat, please, May," Maurice Fitzherbert carried Katy Lodge down the steps of the Moat and into his car.

22

Half a mile to the south-east of Wilhampton, just off the main road leading to Westonbury and nestling in a bend of the River Willon, lay a small hamlet called Netherford. It boasted scarcely more than two dozen habitations, ranging from one large eighteenth-century house—Netherford Grange—to a farmstead by the name of Sweetacres and then to a variety of smaller dwellings, mostly tied cottages occupied by agricultural labourers but interspersed with a few slightly bigger homes of a residential kind, one of which was called the White Hermitage. In the spring of 1932 this, together with Netherford Grange, came up for sale.

The Dowager Lady Fairfax bought the Grange. May Lodge, on behalf of her sister and with the help of estate agents and solicitors, acquired the Hermitage.

May had had a sad, difficult and perplexing time. As was to be expected, she had not fallen down on the charge laid upon her by her late brother-in-law, but it had worried and aged her considerably. Her hair had suddenly turned quite white; her gentle, usually cheerful face was now lined and worn. Nor had her youngest sister's looks fared any better. Katy Mason had become—just as she had after her operations—thin to the point of emaciation.

The young widow had been too shocked to be of any assistance in the winding up of her husband's estate. Her overwhelming distress and melancholy meant that she was unable to make decisions or express any wishes, other than that she did not want to remain at the Moat. May, with no previous experience of legal, business or even money matters, nevertheless found herself discussing all three with both country and London solicitors—for there was the question of the sale of the bookshop—as well as having to deal with curious unexpected problems which daily presented themselves. Every night she went down on her knees to give thanks for the never-failing support and advice of Maurice Fitzherbert who, on realising that Katy's condition was becoming worse rather than better, suggested May should be given a full power of attorney.

Another form of help, for which she was more than grateful, came from the Swaynes who, from the time of the tragedy had immediately swept Emily up and taken her into their rambling, loving, happy home at Bulbarrow, insisting that she must remain with them for however long it was necessary and especially over Christmas.

May had also derived further comfort from a third and completely unexpected source: Edith. Hitherto, her middle sister had kept well away from the Moat. Katy's new lifestyle, though never having made Edith envious—for that was not her nature—had certainly overawed and inhibited her, particularly in front of Philip. She had therefore rarely visited the house but now, knowing that May and Katy were in trouble and living there alone, she often popped in for half an hour or so when she could spare the time from the demands of her family; but, tactfully, she refrained from suggesting that Emily might sometimes visit her cousins on downside.

The child had taken the news of her father's death far better than May had expected. Although at the inquest a verdict was brought in of 'suicide while the balance of his mind was disturbed', Emily had been given to believe that Philip had been taken ill and drowned accidentally while trying to walk home after his car had broken down. The note he had left—thanks to Maurice Fitzherbert—was never read out in court and when the coroner asked May if she knew of any trouble or difficulties her brother-in-law might have had which would have forced him to take his life, she had replied in clear definite tones, "No"—even qualifying this by adding that she understood her sister and her husband to have been extremely happy at the time of his unfortunate death.

And that was true, May remembered thinking, as she had stood in the box. It had been quite embarrassing the way Katy and Philip seemed only to have had eyes for each other during those last few weeks. It had hardly seemed right to her that a couple who had been married getting on for eleven years should make the mutual physical attraction between them quite so obvious. It made May sorry for Emily, who she sensed felt both distressed and shut out. Still, she was glad now to think that her sister and brother-in-law had had that brief seemingly idyllic period and no power on earth was ever going to drag from May

Lodge the fact that, some days after Philip's body had been found half a mile downstream from the mill-race, she had answered the telephone at the Moat and a deep husky female voice had asked to speak to Mr Mason. When May had said, "I'm sorry, I'm afraid Mr Mason passed away last Tuesday," there had been a click and the line had gone dead. Naturally, she had said nothing to Katy and, fortunately, there had been no further communications of that sort. May did not suppose that anyone would ever know the full story. She had simply sensed that it was a long-distance call and it was highly likely she had been talking to the 'mannish' lady agent in London, to whom her sister had once referred so disparagingly. The more she reflected on it the more May felt that her brother-in-law must have got himself into a mess from which the desperate course he had chosen seemed, sadly, the only way out.

It was Cyril Butt who had actually started her thinking in earnest about Katy's future home, when she had met him one cold January day on her way to post yet another of the interminable complicated documents on which her signature was constantly required.

"Katy will be selling the Moat, I suppose, May," he had remarked, soberly.

"Why, yes, Cyril. She's no call to stay there now," she had replied, rather surprised that he should have brought the subject up at all.

"Quite so." May could recall how Cyril had then puffed out his cheeks, moved his thumb stick a little closer and, leaning forward confidentially, had continued, "This isn't common knowledge, May, but there's a small place at Netherford coming up for sale. Pretty. Compact. In good condition. Might suit her down to the ground."

"Really?" At once May had become interested. She knew that a tip from Cyril was not to be ignored. He had then proceeded to tell her all about the White Hermitage, advising her that if they wanted to know more it would be worth while quickly getting in touch with Gordon Brewer, who saw to all the house property at Butt and Swanton.

Tentatively, that same night, May had broached the subject with Katy. She found her sitting, as she so often did of late, smoking the inevitable cigarette and staring into the fire.

"It's for you to say, May," she had replied, indifferently, after hearing what Cyril had said.

"But, my dear, it would be *your* home, yours and Emily's."

"And yours."

For the first time since Philip's death, May felt an exasperation which was difficult to hide. Surely Katy could 'take on' a little now, if only for Emily's sake.

"You mean you want me to live with you?" she had queried, somewhat tartly.

May was quick to note a flicker of astonishment in the large grey eyes as Katy answered, simply, "But of course."

Although it had never been mooted before, May had suspected that this was what had been in Katy's mind all along, so far as she had anything in mind these days, other than Philip; but the calm assumption that May would automatically give up Number Three, Cob Lane, together with her independence, and take care of Katy and Emily for as long as she was required was a little hard to take. May knew that she *would* do it and part of her would find great happiness in living in the same house as her much-loved niece. But it would have been nice to have been *asked*. Besides, one never knew; one day her youngest sister might marry again and where would she be then, with no Cob Lane to which she could retreat?

Doing her best to ignore Katy's last remark, she had said, quietly, "The White Hermitage would be very convenient from the point of view of Emily's schooling. She could still catch the same bus as Helen at the Netherford stop."

"I suppose so . . . although it might be best if she became a boarder."

"A *boarder*?" May had been genuinely shocked. "But I thought you and Philip always vowed you'd never let her do that."

"But Philip . . . isn't here any more. And I'm no good to her now, am I?"

This time May had not been able to refrain from speaking out. "Look Katy, you'll have to pull yourself together. Emily needs you now more than ever. She's been at the Swaynes long enough. Besides, it's wrong of us to go on imposing on Dick and Dorothy's good nature. Oh, I know they're kindness itself and it was all I could do to get them to take anything for Emily's keep, but the child asked only last Sunday when she was coming home."

May had watched Katy stub out her cigarette and light yet another one. She could remember the stillness in the room, alleviated only by a cinder or two falling from the grate and the wind getting up outside. In order to relieve the tension, she had picked up some knitting. Other than managing to execute her outstanding orders, May had done no sewing of late. She wished Katy would answer her but apart from remarking, "I expect the Hermitage would be as good a place as any," her sister had lapsed into silence and withdrawn into that private world of hers for the rest of the evening.

In the ensuing months, while Gordon Brewer negotiated the sale of the Moat and the purchase of the White Hermitage, May often thought about her little dressmaking business and how it would be bound to suffer. She was not so concerned about the financial aspect for, by going to live with a sister who had been left comfortably off, this did not in itself present a problem, other than the very real emotional one conerning May's abhorrence of becoming dependent. She supposed she would still do work for a privileged few such as Lady Fairfax and some long-standing clients which, with the dividends from her small savings, would bring her in a little income. But the thing which really bothered her was feeling that the special link which, through her work, she had forged with the life of Wilhampton would be, if not exactly broken, certainly weakened. She was so much a part of the little town; she had been the recipient of so many confidences as, discreetly, she had slipped a tape-measure round a waist or, pins in mouth, knelt to adjust a hemline. Ever sensitive to the feelings of others, she had shared in their sorrows, rejoiced in their happiness. True, the market-square was but twenty minutes walking distance from Netherford and it had even crossed her mind that she might learn to drive. But in her new life there would not be the daily contact, the constant exchange of news. She would still be on home ground, as it were, yet on its periphery. May Lodge who, for over twenty years, had sent out bills, written in her immaculate script, firstly from *The Mill House* and latterly from *Number Three, Cob Lane, Wilhampton*, felt in some inexplicable way that, by going to Netherford, she was letting the side down.

The move took place one late April day, when patches of primroses bloomed in the hedgerows and clumps of daffodils flowered gaily in all the gardens of the little hamlet, while the chestnut trees were in full bud on either side of the high wrought-iron gates to the Grange. All around, the countryside was bright with the promise of new growth, the water-meadows by the Willon lush with early grass, the fields of corn a rippling sea of silvery green—for Robert Farley at Sweetacres had not, like Dick Swayne, been forced to give up arable farming.

With the eagerness and optimism of youth, Emily, carrying a basket containing May's cat, hurried up the path of the Hermitage ahead of her mother and aunt, thrilled at the prospect of living in what she called a fairytale house. And, with its thatch and whitewashed walls, May could not help thinking that their new home did have that quality about it. She hoped Katy would start to pick up a bit now that she was in different surroundings. May knew it would be uphill work but she was determined to do all she could to help her. After all, life had to go on. They had Emily to care for. Whatever happened, the child mustn't be allowed to suffer.

"Why, look, Katy," she said, as they approached the front door. "That honeysuckle over the porch is going to look lovely in a month or so's time."

Her sister simply nodded and went quickly inside.

23

After Maud Fairfax and May Lodge had been living in Netherford for a year or more, a subtle change became noticeable in their relationship. The older woman was now ageing fast. She no longer needed the clothes which she had been accustomed to ordering when her husband had been alive, having become far less active both in her public and private life. Though she had by no means taken to widowhood as hard as Katy Mason, she nevertheless concentrated on interests of a much more personal kind: her grandchildren—especially John William—the upkeep of her new home, and a few close friends and associates of long-standing, amongst whom she regarded May with particular affection.

Sometimes, if they happened to meet of an afternoon while she was taking an increasingly leisurely stroll with her equally slow and ancient spaniel, she would suggest that May might like to come back for tea at the Grange and, on one of these occasions, the subject of Katy's almost total withdrawal from life came up—as it so often did—in their conversation.

"Could you not get her to *join* something, May? It's so unnatural for a beautiful young widow to remain quite such a recluse at this stage. I don't necessarily mean going in for 'good works', as Alicia's husband puts it so disparagingly, but Katy was very fond of the theatre once, wasn't she? I believe Westonbury has a very flourishing dramatic society nowadays."

"I've suggested something of the sort many times, Lady Fairfax"—May no longer said 'Your ladyship'—"but she simply doesn't appear interested . . . in anything."

"Not even Emily?"

"Well . . ." May hesitated. "I suppose, to a certain extent. Sad as it seems, the fact that the child has become slightly short-sighted has possibly helped to take her out of herself a little. She's agreed to her riding more. In fact, I've just about persuaded her to let Emily have a pony of her own. I'm sure Robert Farley up at Sweetacres would let us some grazing. And it's not as if there would be any question of stabling because it could sleep rough all the winter. A pony would only need a little hay and a daily inspection. I'm sure there would be no problem."

"What a very good idea, May. You *must* pursue it. With the long summer holidays coming along, Emily could be out riding every day, especially with Helen Swayne for company. I hate to think of the child's eyes suffering from too much close study." The Dowager Lady Fairfax knew little about defective vision. Her own and that of her family had always been perfect. It was true that she had taken to using her lorgnettes more frequently of late, but the idea of a pretty little girl of Emily's age having to wear glasses was hardly to be countenanced. It was bad enough seeing them on the face of poor unfortunate Miriam, who was now working as kitchenmaid at the Grange; although her employer could not help reflecting that there was certainly one advantage in this case. Miriam was living proof of Dorothy Parker's "boys never make passes". She was not likely to attract 'followers'.

It therefore came about that a few days later, Katy—having been given a detailed account of her sister's recent tête-à-tête with the Dowager—set off to call on the Farleys. Because of her dislike of meeting people, she was apt to take the car on the shortest journey, but this evening she elected to walk. It had been a glorious June day and the scent of hay in the air remained almost overpowering, even though it was long past sundown. Katy had been well aware that Robert Farley would have been working so hard that she could not expect to find him at home until nightfall—one of her chief reasons for deciding to go on foot—but, as she walked up the driveway to Sweetacres, she hoped that she had also left it late enough for him to have had his supper.

"He's just finished, Mrs Mason. Do come in," his wife, Frances, replied in answer to Katy's initial question, as she ushered her into a dark, heavily-furnished sitting-room, not unlike the Swaynes'. Had it been May paying the visit, Katy knew that her sister and Robert's wife would have been on christian name terms, for May had an extraordinary capacity for getting to know all and sundry with a friendliness which neither overstepped nor fell short of the required mark. She sat down and waited anxiously while Frances went away to fetch her husband.

When Robert Farley came through from the kitchen—his wife excusing herself on the grounds of having to shut up the hens—Katy was struck by this big burly man's aura of utter dependability and kindliness. In manner, he reminded her of Dick Swayne and Maurice Fitzherbert. In their separate ways they were all as different from Philip as chalk from cheese, yet each had about him something for which part of her longed, even though neither possessed that particular quality in his make-up for which, over eighteen months after her husband's death, she still felt a physical ache. She looked across at the man opposite her, his strong weather-beaten face illuminated by a single oil lamp—for Netherford, as yet, boasted no main gas or electricity—and listened with gratitude as he responded with such wholehearted enthusiasm to the proposal she had put before him.

"But *of course*, Mrs Mason. I'd be only too pleased to help. You could have the grazing in the paddock at the back of the White Hermitage where I keep my own mare for most of the year, and then we could put the pony into the Daisy Field at other times. I usually keep a bit of hay in the nearby skilling and maybe Emily would like to put her tackle in the shed at the end and use the place for saddling up."

"It's very kind of you . . . Please, you must let me know whatever you feel it is worth . . . I am so grateful."

For the first time, Robert Farley seemed embarrassed. He did not reply at once, and then he said, "Oh, hardly anything . . . I mean, it'll be nice to have a child with a pony around again, now all our youngsters are grown up."

"But I insist, Mr Farley. You don't know what it will mean to us . . . to Emily."

Again he paused before answering. She knew that the Farleys were not as up against it as the Swaynes but, all the same, times were still hard for farmers. Presently, he said, quietly, "Well, would half a crown a week be acceptable? That's with the hay thrown in, of course."

"But that's far too cheap." Katy might have been brought up at the Felt Mills, but she knew enough about farming to know that such a bargain was overwhelmingly to her advantage. Yet he shook his head at her reply.

"No, it'll be a pleasure, I assure you. It was a sad day when we had to sell the children's pony. Have you anyone in mind you're thinking of buying from?"

"No . . . I wondered if you could give me a little advice about that."

"Shorty," he answered, promptly. "Shorty Miller over at Little Meysey. He's a bit of a rogue but if you mention my name and how the pony will be kept at Sweetacres, he won't do you down. Tell him you want a safe little mount, about thirteen hands, I should say. Emily's getting tall now, isn't she? A bonny lass. Tell you what, would you like me to have a word with Shorty?"

"Oh, *would* you?" Almost, he was beginning to infect her with his own enthusiasm. "Thank you *very* much."

She rose and Robert Farley stood also: tall, infinitely reassuring and wise, not in any scholarly way, but in a much more important one. It was impossible to define. She only knew that the man before her was what her father would have described as "a good 'un". He possessed a countryman's innate common sense which had been handed down to him through a long line of forbears. As he accompanied her to the gate of Sweetacres, they met his wife coming across the yard from the chicken house. Katy shook hands with them both, envying them—though not in any jealous way—their completeness, their mutual satisfaction in their life together.

The moon had risen as she started to walk the quarter of a mile home. Already squares of dim orange light showed in the upstairs windows of most of the cottages. It was a busy time and Katy knew that most of the farming fraternity would soon be asleep. She also knew that even a little later on in the year, in that traditional lull between haymaking and harvest, they would still be going to bed by nine or nine thirty. After all, she reflected a little wrily, that was what was known as 'honeymoon time'.

An owl swooped low across her path and disappeared into the grounds of the Grange. Once or twice a moth fluttered close to her face or some small animal made a rustling noise in the hedgerow. The only house which showed a glimmer of light downstairs was Greenways, the home of Gordon Hillier, a somewhat unaccountable figure who she believed had left London and settled in the neighbourhood some years ago. As she came almost level with the front door, she noticed him sitting in his porch, smoking a cigarette.

"Good evening, Katy." His voice was soft yet it had a curious vibrance. She was surprised that he had addressed her by her christian name, for she had scarcely spoken to him since coming to Netherford.

"Good evening, Mr Hillier." To her dismay, she saw him get up and amble towards his gate, so that she was obliged to pause.

"A lovely day it's been," he remarked, casually, by way of an opening gambit. He was quite close to her now and she was aware of his short, thick-set body and bald head and the way his eyes under their shaggy eyebrows stared at her, intently. She had never given him much thought before, other than that he appeared to be rather an ugly man who, according to May, did not mix much in the local community. "He goes in for those Bloomsbury types," her sister had said, scornfully. "You know, the ones who used to visit Maggie Fortescue at the Moat. Only his friends aren't so nice as hers were. It's my belief half of them pretend to be married for the look of the thing, but I swear that the whole boiling are no better than they should be."

Remembering May's words, Katy answered almost primly, "Yes, it's certainly wonderful haymaking weather." She felt suddenly uncomfortable and wished that she had not allowed him to waylay her so that she had been forced to exchange pleasantries. She started to move away but he said, quickly, "You wouldn't care to join me in a glass of mead, would you? It's what I happened to be drinking when you came along."

She was astonished. Did he really think that she would go, alone, into his house—or, at any rate, his porch—at this hour? What did he take her for? May was right. Probably all his friends were no better than they should be.

"Oh, no," she replied, curtly, just remembering to add "thank you" before continuing, "I . . . have to be getting back. My sister will be expecting me."

Did he give a slightly sardonic smile after saying, "Another time, maybe?" She wasn't sure. She only knew as she left him that whenever she had occasion to walk to Sweetacres again, she would take another route.

It was only later, much later that night, when she woke from a troubled sleep, her body throbbing, and Philip's name on her lips, that she realised, to her horror, that the person who had been making love to her in her dream was not her late husband, but Gordon Hillier.

24

"When are you going to have Toby clipped?" Phoebe Moreton, immaculately turned out, as usual, in a heather-coloured tweed coat and beret to match, was surveying Emily's pony over the top of the paddock gate.

"He's not going to be clipped. He's got to sleep rough." Emily slipped another lump of sugar into Toby's mouth and coloured slightly. It was mid-October and Phoebe, together with a new French governess, had been sent to convalesce at the Grange after a recent attack of scarlet fever. She turned her small, proud, sharp-featured face towards her companion, a mixture of astonishment and condescension in the pale blue eyes.

"But what about the opening meet?"

"I . . . I don't hunt. So far I just have lessons with Miss Cory or go for rides with Helen Swayne or Mr Farley."

"Oh." Phoebe plucked a blade of grass from the nearby hedgerow and sucked it, thoughtfully.

Emily had been wondering whether she would have to offer Phoebe a ride on Toby and was relieved when her guest had not arrived in jodhpurs. She felt sure now that such a thing was not desirable from either of their points of view, especially after Phoebe's next remark.

"I'm going to the Hall tomorrow to ride with my cousins. You know, Belinda and Gillian."

Emily did not know—at least, only of them. This time it was her turn simply to say, "Oh." She was beginning to wish very much that her mother and aunt had not insisted that Phoebe must be asked back to the White Hermitage, in return for a rather tedious tea-party which she had been obliged to attend at the Grange the previous weekend. She also wished sincerely that Helen Swayne was not in bed with a bad cold today and therefore not available to give her some moral support. The nights were drawing in fast and she could not imagine how she could entertain Phoebe until Mademoiselle Hervouët came to take her away at six o'clock.

But fortunately her guest settled the problem herself by

asking after tea whether she could look at a new book of Lionel Edwards's drawings, which she had noticed lying on a side table.

"I believe he lives round these parts, doesn't he, Mrs Mason?" she said, for all the world as if she were forty-five instead of twelve years old.

"Yes, Phoebe," Katy replied, wondering if the child always behaved like this. She said as much to May, as they retired to the latter's small workroom, leaving the two children to get on as best as they could. But if Emily was dismayed by their departure, Phoebe appeared totally indifferent. She sat herself down on the mat in front of the fire and studied the book silently.

After a while, she said, "Did you know that John is going to be an artist when he leaves school?"

"No." Although Emily's dislike of Phoebe Moreton was growing stronger every minute, she was aware that she had little time for her brother also. She supposed he was just the sort of boy who *would* prefer to go out with a sketch book rather than with the hounds.

"Well, that's what he *says*," Phoebe went on, in the same condescending grown-up fashion, "but Daddy's sure Eton will knock that out of him." Suddenly bored, she shut the book and said, peremptorily, "Do you like school?"

"Yes, very much."

"Sometimes I think I'd like to go but . . . I don't know. It would interfere with hunting so much. And I wouldn't want to wear glasses. Ma'amzelle says girls often do when they go to school. I suppose that's what happened to you. Do you wear them riding?"

"No." Emily's eyes strayed towards the clock on the mantelpiece. There were seven minutes to go.

"Does John like Eton?" she asked, desperately trying to be as polite as possible.

"No. He hates it. But Daddy says it'll get better as he gets older. He's still at the fagging stage."

"Fagging?" Emily was at a loss. She noticed Phoebe frown and the look of astonishment and condescension creep into her eyes again.

"Yes, you know. The younger boys have to run about doing

errands for the bigger ones. I must say I shouldn't like that sort of thing myself. It sounds perfectly ghastly."

"Oh." With relief, Emily heard the click of the garden gate and then, mercifully, her mother coming downstairs to answer the knock at the front door.

"Ah, ma chérie! T'es-tu bien amusée?" Mademoiselle Hervouët seemed to fill the whole sitting-room with her bulk and excited volubility.

After Phoebe had given an almost inaudible, "Oui merci, Ma'amzelle," Emily shook hands and wished them both goodbye.

"Please, Mummy," she said, after the front door closed, "not again," to which she was glad to see that, for once, Katy actually smiled.

Later on, when she came to think about it, Emily realised that her mother had been altogether less sad and serious during the past few months. She could not help wondering whether Toby had something to do with it, for ever since his arrival Katy had certainly been out and about more, coming down to the paddock, helping her to saddle up and chatting to Robert Farley if he happened to be around; and one night, she had even gone out alone somewhere, although when Emily had asked Aunt Chip where, she had been rather surprised to receive a short and somewhat evasive reply, which she knew better than to pursue.

Some two or three weeks after Phoebe's visit, Emily was further surprised to be told that there was a party taking place at Greenways that Saturday evening to which her mother had been invited and, a little before seven o'clock, Katy came downstairs in a smart black crêpe tiered dress which neither her sister nor her daughter had seen her wearing for a very long time. She had obviously had her hair professionally set that day and, with just the right amount of jewellery—some small pearl-drop earrings and a necklace to match—there was something mysterious, almost magical, about her as she went out of the door, wrapped in the black cloak which May had made her many years ago.

"Mummy looked lovely, didn't she, Aunt Chip?" Emily said, as they heard the sound of her high heels receding down the garden path.

"Yes, dear."

"She looked just like she used to when she went off to dance at the theatre. What time will she be back?"

"I really don't know."

"Can I stay up and hear all about the party?"

"Oh, no." May said quickly. "You'll be asleep long before it's over."

"Who else will be there?"

May paused. "Hard to say. No one from these parts, I should think. I believe Mr Hillier has guests from London staying at Greenways. Now, Miss, it's time you stopped asking so many questions and also put away that book. You know you aren't meant to use your eyes too much in artificial light."

"Is lamplight artificial, Aunt Chip?"

"Yes, of course. Anything that the good Lord doesn't give us is artificial."

When May had seen to Emily's supper and at last chivvied her, reluctantly, to bed, she wondered whether she herself would now do exactly what her niece had wanted to: stay up until Katy returned. But soon she decided against it. Her sister was a married woman—or, rather, widow—of thirty-one. She was not the young girl of eighteen whom May had waited up for at the Mill House back in the November of 1920 when Maurice Fitzherbert had taken her to her first dance. May's reasons for staying up then were both natural and understandable. It had been simply a pleasurable duty combined with a genuine desire to know that her youngest sister had enjoyed herself. She had had no fears of Katy not returning safely as soon as the dance ended. She knew Maurice Fitzherbert and his family far too well for that. But tonight it was different. She was worried on more than one score. Ever since Gordon Hillier had suddenly rung up a few weeks back and asked to take Katy to the pictures in Westonbury to see Fred Astaire and Ginger Rogers—an invitation which, to May's surprise, her sister had accepted—she had noticed a subtle change in her. And while ordinarily she would have welcomed almost anything and anybody who brought this about, Gordon Hillier was the exception to such sentiments.

To try to take her mind off her anxiety, May picked up some sewing and turned on the wireless; but even that well-known reassuring voice ordering London to "Stop" for *In Town*

Tonight failed to hold her attention. Presently, she got up and made herself a little soup from the stockpot which was still kept in exactly the same way as it had always been in Sarah's days, and then, after drinking this and filling two hot-water bottles, she went upstairs, placed one in Katy's bed and one in her own and retired for the night.

Yet sleep eluded her. Very faintly, over the cold clear air, she heard the clock above the Wilhampton town hall strike eleven, twelve and then one. "She's having a good time," she kept saying to herself. "And so she should. She's beginning to pull out of it. It's nice to see her getting out, meeting people. Philip would have wanted her to. She's been leading the life of a nun too long." Yet at the thought of nun, May's uneasiness increased. Gordon Hillier was no monk. She felt certain of that. Neither would she have thought that he was a marrying man. Did Katy not realise what she might be letting herself in for?

At last, just after two a.m., she heard the sound she had been waiting for: footsteps along the lane. They grew louder slowly, not one person's but two. Again she tried to tell herself that that was only to be expected. No gentleman would allow a lady to return home alone at this hour. All the same, May felt that there seemed to be silence for an inordinate length of time at the garden gate until, at last, she heard Katy's footsteps alone coming up the path and her key turning in the lock. Suddenly, she was unable to refrain from putting on a dressing-gown and going down to greet her.

"Oh, May! You're not asleep. You haven't been worried, have you?" Katy said, apologetically, blinking in the light of the lamp which her sister had turned up high and dismayed to see the anxious face, shiny with cold cream, its features slightly distorted by a tightly-fitting lace and crêpe de Chine boudoir cap.

"Well . . . a little. You know how it is. I thought it was getting rather late."

"I'm sorry . . . But it was *such* a good party. Wasn't it a coincidence? Gordon had some people staying with him who I'd actually once met in London when . . . I was in that revue."

"Really?" May noted the flushed cheeks, the bright eyes, the way her sister's whole being seemed to have come alive again, as she threw off her cloak with a casual graceful movement. She herself felt a spoilsport, a silly old Mother Grundy or 'Mother Mothballs', as she used to call Maurice Fitzherbert's mother, well aware how anxious she had been that her son should not marry Katy Lodge.

"I'm glad you had a good time, my dear," she said, quickly. "Would you like a hot drink before you go up?"

"Oh, no thanks. Gordon gave us all some mead to finish up with. I must say it was very good."

Without saying more, they went upstairs quietly, careful not to wake Emily, and parted on the landing. May got into bed again and pushed her feet down the feather mattress to where her hot water bottle was still warm. But it was quite a while before she drifted off to sleep; and when she did so she found herself thinking the same thought which so often came to mind: if Katy had married Maurice Fitzherbert, none of this sort of thing would ever have happened.

25

"There's been talk, May." Edith picked up the tea-pot from her kitchen table and poured out a second cup for her sister and herself. "No sugar today, then?" she enquired, as an afterthought.

"No thanks, Edie. I went on the scales in the chemist's only an hour or so ago."

It was a few weeks after Christmas and May, who had now learnt to drive, was visiting Edith after doing some shopping in Wilhampton. She was by no means as expert at the wheel as Katy, but Arnold Parker's son, who had given her lessons over a year ago, had pronounced her perfectly safe to go out alone, even if reversing into small spaces was not exactly her forte. As with the wireless, driving a car had given May's life another extra dimension. She was delighted to be able to transport herself hither and thither in such an independent way. She went slowly and carefully, gave all the correct hand signals, could double-declutch and did not feel at a disadvantage because she found it easier to negotiate the Wilhampton streets rather than the Westonbury ones; for, as far as May was concerned, her home town was almost always where she wanted to go. In her eyes there was and never would be anywhere quite like it even though, with her customary cheerful resourcefulness, she found Netherford and its inhabitants a pleasant place in which to live—that is, if it were not for Gordon Hillier.

"Where did you hear it, Edie?" she now asked, stirring her tea from force of habit, even though there was no sugar in it.

"Where do you think? In Lilian Perrick's shop. She was serving Phyllis Hopkins when I went in to buy our Georgie some sherbert." Here, Edith broke off and told her youngest son to run round the back and go and play next door. As soon as he had departed, she continued, "It was the words 'merry widow nowadays' which caught my attention and the way they stopped talking suddenly when I appeared. As soon as Phyllis had gone out—I must say she's a dour one if ever there was one—I asked Lilian if it was Katy they'd been discussing."

"And what did she say?"

"Well, she hedged a bit and went rather red. You know what Lilian is. I know for a fact she gossips about our Della. Calls her a honeypot for the boys. I must say myself that I wish Della was like her twin sister. Debbie's much more serious-minded. But that's by the way. To get back to Katy. There was Lilian smirking behind the counter and eventually she came out with, 'Well, Edie, your youngest sister's always been a bit on the flighty side, hasn't she?' 'Flighty?' I asked her. 'How dare you talk like that, Lilian. Just because she's pretty and has lived in the west end of London doesn't mean she's flighty. She's been through a lot lately, poor girl.' And then Lilian gave one of those shifty looks of hers and said, 'Oh, I *know* but she's making up for lost time now, by all accounts. I'm not saying there's anything wrong in it, mind, but you'd think she might take up with someone, well. . . more her own age. Besides, folks say a lot of funny things go on at Greenways'."

May was silent. She knew that she would have to have a really serious talk with Katy when she got back. It wouldn't be the first time. But whenever she had tried to broach the subject, her youngest sister had simply opened those enormous grey eyes of hers and said, "But May, where's the harm? Gordon's got such an original mind. More like Philip's. He makes me laugh. I'm not hurting anyone by seeing him sometimes."

When May had pointed out that she did not know what effect it might have on Emily, Katy had replied that her daughter seemed happier now that she was happier. In a way, May knew this to be true, but she wondered how long it would last. Emily, at the moment, for all her intelligence, was extremely immature and naïve. She was what the Dowager was apt to refer to as: "A typically nice English girl—late in growing-up". But one day, not too far ahead, they were going to have to tell her about the start of menstruation and the facts of life. It wasn't like it had been in May's day. Not a word of enlightenment had ever come from Sarah; only, oddly enough, from Lilian Perrick, who had lent her a curious book called *The Cradle Ship*. May had been thirteen at the time and, with its allusive prose and whimsical drawings of some mother-to-be going around in long floating gowns with her husband always hovering anxiously in the background, the whole subject had seemed somehow more shameful and shrouded in mystery than ever. Of course, now that Emily was so often riding or running about on at least two farms in the neighbourhood, May felt that she had probably assimilated quite a lot of knowledge concerning procreation; moreover she supposed that there were certain girls at school willing to impart some extra clumsy and inaccurate information. But it would be so much better if her mother, at the appropriate time, could talk to her naturally and sensibly about the subject. Yet would Katy be able to do that at the rate things were going? It was even possible that Emily would soon start asking awkward questions about her mother and Mr Hillier.

"She's always been different, hasn't she?" Edith went on, breaking in on May's thoughts. "I mean, Katy's had grand ideas. She's never been quite one of us. No more than Philip."

"Yes, I know what you mean."

"I often feel sad she couldn't have fallen for Maurice Fitzherbert like he did for her. I know you do, too. D'you see much of him these days?"

"Not a lot. Although, as a matter of fact, I'm gong to call in at East Lodge on my way home."

"Oh, *May*. Nothing serious, I hope?" Edith looked concerned. Her eldest sister was the mainstay of the family. She hated to think of her ill.

"No. Probably just the change of life. But I keep getting a rash come up on my face and neck." May could actually feel it now beginning to trouble her. "I'd best be getting along, Edie. I want to have a look in on Ethel Sharman, too, if I can. She's a bit lonely since I left Cob Lane."

On Katy's insistence, May was no longer a panel patient of Maurice's and therefore, just before five-thirty, she drew up at the front door of East Lodge, got out of the car and rang the bell. Gone were the days when no female patient would dream of visiting the doctor without some other female to accompany her. To May's surprise the door was answered by Clare Fitzherbert herself who explained, none too graciously, that owing to certain temporary domestic changes, she was having to act as parlourmaid.

What a strange choice of wife, May reflected, as she sat in Maurice's sombre old-fashioned drawing-room. Of course, he had been caught on the rebound. No doubt about that. And if one did not look too closely at Clare's face, her actual physique was vaguely similar to Katy's. She was small and thin, with a mass of the same light brown hair. But after that, the likeness stopped. May believed that Maurice's wife had been a little more charming and attractive during their courtship, but something must have gone seriously wrong soon after the wedding. Was it, May wondered—albeit feeling guilty for even harbouring such a thought—a problem of sex? After all, there had never been any children. Presumably the marriage bed wasn't happy.

"May?" Maurice had come into the room so quietly and she had been thinking so hard that she had not heard the door open. She stood up, flustered. The rash was quite evident now and there was little need to explain why she had come, when she found herself seated in his small consulting room at the back of the house.

After he had examined her carefully and asked a few questions, he pulled a piece of headed notepaper towards him and started to write out a prescription. "This ointment should help, May," he said, handing it to her. "But I can't guarantee it. You see, I think . . . the trouble is probably . . . well, of nervous origin. You've been carrying quite a load the last few years, haven't you, my dear."

To her mortification, she found tears beginning to well up in her eyes. Embarrassed, she opened her handbag and fumbled for a handkerchief. It was ridiculous. She ought not to be crying like this. True, she had cried once before in front of him, when she had first heard how ill Katy was and that she would probably have to undergo a second operation. But there was nothing like that now. Katy was, on the whole, very much better than she had been for some time. Emily might have had to take to wearing glasses but she was getting on well at school and, with a pony of her own, she was in her seventh heaven. Compared to many people, they were not worried financially. And being able to drive a car had given May so much more freedom. There was nothing to cry about.

Yet she was aware of the deep concern in Maurice Fitzherbert's eyes; how he almost, but not quite, put out a hand to comfort her; that of all the people in the world—even before any blood ties—she felt much more kinship with this gentle compassionate man who so easily might, many long years ago, have become her brother-in-law.

"You couldn't get away for a while, could you, May?" she heard him say, quietly. "A little holiday would do you good."

"Away?" She looked at him, askance. "Oh no, Maurice." How could she possibly go away? Anyway, where could she go? There was, she supposed, her brother up in Catterick, but she saw him so seldom that they had grown apart. She knew that Henry would be only too pleased to have her, but she was not so sure about his wife. Poor Marianne had been given the cold shoulder by Sarah, all right, back in 1919, when she had given birth to Frank François only seven months after the marriage. No, it wouldn't be any good going to visit Sergeant Henry Lodge and his wife. Besides, she was very much needed where she was just now, although she couldn't tell Maurice why. He evidently had not heard anything or surely he wouldn't have suggested her leaving Netherford? Or had he? Maybe he thought her absence might make Katy behave more responsibly. One never knew how much a doctor, or a rector, for that matter, was aware of what was going on. The Reverend Donaldson and Maurice's father had had an uncanny knack of keeping their fingers on the corporate pulse of the neighbourhood. She suspected that Maurice had inherited the same ability. All the same, whatever he felt, she wasn't going to risk any kind of holiday. There was Emily to consider. She came first.

"If you won't go away, May," he said, as she got up to go, "try to take things a little easier. I hope the ointment helps but, in any case, come and see me again in a couple of weeks. How's Emily, by the way?"

She had recovered her composure now and was able to answer him quite cheerfully. "Oh, she's fine, thank you Maurice. And of course she positively worships that pony of hers."

He smiled and wished her goodbye. Only as she was driving home did it suddenly occur to her that for the first time she could ever remember, he had not actually asked after Katy.

26

There was no harm in it, as she kept telling May. Her involvement with Gordon Hillier really only amounted to a visit to the pictures and dinner at the White Lion in Westonbury about once a week, or possibly supper at Greenways, when there were always others present. Gordon had behaved quite decorously—apart from one or two occasions when Katy felt that he had been on the verge of doing or saying something just a fraction more intimate, such as on the evenings when he had walked her home or the time when she had looked up suddenly from where she had been sitting on his sofa, listening to his friends discussing the theatre, and found him watching her, carefully. But she was no longer apprehensive about him. The leisurely pace at which he seemed prepared to let their relationship develop had allayed any initial fears. She knew that he admired her and enjoyed her company and for this she was grateful. It was so long, so very long, since a man had made this quite so obvious. But that was as far as the whole thing went or was going to go. She wished that she could get May to see this.

One evening towards the end of April, Katy was in her bedroom geting ready for a slightly different kind of outing with him. It had been a cold late spring but, during the past few days, one of those quick-change acts which only the English climate seemed able to perform successfully pushed summer on to the forefront of the stage. Robert Farley's arable fields, which had hitherto worn only the thinnest of green sheets over the brown earth, suddenly appeared to be covered by a thick emerald quilt; the foliage of the trees, which had been but flimsy lace mantles, was now dense and luxuriant; the blackthorn might still be in the hedges, but the sun was warm and Emily's pony occasionally kicked up his heels and tore round the paddock for sheer joy of living.

Gordon had said that it seemed a shame to waste such lovely weather by sitting in a stuffy picture-house and proposed taking a picnic and driving Katy some twenty miles over to Great Ridgeford. It seemed an admirable suggestion and, having got him to agree to her at least providing the food, she found herself very much looking forward to the expedition. She had never been to the Ridgeford villages, but she had heard that on a clear day from the downs above them it was perfectly possible to see the English Channel.

Now, having put on a cream tussore blouse and a light-weight grey flannel skirt, she sat at her dressing-table, carefully applying vanishing cream and powder and just a touch of lipstick and rouge. Katy had no desire—nor, she knew, would it be suitable—to emulate those fashionable ladies, the photographs of whom she had just begun to study again in the popular press, particularly the two she had noticed in the latest edition of May's *Britannia and Eve*: Barbara Hutton and some woman called Mrs Simpson. With their almost black lipstick and heavy eye-shadow, they seemed to her to have turned themselves into clowns. All the same, she did not believe in leaving her looks entirely to nature, as did Frances Farley and Dorothy Swayne. Even May approved of a little make-up, although lately she had had to refrain from using any at all owing to her unfortunate rash. Poor May. Katy knew that she had given her a bad time the last few years. It seemed so ironical that just when she herself was beginning to pick up the threads of life once more, she had burdened her sister with a different kind of anxiety altogether. It often made her feel guilty, yet she was loth to give up her new friendship. If only she could get May to approve of Gordon Hillier. She would like to have asked him to the White Hermitage. After all, it was *her* home, but she did not want to incur further trouble—something which she felt he understood—and therefore, so far, he had not set foot inside the door.

Presently Katy got up, took out a grey swagger coat from the wardrobe, collected her handbag and went down into the garden to find Emily putting Toby through his paces in the paddock, while May was watching from over the fence. The child had erected some sticks, through which she was preparing her pony for the bending race at the Wilhampton gymkhana later in the summer. Emily, flushed with triumph at Toby's last effort, pulled up and shouted, "Did you see that, Mummy? He's coming along beautifully. We could even *win*. Toby could get a red rosette."

Katy laughed. "That would be wonderful, darling. But isn't it time you gave over now?" She would like to have seen her daughter safely dismounted before leaving.

"Shan't be long. Just another few tries." Emily waved gaily and trotted the pony to her improvised starting line, while the sisters exchanged quiet goodnights. Both knew that it would be doubtful if Katy returned much before eleven.

The drive to Great Ridgeway gave Katy not only pleasure but a great deal of interest, making her realise how comparatively little she knew of her home ground other than within a five or six-mile radius. She had dim recollections of being taken further afield by train when she was a child in order to visit both her maternal and paternal grandparents; but such occasions were rare and, through going to work in London at so young an age and then living there immediately after she married, there had been little opportunity to explore the west country. True, the advent of buses and motor-cars had made travelling a great deal easier during the few times she had stayed at the Mill House, but it was not really until she and Philip had come to live at the Moat, and sometimes of a Sunday afternoon he would take her and Emily out in the Morris, that she began to appreciate their all-too-brief journeys into the New Forest or the Blackmore Vale. Since her husband's death she had only used the car for purely practical purposes.

This evening, as Gordon drove her up over the Dorset Downs and stopped by an old barn situated on what seemed like the top of the world, she drew in her breath and then gazed silently at the scene all around her for quite a while.

"It's like a . . . sort of glory, isn't it?" she said, turning to him at length.

He smiled at her choice of phrase. "Yes, I thought you'd like it. Shall we take our picnic over to those trees? That's where we should just be able to see the Channel."

She nodded and got out of the car, waiting while he extracted the hamper and a rug from the boot. Slowly, they made their way over to a small clump of beeches, where he spread out the rug at the base of one of the largest and they sat down facing due south. In the distance, where the greeny-blue horizon dipped slightly, there was a patch of deeper blue. It seemed perfectly natural for him to pick up her hand as he pointed it out to her. "The sea, Katy," he said, softly.

She had never thought about it very much before but now,

still looking ahead, she replied, "Do you know, Gordon, I've only been to the seaside once." She did not add "on my honeymoon".

"Really?" He did not seem altogether surprised. He simply continued, "Well, perhaps we could put that right this summer . . . Besides a lot of other things."

She was in his arms then. She kept telling herself that she hadn't meant it to happen, that she hadn't expected it to, but soon she was being given little time to think. She was being pushed backwards, gently but expertly, until she finally found herself stretched out full length on the rug and responding eagerly to something of which she had long been starved. In between his kisses, she was vaguely aware of the leafy tracery above her. She could have been once again on Putney Heath or Breconbury Down with Philip. She might not feel for Gordon Hillier in the same way as she had for her husband, yet his love-making was something she understood, wanted and needed. She felt his hands start to unbutton her tussore blouse and she did not restrain him.

"I always suspected," she heard him say, "that you might be rather good at this sort of thing, Katy." His voice was lazy, bantering.

She blushed and turned her head away.

Katy never knew exactly when or how she managed to stop what had seemed like the inevitable taking place. One minute she was prepared to give in to an overwhelming physical urge, the next it was as if some bell in her inner consciousness was ringing loudly, insistently; and as if in some inexplicable way it was unmistakably connected with Emily. She sat up quickly, so quickly, in fact, that Gordon Hillier was left lying beside her, bewildered and frowning.

"What is it, Katy?"

Agitatedly, she buttoned up her blouse. "I'm sorry . . . I shouldn't have let you . . . Forgive me."

"But you were enjoying it, my dear, just as much as I."

"Yes . . . No. I mean, it was wrong of me."

He propped himself up on one elbow. "Hardly fair, was it?" he said. "After all, it isn't as if you're . . . inexperienced. Is it your habit to lead men on and then hold out on them? There's a word for that kind of woman, you know."

"Yes . . . I know. I've said I'm sorry. I can't explain."

"Is it because you weren't . . . prepared? I'd have taken care of all that, you know."

"Yes. I'm sure."

"Well then . . ." He attempted to pull her down beside him again, but she struggled free.

With a shrug, he sat up also, opened the picnic basket and began looking inside. Presently, he handed her a glass of white wine. "I have never," he said, as he slowly sipped one himself, "entirely understood women. Possibly you take more understanding than most."

It was not even ten o'clock when they came over the Barbury turnpike and dropped down into Netherford. Katy was surprised to see a car parked outside the Hermitage. As they drew closer, she recognised it as Maurice Fitzherbert's.

"Oh, my God!" She clenched her fists together, staring at it in horror.

"Don't worry, Katy. It may be nothing." He dropped a hand on to her knee, but it was a purely avuncular gesture.

Angrily, she brushed it aside. "How can it be nothing, Gordon. Maurice wouldn't call at the Hermitage at this hour for *nothing*."

Her voice had risen, hysterically. He stopped at the gate. Before he had had time to reach across and open the door, she was out and flying up the garden path.

27

For over a fortnight, May and Katy between them kept an almost round-the-clock vigil by Emily's bedside in Westonbury Infirmary, where she was taken after being thrown from her pony. One evening, towards the end of that time, the child opened her eyes and asked for her mother. Ever afterwards, Katy thanked God that she had been the one who was there. Yet it was but the beginning of a long, slow and painful recovery. Even at the end of it, Maurice Fitzherbert warned Katy that it was possible Emily might always walk with a slight limp.

During those first agonizing two weeks, Katy did something which she had not done for a long time: she prayed. In their separate ways, both sisters felt responsible for the accident: May, because she had been the prime motivator in Emily's having a pony; Katy, not only because of her absence from home at the time of the fall but because of what she had been doing during that absence. The memory haunted her, tortured her. That early, harsh indoctrination concerning good and evil from which she felt she had managed to escape now seemed to re-establish itself more firmly than ever. Her parents' warnings and strict conventional attitudes—especially Sarah's condemnation of any woman who, in her eyes, was no better than she should be—kept repeating themselves in her tired brain; while she was constantly reminded of those terrifying, doom-laden texts which were even now still pinned up outside the chapel on the corner of East Street and to which, in her youth, her eyes had been inescapably drawn: *Be sure your sin will find you out*, *Enter not into temptation* and *The sins of the fathers* . . . Only in this case, she thought grimly, it was not an errant father who had visited his sins upon his children but a wanton mother. Her personal castigation knew no bounds. What ever had *induced* her to go on a picnic with Gordon Hillier? She had known deep down, hadn't she, that it was asking for trouble?

In the long hours of watching and waiting, Katy recalled that other picnic with Philip on Putney Heath soon after they had met which, though of a more innocent nature, had nevertheless been followed by retribution. In many ways, she felt that there was a definite similarity between that which had taken place in the early summer of 1920 and that which had so nearly happened in the spring of 1934. Because even then, there had been the same initial abandonment, the sudden halt she had put to proceedings and the shock of her return when she was told that she was wanted immediately at the Mill House, because her mother and her eldest sister were seriously ill. Did one's life path always follow the same pattern, she wondered? Was a person conditioned to make the same kind of mistakes over and over again which gave rise to the same sort of tragedy and remorse? She supposed that she was being morbid; for, in the light of experience, she knew, logically, that her actions could not possibly have caused her mother's or Flo's or Emily's misfortunes; yet she was unable to rid herself of the idea. There were, as Sarah used to shake her head and mutter, "More things in heaven and earth . . ."

Emily did not return to the Hermitage until the end of July and when she did, there was a very great change in her. Physically, she was pale, weak and a little uncertain on her feet. Moreover, during the time she had spent in bed she seemed to have grown several inches and was now taller than either her mother or her aunt. But it was mentally that the alteration was most apparent. There had fortunately been no brain damage, even though she had suffered a fractured skull; yet the child had been through a lot and this manifested itself in a quiet, curiously detached attitude to the world around her.

It had been agreed by May and Katy that Toby should be sent temporarily, and in all probability, permanently, to one of Frances Farley's nieces; and this Emily appeared to accept quite naturally. She did not refer to what had happened. For one thing, mercifully, she could remember nothing of the fall, how, in her excitement, she had turned the pony too short and he had gone down, throwing her between him and the side of the skilling on which she had hit her head. That scene was imprinted, indelibly, on May's mind only. She could recall the sudden fear, the bundle of yellow jersey and fawn jodhpurs lying on the ground, running towards it and kneeling down, the miraculous arrival of Robert Farley and how he had taken off his jacket and placed it gently over the inert form, while warning May not to attempt to move the child until the doctor came; and then there had been the waiting until, suddenly, she was aware of Maurice Fitzherbert's quiet voice and the ambulance backing into the paddock. Once they had settled Emily inside it, May had been allowed to accompany her niece on that slow harrowing drive to the Infirmary, where she found Maurice already standing at the entrance to receive them, after which he promised to return to Netherford in order to bring Katy to the hospital as soon as possible.

Naturally, neither sister spoke very much of all that had taken place that night; and the fact that Emily herself never enquired made it that much easier. What was soon to prove more of a problem, however, was the child's education. Maurice Fitzherbert did not consider Emily fit enough to return to Wickfield House for some time and the services of Ethel Sharman were therefore called upon once more. While doubtful that she was up to the teaching standard required, Ethel was only too pleased at the thought of being in contact with her favourite pupil again and it was agreed that, with the help of all the books listed by the school which Emily would have been studying had she been there, Ethel would come to Netherford three afternoons each week, transported to and fro by either May or Katy. As the nights drew in, the little ménage at the White Hermitage settled down into a different, calmer and, in many ways, less troubled routine than it had had for some time. It might have been a house of women, but at least they were all in accord and the simple, if cloistered, atmosphere seemed to give each one of them a necessary period of reparation.

Gordon Hillier had written Katy a kind and sympathetic letter soon after the accident to which, in due course, she replied. He did not attempt to ask her out again and she naturally had no wish to go. By mutual tacit agreement, their affair—if such it could be called—was over. May, with commendable restraint, never mentioned it. The rash on her face and neck, like Emily's condition, slowly improved, as she set about making her sister, her niece and herself new winter dresses. Such an undertaking was not without forethought because, on the advice of Maurice Fitzherbert, Katy had booked up to take the three of them for a week's holiday at the end of October to a hotel on the south coast and the thought of this began to rekindle some of Emily's former animation.

"Will I stay up to supper with you and Mummy, Aunt Chip?"

"It depends," May answered, guardedly. "And anyway, Miss, it's called dinner at the Boscombe Towers."

"Oh. I bet that's why you're making me a new dress, though."

"Perhaps. But a nice blue velvet frock will always come in useful. I believe Phoebe Moreton and her brother will be spending Christmas at the Grange and there could well be a party."

Emily became pensive. She had not seen Phoebe since she had come to tea at the White Hermitage the previous year, when she had found her precocity appalling. To meet her again would probably mean being asked awkward questions about Toby and riding, something which Emily preferred to forget. "I'd rather stay up to dinner than go to a party at the Grange," she said. And there the matter rested.

Although the visit to the seaside was taken out of season, it proved to be an unqualified success. May, having never spent a night in a hotel before, took particular pleasure in studying the other guests, casting a discreet but knowledgeable eye over every detail of their apparel. "I haven't seen anything that's a patch on Emily's velvet or our wool georgettes," she would say to her sister, with satisfaction. "And as for that old crone in the corner. Did you ever see such an ill-fitting reach-me-down?" And Katy, pleased that the week was going so well, would smile and agree.

As for Emily—although her wish to remain up for dinner was granted—she found her chief source of delight at teatime, during which an orchestra played Viennese waltzes and some of the latest Cole Porter and Noel Coward hits, *Night and Day* and *I'll Follow My Secret Heart* being her two favourites. She would sit entranced, absentmindedly stuffing herself with cucumber sandwiches and chocolate éclairs until, to her regret, the musicians packed up and went away at five-thirty. When, on the last night of the holiday, May and Katy took her to a production of Dodie's Smith's *Autumn Crocus*, she decided then and there to become a playwright, expecially when she heard that this particular play was written by a shop assistant. It must be quite easy, she felt, and went back to Netherford with her imagination fired and her head full of promising ideas.

In a sudden burst of confidence, she said as much to John Moreton one afternoon during the Christmas holidays, when they cycled over the Barbury turnpike together while Phoebe had gone riding with her cousins. Emily no longer found he was quite the object of scorn which she had once considered him to be. He had shown her, diffidently, some of his drawings, and she could not help feeling that they were rather good. He was so totally unlike Phoebe that it was hard to think of them as brother and sister; certainly, he was much easier to talk to.

"Do you," he said, on the way home, "ever ride now?"

"No. I had this accident, you know."

"Yes, my grandmother told me. Do you . . . mind? About not riding, I mean?"

"Not really. I . . ." She hesitated. Colour flooded her face and she hoped he would not notice. "I'm rather scared of horses now," she went on, with a rush.

She was relieved at his matter-of-fact reply.

"Quite understandable. I've always thought them stupid animals, as I believe I once told you. I wish my sister wasn't so mad about them. She doesn't think of anything else and there are so many other things to do with one's time."

She wondered whether to risk her next question and decided that, as he himself had switched the conversation on to such personal lines, he would not mind.

"Do you like Eton better now?" she asked.

"It's not so bad. I enjoy cricket. And art. And I've just taken up photography. Incidentally, doesn't one get a marvellous view of the valley from here."

By mutual consent, they slowed down and dismounted, studying the scene before them and the silvery course of the Willon, so much easier to discern now that the trees were bare.

"It's a bit like being in an aeroplane up here, isn't it?" he continued. "It reminds me of something one of our English masters said the other day: when you look down on a river from a great height, instead of just sitting by its banks, it's as if you can see the past and the present and the future all at once."

"Yes, I . . . suppose it is."

"Look," he said, suddenly pointing. "There's the Felt Mills. Do you remember that time I first met you when you were staying there with your mother and she took us to see the mill-race? D'you ever go there now?"

She looked away and he could have kicked himself. That was where her father had drowned, hadn't he? He seemed to recall there having been some sort of mystery.

"I'm sorry," he went on, quickly. "I . . . was forgetting."

This time she turned to face him. "It's quite all right," she replied, quietly. "It was a long time ago."

And so it was, she thought, as they remounted and free-wheeled practically the whole way home. Her memory of the tragedy had always been shadowy and confused. She had never known much about what had happened, other than that neither her mother nor her aunt wished to talk about it. Gradually, she had begun to sense that there was something not quite straight-forward—even shameful—connected with her father's death. In some curious way it became linked in her mind with those puzzling, secretive, nocturnal goings-on from which she had been excluded as a child. Once or twice, as she grew older, she had been on the point of asking May a few questions, but at the last moment she had refrained. Perhaps, after all, it was better not to know. She liked things the way they were: just her mother, herself and Aunt Chip. She would never have breathed a word to anyone about it, not even Helen Swayne, her best friend, but somehow life seemed easier without her father about the place.

At the gate of the Hermitage, John raised his cap and wished her goodbye, remarking that he was looking forward to seeing her at the tea-party his grandmother was giving the following afternoon. "She's hiding clues," he added, with a smile. "That's why she and Phoebe's new governess wanted us all out of the way today. As far as I can make out, Granny has been organising treasure hunts all her life. I don't know how she still does it now she's confined to a wheel-chair."

Emily went indoors, any sense of embarrassment which had overcome her a little while ago having been completely swept aside by his gentle apology. Now that she had got to know John Moreton better, she felt as if she would have some ally at the forthcoming party at the Grange. She had ceased to dread it. She would be quite interested to take part in a treasure hunt. She wondered whether she would need to wear her spectacles for it. She certainly wasn't going to keep them on at tea. It was perfectly possible, by dint of a few little tricks such as screwing up her eyes, to get by without them when she wanted to, even if the world did seem rather on the hazy side.

28

"I'm glad Doctor Fitzherbert thinks Emily can start again at Wickfield House in the summer term," said Ethel Sharman, one late March evening the following year when May was driving her home. "Not that I won't miss my visits to the Hermitage more than I can say. But the child needs companionship of her own age now, May. She's been with grown-ups too long."

"Yes. Yes, I daresay you're right, Ethel." May drove slowly, keeping her eyes on the narrow Netherford lane. She never, in fact, went very fast and rarely got up to even thirty miles an hour, the speed limit recently imposed in built-up areas by the young go-ahead Minister of Transport, Mr Hore-Belisha. Tonight she was taking extra care, because a mist had formed in the water meadows by the Willon and she would be thankful to reach the main road where she always found the new cat's eyes such a blessing after dark. It was a relief when her passenger, possibly sensing her need for concentration, lapsed into silence.

But just before they reached Cob Lane Ethel suddenly clapped a hand on her forehead and burst out, "Oh May, I quite forgot. I meant to mention it before. Would it make any difference, do you think, if I made my final session with Emily next Tuesday instead of Monday. I've got Edwin coming to lunch that day. You remember, my cousin at the Air Ministry."

"No, of course not, Ethel. How is he, by the way?" May knew that Ethel had a high regard for Edwin, who appeared to be her only relative.

"Well, he's worked off his feet, poor thing." Ethel's voice became subdued. "And you know, May, from what he says in his letters, you can't help *wondering*."

May negotiated the tricky turning into Cob Lane and drew up outside Number 7 before answering, "Wondering what, Ethel?"

"About this conscription that's just been introduced in Germany. This man Hitler . . . You don't know what to think. He's got such a shifty face. I mean, what's he re-arming *for*? That's what I should like to know."

"Not another war, Ethel. That's for certain. And anyway, there couldn't be. The League of Nations will see to that."

"Please God you're right, my dear. But I just don't like it somehow. You should have seen the photographs in the last issue of the *Illustrated London News*. Edwin sent it to me. I'll bring it along next time I come."

After she had wished Ethel good-night, May backed the car and turned round—not without a little difficulty—and then, glancing somewhat wistfully at her old home, drove back to the Hermitage. The trouble with Ethel, she reflected later on that night when she was in bed, was that she would keep reading the more serious papers and magazines. They were all right in their way, but it didn't do to dwell quite so much on the possibility of wars or the blunders of politicians. It was so much better to look on the bright side and, personally, May felt she had a lot to be thankful for just now: Emily's return to health (her niece hardly ever limped except when she was very tired); Katy's less self-absorbed and altogether more mature attitude to life, which she was forced to admit was thanks—agonizing as it had been—to the child's accident; then there was the miraculous disappearance of her own distressing rash and, what was more, a very special summer to which they could all look forward.

To May's surprise and delight the Dowager Lady Fairfax, unable to take any active part in proceedings herself, had put forward May's name as a suitable candidate to sit on a committee to organise the forthcoming Jubilee celebrations and, after her election, it would have been hard to find a more energetic and enthusiastic member. Along with the Dowager's daughter-in-law and various other lady parishioners, including Dorothy Swayne, May found herself discussing a variety of ideas with the Reverend Morgan—the new young rector of Wilhampton—Maurice Fitzherbert, Cyril Butt and Robert Farley; for Netherford, being so close to the small town, always joined forces with it at times like these. The proposals most favoured to do justice to the occasion ranged from a pageant, a tree-planting, a children's tea-party, a torchlight procession, an ox-roasting in the market-square and a concert by the Wilhampton brass band.

"You can't have them all, May," Maud Fairfax had said with a smile, one evening when she had gone to the Grange to report proceedings. "Personally, I should think a children's tea-party, a tree-planting and a torchlight procession would be best. A nice Jubilee oak on Breconbury Down at the top of Dick Swayne's farm would seem most appropriate. I feel a pageant would be too much of a problem. I remember the one poor Maggie Fortescue arranged at the time of the Coronation. Such *bickering*, May. You've no idea. They wanted poor Dick Swayne's father and mother to dress up as George III and Queen Charlotte, but Mrs Swayne, bless her soul, said that nothing would induce her to do that because, although George III was known as the farmer king, he was also as mad as a hatter and her husband was the sanest person she knew!"

May had not been able to refrain from rocking with laughter and saying, "Oh, chippatoo!" until the Dowager had gone on a little more seriously, "If only Alicia were here instead of Rachel, it would all be so much easier, but I'm afraid my daughter in-law isn't quite up to . . . well . . . taking charge of a *pageant*."

It was not often that Maud Fairfax went as far as to voice the slightest regret that the young woman who had stepped into her shoes was in any way a disappointment to her. But May had known long ago, without being told, that the Dowager was more than a little unhappy at the way things were run at the Hall these days and the fact that her son was so often abroad. The uncertainty as to whether he would even be at home on the 6th of May had already precluded his being asked to chair the Jubilee Committee, which duty was now being undertaken, well-meaningly but ineffectually, by his wife.

The next morning May decided to pay one of her visits to the Grange, not so much this time to tell the Dowager what progress was being made, as to elicit further advice from her before the next committee meeting which was due to take place that Friday. Although May was not without her own ideas and opinions and was now quite able to put them forward to good effect, she well knew that Maud Fairfax had a lifetime's experience behind her and that, whatever pronouncement she made on such matters, it was not only sound and sensible but in some curious way she was still in remote control. She might be confined to a wheel-chair but there was not much of importance that escaped the former chatelaine of the Hall. She might never have had, like the Reverend Donaldson and Maurice's father, quite such close day-to-day contact with the local inhabitants, but she had always had her own particular ways of finding out about them and showing concern for their well-being. Even now, handicapped as she was, while she obviously enjoyed May's visits for their own sake, the latter was not unaware that her hostess put them to good use from the point of view of keeping in touch with all that was going on in the neighbourhood.

Yet, on her arrival that day, May soon discovered that there was something which had pushed the Jubilee committee—at least, temporarily—right into the background.

"I've sad news, I'm afraid, May. Nanny Barlow died last night. Of course, we've all expected it for a long time, but, nevertheless, when death finally comes . . ." The Dowager sat very erect in her wheel-chair and for once she did not end her sentence. Her eyes had an unusually faraway look in them and May knew at once what she was thinking. The woman before her was older than Nanny Barlow. She must know that she could not have many more years ahead of her. Then, after a little while, she seemed to return to the present and her customary efficient and practical way of dealing with things.

"Nanny expressed a wish to be buried in Wilhampton, May. So Alicia is making arrangements her end. I should think the funeral would be some time in the middle of next week. Not many relatives to inform. A niece and her husband—but I think they were rather a disappointment to her. Other than them, well . . . we seemed to be her life." She paused and then went on, "I suppose, in these days, some people might consider that wrong. But . . . I don't know. I believe Nanny wouldn't have had it otherwise. There'll be an announcement in *The Times* and the *Telegraph* tomorrow. I've already telephoned the *Westonbury Journal*. And I'm getting on to the Reverend Donaldson. I'm sure he'd be only too glad to come back and give the address. And we must sing *All Things Bright and Beautiful* at the service. It was her favourite hymn."

May felt the tears beginning to come. Hastily, she pulled out a handkerchief. She knew that people like the Dowager hardly ever cried in front of others, although she suspected that they probably cared just as much in their controlled, dignified way.

"I'm sure Nanny Barlow would like that," was all she managed to say.

As she left the Grange, the Reverend Morgan, young, fresh-faced, eager to please, was coming up the steps. May knew he would do his best. But how could he possibly *know*: about the Fairfaxes, their Nanny, their children and their grandchildren, and the curious inter-relationship between their family and that of the Lodges from the one-time Mill House, Wilhampton? It would take a lifetime to explain that—if it was possible to explain, which she doubted. One had to live in a place, love it, cherish it, even. It had to become part of one so that one's life was inextricably bound up with it, just as the River Willon threaded together all those little towns and hamlets through which it passed on its omnipotent way to the sea. Quietly, May wished the Reverend Morgan "Good morning", and hurried back to the Hermitage.

After much deliberation, especially on Katy's part, it was agreed that Emily should attend the funeral the following week. "I think she's old enough," May had said. "And it isn't as if she was all that close to the old soul, as you were once. That's all to the good, really. And I expect Phoebe and John William will be there, especially as he's likely to be home for the Easter holidays."

May felt her opinion in the matter to be justified when the three of them sat half way up the front aisle of St. Mark's the following Thursday afternoon. She watched both the Moreton children walk up to the front pew beside their parents—John in his Eton uniform and Phoebe in a smart navy coat and beret—where the Dowager was already waiting in her wheel-chair, with her daughter-in-law beside her. There was no sign of the present Lord Fairfax.

"I don't like it," May said to her sister later that night when Emily was in bed. "His poor wife. She does her best. It isn't her fault. They say he's in Monte Carlo. Perhaps you couldn't expect him to come back for his old Nanny's funeral but I hope to God he'll be here for his mother's."

Katy looked at her sister in some surprise. It was so unlike her to speak so vehemently, although she knew that May was becoming a force to be reckoned with. She felt that she might even end up on the local council at the rate she was going.

29

Although, despite her long absence from Wickfield House, Emily found that she was put in the same advanced form when she returned there that summer, she decided of her own volition to do a few extra studies in English Literature during the forthcoming holidays. As long as such an undertaking was done in daylight and not carried to excess, Katy felt there was no harm in it, especially as no deterioration in her daughter's short sight had been found during a recent eye-test. She was glad that Emily shared her love of reading and therefore, while she herself was enjoying Scott Fitzgerald's latest novel, *Tender Is the Night*, which she had just borrowed from Boots' library in Westonbury, Emily was becoming enthralled by *Wuthering Heights*.

At first, Katy had been reluctant to let the child read this particular book, which she always kept in a drawer by her bed, but when Emily explained that it had been listed by the English mistress at Wickfield as 'recommended reading', she had given in and handed it to her.

"You'll take great care of it, won't you, darling. If it hadn't been for *Wuthering Heights*, I might never have met your father and you wouldn't have come into the world." Katy had just begun to talk about Philip quite naturally, something which May noted with pleasure and relief.

"Yes, Mummy. Of course."

Emily took the book eagerly. She already knew the story of how her mother, as a young nursery-maid in London, had been looking at some good, albeit damaged, editions which were for sale in a trough in Masons' doorway, and how her father had practically forced his future wife into buying one because he desperately wanted to get to know her better. Emily had considered it highly romantic and the knowledge that when she had been born her parents had decided to call her after the authoress of *Wuthering Heights* had naturally only increased her interest in it. It had always been a disappointment to her that, until now, she had not been considered old enough to read it.

She could think of nothing better, she decided, when, on a

second sunny August day running, she settled down with the book, leaning back against her favourite willow tree at the end of the overgrown lane leading from the Hermitage to the river. To her right, she was aware of the thrumming of Robert Farley's tractor and binder as it circled a field of golden wheat; on the opposite bank of the Willon she could see his herd of shorthorns moving slowly towards the gateway of the meadow where, with a gentle "Coop . . . Coop", his dairyman, Fred Cutler, called them for the afternoon's milking; while half way up the downs in the distance, she could just discern a small group of ant-like figures stooking oats. But soon her surroundings were lost to her. Emily was back in time at another farm owned by another man, where it was winter, not summer, and the heroine was returning from a different Grange from the one she knew at Netherford. Emily had just got to the place where Cathy, still dressed in all her finery, rushed to embrace Heathcliff when, to her extreme annoyance, she was brought rudely back to the present century by several shrill "Cooees" coming from somewhere close at hand. There was then the sound of parting rushes and Mavis, Edith's youngest daughter, stood before her.

"Hullo, Em." The girl spoke half defiantly, half mockingly.

Mavis was a month younger than Emily, but she looked older in every way. There was a curious provocative maturity about her. She had a pale pert freckled face, albeit somewhat redeemed by a wealth of auburn hair, similar to her mother's at the same age. Her body was short but shapely and now, with both hands held firmly behind her back, she looked almost as if she wished to draw attention to it and the way her thin blue cotton dress strained over her small thrusting breasts.

"Hullo, Mavis." Emily blinked a little behind her glasses and kept a thumb on the page she had been reading. She knew that her Aunt Edith was expected to tea but had imagined that she would come, as usual, alone.

"I was going to stop home and mind Georgie," Mavis volunteered, "but when he got asked next door I decided to come along. It's not a bad walk, is it? In summer, that is."

"No." Emily was always at a loss to know how to deal with her cousins and she knew that they knew this. She often pictured them giggling behind her back and, although she had no desire to be like them, she wished that she could behave more spontaneously in their presence instead of so often being, as now, tongue-tied.

Certainly no such problem ever bothered Mavis. Suddenly, she flung herself down on the grass beside Emily and burst out, "Mum's in a terrible way. I'm not meant to know. That's why I've been sent down here to find you. She wants to talk things over privately with your Mum and Aunt May."

"Oh." Emily could not think what was the matter unless, perhaps, it had to do with her Uncle Herbert's health. Many was the time she had overheard whispers to the effect that he was unlikely to "make old bones".

"Don't you want to know what it's all about?" Mavis enquired, obviously slightly put out that her initial information had not elicited a more forthcoming response.

"Yes . . . But . . . I mean, you said you weren't meant to know."

Mavis's pale blue eyes opened wide in astonishment. If her cousin was that much of a prig, she felt it was time to shock her well and truly out of it.

"Della's in the family way," she announced, loudly. "She's *three months gone*."

Emily remained staring straight in front of her. The sun had momentarily passed behind a cloud and it seemed as if all the enchantment of the afternoon had gone with it. She knew what Mavis meant, even though it was knowledge which had scarcely been assimilated. As far as she was concerned, it was a subject which one simply never thought—and certainly never talked—about. It was disgraceful, frightening and had to be hushed up. Della had done something wicked, which was connected with a man. Just what, Emily had no idea, except that it resulted in a baby. How this came about when one was not married was a complete mystery. In her mind, giving birth was synonymous with marriage. After all, her mother had implied as much when she had given her a little talk on the subject not long ago. And whatever it was that men and women did together which resulted in a baby, while it was shameful if they were not man and wife, it was apparently perfectly acceptable—even creditable—if they were.

Or was it? Into her mind, unwilling and unbidden, came the

recollection of those nights in Davies Street long ago, when she had been suffering from nightmares and occasionally overheard something which she did not understand taking place in her parents' bedroom. Even if it were not shameful or wicked, it had definitely seemed very frightening and was obviously something which had embarrassed her mother, who had tried to pretend it hadn't happened. Emily had done her best to forget about it, as well as the guilty knowledge that when, after her father's death, she had suddenly realised that nothing like that could happen again, she had felt immensely relieved. It had never occurred to her that her mother might ever remarry. She supposed that Katy's friendship with Gordon Hillier, owing to his age, had simply come about through a mutual interest in the arts, although she had sometimes wondered why they now saw so little of each other.

"It was the torchlight procession on Jubilee night that was at the bottom of it." Still aggrieved and aggressive, Mavis broke into her thoughts. "I could have told Mum all along," she continued. "We lost Della towards the end. Debbie thought she'd gone with the Pearsons next door, but I knew better. I saw her slip away with . . . well, p'raps I'd best not say who I thought she was with." Even Mavis seemed to have some sense of obligation at this point. "Anyway, whoever it was, I knew what she'd probably be up to. You see, she's not the same as Debbie. I know what Della likes."

Part of Emily wanted to scream and ask Mavis to stop, yet part of her wanted to know more. *What* did Della like? What was Mavis getting at? She did not have to ask. Her cousin, obviously enjoying herself, seemed to be in full spate now.

"You see, my brother Donald . . . well, when they were growing up . . . I used to watch them through this little hole in the bedroom wall . . . when Mum and Dad were out. That wasn't often, mind you, but just sometimes they used to go to the pictures when Dad felt they could afford it and p'raps there was a Laurel and Hardy film on. Donald and Della used to take off all their clothes then. Of course, I mean, he never *did* anything. After all, she was his sister. But, you know, he . . . mucked her about."

Emily felt as if she were going to be sick. She wished Mavis would go away. For some unknown reason, she found her glasses misting up and she tried to fight back the tears. This, surely, wasn't what happened? The way grown-up people went on? The way her own mother and father behaved? The way she herself had been brought into the world? There must be some mistake. Mavis, after all, was just a silly and not particularly intelligent girl who had got hold of the wrong end of the stick. Yet she seemed so assured, more enlightened, it would seem, than Aunt Edith if, as she maintained, she knew what her sister had been up to on the night the Jubilee oak was planted.

Presently, conscious that she had made her point, Mavis sat up and, slightly changing her tactics, said, "Have you started yet?"

"Started?" Emily was confused, still miserable.

"Oh, Em. You know what I mean. I had the curse two years ago, but I had a feeling you hadn't."

"No," Emily answered, this time quite calmly. "And I do wish you wouldn't go on about these sort of things, Mavis."

"All right." Suddenly and quite naturally, the girl beside her put out a hand in a friendly gesture. "I know you're different from us," she continued. "Mum always said that. Just like your own Mum was. Reckon you'll make a good match one of these days. Nothing like what's happened to our Della will happen to you. D'you know what Dad said a little while ago? He said, 'Katy and her kid have class'. Funny, i'nt it, when you come to think of it. Here's you staying on at school for quite a while yet, I suppose. But I'll be leaving after Christmas. I think Mum's hoping to get me a domestic job over Baverchalke way where I'll live in. It'll make things easier at home. A bit more room for Della and her brat, that's if Bob Swayne don't marry her." Hastily, Mavis clapped a hand over her mouth and then added, apologetically, "Sorry, Em. I've properly let the cat out of the bag now, haven't I?"

"*Bob Swayne*?" Emily turned, white-faced, and stared at her cousin. "Bob Swayne," she repeated in a whisper. "Oh no, Mavis . . . you can't mean it. He's Helen's brother. It's not . . . possible."

"It's possible all right, Em, even though . . . well . . . he's several cuts above us, so to speak. Mind you, I'm not saying for sure it was him. Della likes the boys, as I said. And they like her. There's been plenty after her lately." She stood up. "I wonder if they've stopped threshing out what's going to happen to her back at the Hermitage. P'raps I'll go and see."

After she had left her, Emily remained by the willow tree, *Wuthering Heights* still open in her lap. But she did not read again that afternoon. She sat, unsure, bewildered and feeling somehow besmirched. It crossed her mind that her Aunt Edith would soon have not six but seven young things to care for in that small, hopelessly inconvenient house on downside, that is, if she did not get Mavis away to Baverchalke. Or would whoever it was who had done this terrible thing to Della marry her and make whatever was so disgraceful altogether respectable again. It would be nice to think so. Emily did not particularly care for any of her cousins, but she did not wish them any harm.

Still she sat on, reluctant to go up to the house, watching the Willon flowing gently along in front of her. Presently, the cows started meandering back into the opposite meadow, the afternoon's milking over. After a while, a fisherman came into view, leisurely casting downstream. Gradually, the unhurried peace of her surroundings began to soothe her shattered senses.

It was, perhaps, an unusual thought for one so young but when, at last, she walked slowly back up the narrow pathway and climbed over the little stile into the Hermitage garden, she was comforted by a feeling that whatever happened, she would always have herself, that as long as she remained alone and never married she would be all right.

30

During the rest of the holidays, for the first time since she had known her, Emily was reluctant to remain very long in Helen Swayne's company. But gradually, with relief, she came to realise that whoever had got Della into trouble, it was certainly not Bob Swayne. Whenever she went to Bulbarrow there was just the same easy friendly atmosphere as there had always been. Helen's parents were their usual charming selves and Bob, who she had to admit was strikingly good-looking, did not behave as if some cloud was hanging over him. Besides, Emily was conscious enough of class distinctions to know that it was most unlikely that he would have anything to do with a girl living on downside. Dorothy and Dick Swayne had made tremendous sacrifices to send him and his younger brother Tim away to a minor public school catering specially for the sons of farmers, and now Bob was destined—at least, for a year or two—to help his father at home on the farm. As for Helen, she appeared to be perfectly happy, full of plans for something she called landscape gardening: making a rockery and pool in a small corner of the Bulbarrow garden which had been given over to her.

Yet the stigma hanging over Emily's own family was, she knew, still there and becoming more oppressive and threatening every day. She could see the worried preoccupied look on her mother's and aunt's faces, however much they tried to appear normal in her presence. She occasionally overheard snatches of conversation which were hastily broken off whenever she entered the room, such as "Pity Edie wasn't stricter . . ." "Needed Sarah's hand . . ." or "D'you think Henry might . . . ?" But whatever her Uncle Henry might or might not do was something about which she could only make private conjectures. Mostly, such remarks came from May, Katy's remembrance of the recent far from creditable occasion in her own life possibly inhibiting her from being quite so openly censorious.

Emily was angered that everyone seemed to imagine that she herself knew nothing of the situation and, in consequence, she was obliged to keep up some kind of pretence. But one day, just before the start of the Wickfield autumn term, there was an incident which was so bewildering that it made her conscious of how very little, in fact, she did know. She had gone to Westonbury alone by bus to collect her school satchel which was being mended at the saddlers. While she was waiting at the stop outside the White Lion for the return journey, two women came along and stood behind her. She had no idea who they were, other than that from their conversation it appeared they were going to visit some family living on downside, "Next door," said the elder of two, "to that poor Edith Lench, the one whose daughter's up the spout."

Emily had felt the same sudden surge of nausea which she had experienced in the meadows on the day when Mavis had launched forth on her hideous outburst of enlightenment. Now, once again repelled but riveted with curiosity—especially by the crude expression which, though totally inexplicable, seemed nevertheless suggestive of something horrible—she heard the other woman reply even more incomprehensibly, "I gather it's a married man, isn't it? Lilian Perrick's son, Archie, by all accounts. He always was a bit of no good. Poor Sarah Lodge. I should think it would make her turn in her grave."

After that the bus had arrived and Emily heard no more. But all the way back to Netherford her mind had been in a turmoil. She was dimly aware that Lilian Perrick, at the Wilhampton sweetshop, had a married son who was constantly on the dole. She was not sure, but she believed that he, his wife and several children lived in one of the new council houses which, sadly, had recently been put up on what was once known as the buttercup field belonging to Bulbarrow Farm. She had not seen him for some time, but her recollection was that of a thin ferret-faced man whom Dick Swayne occasionally employed during haymaking and harvest. She looked upon him as quite middle-aged, at least thirty-five. It was just as impossible to think he was the cause of Della's downfall as it was Bob Swayne. Even more, in fact. For Archie Perrick was *married*. The two old gossips at the bus stop were obviously being just as foolish, in their way, as Mavis had been. Surely everyone knew that once a man was married he could only be the father of his wife's children?

Emily had been back at Wickfield for about a week when she came home one day to find a visitor at the Hermitage. As she entered the small drawing-room, her mother introduced her to her Uncle Henry, whom she had never seen.

She took to him at once. In his khaki uniform with his sergeant major's stripes on his arm he stood up and courteously held out his hand.

"So this is Emily, my youngest sister's child." His weather-beaten face creased into a friendly smile. "I've been looking forward to meeting you."

Solemnly, she shook hands and took off her school board and coat.

"Uncle Henry is staying the night, Emily," May said, quickly. "Run and wash your hands and then we can all have tea."

She sensed immediately why he had come and what they had been talking about before she arrived, although the conversation was now carefully steered into other directions. Henry Lodge began referring, quite naturally, to his present life at Catterick, to his wife, Marianne, who was "getting on a bit like we all are", and to their son, Frank François, who had "sensibly decided not to follow in his father's footsteps". "He's a bit like you, Emily, I shouldn't wonder," Henry Lodge went on. "He's not leaving school till next year and then, if we can somehow manage it, he wants to go into the printing trade. Although," and here she saw her uncle's face cloud over as he continued, "God knows if he won't end up in uniform, after all, the way things are going."

May remained silent. It was Katy who said, "How d'you mean, Henry?"

"Mean? Well, I don't like it. Baldwin got in at the last election in June because the Conservatives never said anything about the need for rearmament. But, by God, we need to. I've been through one war and I can't see what's to stop another in a few years' time."

"Oh, *Henry*!" Rather as she had remonstrated with Ethel Sharman not long ago, May started reaffirming her belief in the League of Nations but her brother cut her short.

"Don't let yourself be fooled, my dear. Germany left the League two years ago. It's about as much use at stopping a war as . . ." Here Henry seemed to search around for a suitable comparison which would not offend feminine susceptibilities and suddenly came up with, "Well, a mother's meeting. And you forget," he continued, "I've been out in Germany quite a bit. Our battalion was one of the last to leave at the end of the occupation in 1930. This man Hitler means business. Maybe we've only got ourselves to blame. The Treaty of Versailles wasn't just. Although . . . I don't know . . . when you've lost a brother in the fighting . . ." Henry's voice, so certain, so authoritative, suddenly became husky and altogether different.

The conversation was above Emily's head. She had never heard of the Treaty of Versailles. Her form at Wickfield was doing the French Revolution and she was longing for the Scarlet Pimpernel with Leslie Howard and Merle Oberon to come to the Odeon in Westonbury.

Presently, May drove Henry off to downside and, apart from a brief meeting the following morning, Emily did not see him again. By the time she returned from school that afternoon he had gone. She did not learn until almost a fortnight later—and then only by a short statement from her mother which brooked no further enquiries—that he had taken Della with him. She never knew until a long time afterwards that, because of her grandmother's hostile attitude over the so-called premature arrival of Henry's son, he was determined—despite his wife's natural reluctance—to do his best for his sister's child. As it turned out, his good nature was rewarded. Early the following year, just before she gave birth to a daughter, Della—greatly to her family's surprise and relief—married a young lance corporal in Henry's regiment. The news was imparted to Emily in a slightly more forthcoming manner yet, even so, she knew that the subject was not one upon which her mother and aunt wished to dwell—at least, not in front of her.

But in any case, news on a national scale was now occupying their thoughts, so much so that even the pupils of Wickfield House were made to feel its import. On January 20th they were all summoned into the big hall, where Miss Lawrence told them that King George V was dying. Throughout the day the usual clatter and hubbub of school life was subdued. No games were played and when Emily returned to the Hermitage she found Katy and May listening intently to the voice of Stuart Hibberd as he gave out hourly bulletins on the wireless: "The King's life is drawing peacefully to a close". All other programmes ceased and the intervening silence was broken only by a ticking clock, distressingly similar to the sound of a beating heart. At breakfast next morning, Emily was surprised to find how sad her mother and aunt seemed and it was obvious that May had actually been crying. The king had been but a shadowy figure in Emily's own life and the Prince of Wales, so far as she thought of him at all, a much more interesting and romantic one. She wondered whom he would make his queen and hoped it would be some beautiful girl such as those she was constantly drawing in her private sketchbook: tall and willowy, with a dreamy expression and masses of lovely long wavy hair.

May, too, evidently hoped vaguely for something of the same sort. When, during Ascot week, she noticed photographs of Edward VIII in the company of a dark, sophisticated-looking and much older woman than she would have expected, she was clearly upset. May always made a point of carefully studying the Ascot fashions and would come out with many a quick and, on the whole, remarkably shrewd observation on the merits or otherwise of a certain person's attire. In her eyes, Mrs Simpson was "smart, but too *hard*". She would have done better, May felt, to be dressed by Molyneux, as Princess Marina was; but her chief crime was the fact that she was a remarried divorcée, "not at all the kind of woman with whom the king should be consorting".

As the year progressed, although the British press was singularly restrained on the subject, any little item of information which May could glean only served to increase her consternation. She could not understand what had come over the new king, "gallivanting," as she put it, here, there and everywhere, especially on board the yacht, *Nahlin* in the Adriatic in the company of what she called a "a fast set", in which "that woman" appeared to be a fixture. It would never do for Mrs Simpson to become queen of England. Surely Mr Baldwin would put a stop to that.

When, in fact, that December, Stanley Baldwin came up to May's expectations and managed to prevent such an occurrence, May was infinitely relieved. The Duke of York might be shy and stuttering and totally lacking in that rather doubtful aura of glamour which had surrounded his elder brother, but the new Queen Elizabeth looked charming. As for the pretty well-dressed little princesses, all those shocking rumours about Margaret Rose being deaf and dumb were now proved to be clearly without foundation. She felt that the monarchy, as never before, was an institution with which the whole nation could identify. Rather as May's own family problems had been solved earlier that year, she was delighted to think that those of the throne had now been so satisfactorily straightened out.

31

"My grandmother is asking for you, Miss Lodge. I . . . we . . . wondered if you could come."

It was February 1938. John William Moreton, now up at Cambridge, stood on the doorstep of the Hermitage: tall, thin and incredibly handsome. There was something about him, May felt, which was at the same time assured yet vulnerable. With his fair wavy hair and disarming smile, he reminded her a little of a young Maurice Fitzherbert.

"Of course," she said. "Come in one moment while I get my coat."

He had to stoop to enter the front door, rather as she remembered Maurice had once had to do at the Mill House. She saw him look round as if he was expecting to see Emily. Quickly, she explained that her niece was at school, rehearsing in a play she had written for which she had won a prize and, as it meant staying late that night, her mother had driven into Westonbury to fetch her.

"Ah, I see. Is Emily leaving Wickfield at the end of the summer?"

"Yes, John."

"But not to go to university, I hope?"

"No. She's decided to attend the local art school."

"Oh, good. I can't help feeling that at Cambridge girls don't seem . . . well . . . quite right, somehow."

He helped May into his small sports car and they did not talk again until they were on their way. As he turned into the gates of the Grange, she said, gently, "Your grandmother is worse, John?"

"Yes. That's why I drove my mother down yesterday. It's pleurisy as well as pneumonia, I'm afraid."

"I'm so very sorry." May knew what that augured, especially for an octogenarian. To say more seemed somehow superfluous.

As if sensing her thoughts, the young man beside her said, "She's eighty-two, you know. I suppose . . . I mean . . . it's a good age, isn't it? But it's difficult to imagine . . ." He broke off awkwardly, obviously embarrassed at having said more than he intended. May had always known that there had been an unusually close link between the old lady and her grandson.

She could see a light now in one of the bedrooms of the Grange which she knew belonged to the Dowager and, as they came to a halt by the front door, another car came swiftly up the drive and pulled up beside them. Maurice Fitzherbert got out and together they all three went into the house.

While Maurice was shown upstairs, Alicia Moreton came into the drawing-room to talk to May. Her appearance gave the older woman a shock. Alicia's hair was quite grey and there were deep lines under her eyes, which May felt had been there for some time and were not just due to the present situation. She could not help wondering about her marriage. How happy had she ever been? Was Charles Moreton still philandering, chasing after women such as Grace Armitage, the Wilhampton *femme fatale*, with whom it had long been recognised that he had had some kind of liaison when John William had been a baby?

"It's good of you to come, May." Nervously, Alicia picked up a silver cigarette box, held it out to her visitor and then, when the offer was declined, took a cigarette herself, lit it and inhaled deeply. "I don't think Mummy's going to pull through," she went on. "But she's wonderfully brave, as you might expect. She's even on about having some new nightdress made."

When May was eventually shown up to the Dowager's room, Alicia's words proved correct. It appeared that the old lady did, in fact, want a new nightdress, but one for a very specific purpose.

"That silly girl, Miriam, has ruined all my others, May . . . These days they don't understand about washing properly . . . Not a decent one left to be laid out in." Maud Fairfax closed her eyes for a moment. She seemed to be saving her breath for her next startling announcement. "Over there," she said, suddenly, with a touch of her old imperiousness, pointing to a chintz-covered ottoman in the corner. "There's a length of white crêpe de Chine . . . If you slip your hand down the side . . . a muslin bag. Lace," she said, and stopped again.

May went across the room and did as she was bidden, soon returning with both items. The voice from the bed was more feeble now. "The lace . . . is from my first dance dress, May. When I met Jimmy. We weren't . . . well off. Indian civil service . . . But my mother's cousin had this fichu . . . It was given to her by the old Duchess of Roxburghe . . . I know you'll do your best . . ."

A nurse came silently into the room with a small glass of medicine and, equally unobtrusively, May withdrew.

John Moreton was waiting for her in the hall when she came down the stairway.

"I'll drive you home, Miss Lodge."

"It's kind of you, John, but it's only a little way. There's really no need."

"But it's the least I can do." He glanced at May's packages. "I believe my grandmother has been putting you to work." She was struck again by his extraordinary charm.

She saw lights in the window of the Hermitage as soon as they swung into the lane, which meant that Katy and Emily were back. "Would you," May asked, when he drew up at the gate, "care to come in?"

He accepted with alacrity. There was, she supposed, little to occupy him in Netherford at the moment, with a dying grandmother and a mother who seemed so preoccupied and tense.

Emily was standing in the small hallway when they entered, surveying herself in an antique looking-glass which Katy had recently bought in one of Butt and Swanton's furniture sales. She was adjusting an old-fashioned wig with ringlets. Her face still bore traces of the make-up she had worn for the dress rehearsal of her play, *The Princess in Waiting*. As she turned towards them, May felt she was being confronted by a side of her niece that she did not know. She looked beautiful, much more mature, but infinitely lonely.

"Hullo," Emily said, clearly so preoccupied with theatrical problems that her surprise visitor appeared scarcely to register. "I don't think the costumiers have done very well with this." She held out the wig to May. "It's too mousy. My princess was meant to be blonde."

"But I thought you looked most becoming in it." Gallantly, John Moreton did his best. The young girl before him seemed all at once to become aware of his presence and her face brightened.

"Oh, do you think so?"

Katy had by now come out of the sitting-room and May, having explained that she wanted to get on with some sewing, went straight up to her workroom. She knew that there was some urgency about her allotted task. By the time she heard John Moreton leave, she had already cut out his grandmother's nightdress. By ten o'clock the next morning she was on her way back to the Grange with it. But she did not see her client again. Later in the day the Dowager went into a coma and that evening she died.

To May, her passing marked not only the end of an era but the loss of a relationship which had meant more to her than she had ever realised. Often, she would walk past the Grange and wonder what was to happen to it. She knew that Alicia was staying there temporarily, engaged in some necessary clearing-up operations. But, apart from the funeral, she saw nothing of Charles Moreton, nor the present Lord Fairfax. Rumour had it that the latter, having arrived an hour before his mother died, had left for the continent again as soon as she was buried.

When, a few months later, May received a thick white envelope with a London postmark, she was astonished to find, on opening it, that it was from a firm of solicitors, informing her that, under the terms of the late Dowager Lady Fairfax's Will, she had been left five hundred pounds and a cameo brooch "in gratitude for a valued friendship and loyal assistance over a great number of years".

Quietly, she passed the letter over to Katy and pulled out a handkerchief. "1909, it was," she said, "when Flo and I were first summoned to the Hall. You were only seven. I can remember it as if it were yesterday. It was a Wednesday in April, the weather a bit like it is now. Mother made us both wear grey flannel costumes and white blouses. We sat up half the night getting them finished. Maud Fairfax was in her prime then. She wanted some dresses made for Ascot. I was so nervous writing down the measurements when Flo called them out, that when we got back to the mill we weren't sure whether I'd written a thirty-two or a thirty-three inch bust. We had to do the cutting out making allowances and put things right at the first fitting. But she seemed pleased with the result. I mean . . . we always had her custom from then on."

"Yes." Though Katy was not in tears, she was very near them.

"She was a good woman," May went on. "She did a lot for you when you were young. Always sending down things from the Hall when you were poorly. She's going to be missed. There aren't many like her these days. I believe she had quite a hand in keeping the estate together these last few years. Cyril Butt said the agent used to go and see her at least once a fortnight. But now . . . the Lord knows what'll happen. I mean, her daughter-in-law's not much use, although I can't help feeling sorry for her. I suppose, if John William were of age . . . well, there's no male heir, is there?"

"No. But presumably one day John will inherit Bishopsdown from his own father."

There was suddenly silence between the sisters, both wrapped in private thoughts which, had they wished to exchange them, might not have proved so very dissimilar, except that May's had gone as far as to contemplate a cream satin wedding-dress and a veil of Brussels lace.

Later that night, when she was in bed, Katy found herself still mulling over their conversation, the past and the present jostling for supremacy in her mind. She could see Sarah and the Mill House with startling clarity. Having been so young at the time, she could not recall the incident of the white blouses and grey costumes to which May had referred, but her sister's reminiscences had certainly brought back her mother's extraordinary power over her family, the way she had almost always been able to make her children jump to do her bidding. Katy could not help feeling that, tragic though the circumstances had been surrounding Sarah's death, it was a blessing that she had been spared the knowledge of Philip's. It was not that she would have exactly grieved over her son-in-law—only for the wayward daughter who had gone against her wishes in marrying him.

Katy was grateful that she could now, at last, look back a little more calmly and rationally on her husband's suicide. The thing which had invariably upset her most was the fact that, whatever the trouble had been, he had not felt able to confide in her. She knew she would have forgiven him, whatever it was. She had soon realised that it must have been connected with Barbara Woodley yet, equally, she had known that he was speaking the truth when he had said that his affair with her was over. Not until she had eventually started to let her mind open up to all the possible reasons he might have had for throwing himself in the mill-race, did the real one enter into it. If only Philip had not been so impetuous, although, in moments of brutal honesty—such as tonight—she was well aware that this was what had originally attracted her to him. She had never felt the same way about any other man, that is, unless she counted her temporary lapse from convention with Gordon Hillier; and that little episode was, thank goodness, over and done with. At the moment she was glad to be leading a perfectly innocuous existence, yet somehow she knew it was not good enough, especially with Emily growing up. She should be making more of an effort; she should have got to know some of the parents of her school friends. Apart from Dorothy and Dick Swayne she was really only on nodding terms with the rest. Emily needed to move in a wider social circle; even though the child seemed to have attracted the attention of an eminently suitable young man, she was still only sixteen and, for more than one reason, it was difficult to think that anything would come of that particular relationship.

In the distance, she heard the faint sound of the Wilhampton town clock striking one a.m. She turned over, restlessly, reflecting on how she had failed, miserably, whichever way she looked at it. She had withdrawn from life. Unlike May, who appeared to have an inborn facility for getting on with everyone, she was aware that she only seemed able to come alive and respond in the presence of certain people, presumably the kind like Gordon, who were few and far between in and around Wilhampton.

Almost involuntarily, she stretched out a hand to the empty space beside her, wondering if this was to be her lot for the rest of her life. She felt immeasurably grateful to May for all her support, yet just now she would have given almost anything to have had a man about the house, or even one who would simply advise her about Emily's future. The child had become difficult of late. She knew she was talented, more intelligent than clever and that, when she left off her glasses, she was—or would be—beautiful. Her headmistress had been so anxious for her to go to university. She had passed her School Certificate at such a ridiculously young age. But, in consequence, Emily now seemed determined to leave Wickfield as soon as possible and attend the local art school, this desire having apparently superseded any previous ones. Had her daughter, perhaps, inherited her father's impetuosity? Should she, as her mother, have given in to what were possibly no more than youthful capricious demands of the moment?

The obvious person to consult was, Katy knew, Maurice Fitzherbert. He was the one man in whom she could, and probably should, confide. But lately she had begun to hold back more and more from asking anything of him other than of a strictly medical kind. She had always imagined that, as the years went by, he would come to regard her simply as a friend. Certainly, while Philip had been alive she had scarcely given the matter a thought, one way or the other; but nowadays, despite his impeccably correct and courteous manner, she had sensed that his feelings for her remained constant. It would have been so easy, sometimes, to turn one of his professional visits into more of a social occasion: offer him tea or a drink—not that she thought he would ever accept the latter. But whenever he had said, a little reluctantly, that he must be getting on, she had always stood up at once and, almost formally, held out her hand.

She recalled the last occasion when, after showing him out, she had spent the evening wondering why so nice a man who did so much public good was destined for such private sadness, regretting bitterly that she seemed to be the cause. It would have been so much better if she and Philip had never returned to Wilhampton or, after his death, she had moved right away again. But then she had reminded herself that she had been in no position to make such a decision. Besides, May would have hated it and there had been Emily's schooling to consider.

She turned over yet again. As, at last, she drifted off to sleep, a thought which had so often assailed her over the years seemed to float in and out of consciousness: that she was bound, irrevocably, to the banks of the Willon and the place where she had been born and bred.

32

"How much do you think Emily ought to have as a dress allowance now she's left school?"

Katy and May were sitting in the little workroom at the Hermitage while the latter put some finishing touches to an outfit for Ethel Sharman, whose cousin at the Air Ministry was at last—at the age of fifty—getting married to a lady who worked as a secretary in the Foreign Office. Emily had gone to supper with the Swaynes. Although it was a sultry August evening, both sisters had come indoors early, for there had been nine consecutive days of thunderstorms and it looked as if yet another was looming up.

"I should have thought six pounds a quarter, or thereabouts," replied May, snipping off a thread and standing up to put Ethel's simple, beige, wool georgette two-piece on to a hanger. "She should be able to manage on twenty-four pounds a year and it will teach her the value of money before she comes into her own when she's twenty-one. After all, you've promised her a new winter coat for her seventeenth birthday and her underwear is well up together."

The room was suddenly lit by a flash of lightning and for a while May remained looking out of the window.

"Do you remember," she went on, as she sat down again, "when poor dear Mother was alive, how she always came up to the attic if we had a storm in the night and draped a sheet over the looking-glass on the dressing-table?"

"Yes. And then Father would go downstairs and make us all a cup of tea."

"She used to say that the lightning was the devil's writing in the sky and the thunder was God telling us not to look at it. When something nasty happened, even if it was a long time afterwards, she always maintained it was because we hadn't paid enough attention to His warning."

A violent clap of thunder brought their conversation to an end and throughout the rest of the storm they said little. Both knew that just now there was enough potential danger in the world around them for Sarah to have had plenty of reasons for justifying her predictions.

Presently, May switched on the wireless, shaking her head as the evening's news appeared to be even worse. She had never been much of a student of history or geography and had, in fact, had to turn up an old atlas to ascertain the exact position of the country whose name was currently on everybody's lips: Czechoslovakia. It seemed so far away and remote somehow, even though she had recently noticed several advertisements in the press for a fifteen-day holiday there for only twenty-two guineas. These had been accompanied by drawings of young women with plaited hair wearing dirndl skirts and wooden clogs. She felt it must be such a pleasant, quiet, old-fashioned place. If only Germany could let well alone. She could not think why this wretched man Hitler had to keep meddling in other people's affairs, nor why law-abiding people like the British had to be drawn in to keep the peace. It seemed such a pity that her favourite politician, Mr Eden, hadn't been able to do better with his League of Nations. Her belief in it had been sadly undermined now that Germany and Japan and Italy were no longer members. There was so much going on that she did not understand—and most certainly did not like. Only that morning she had received a letter from Henry, informing her that he was being sent down to Salisbury Plain immediately—as an instructor on some training exercises—and, although she was pleased to think that this might mean an opportunity of seeing him, she felt sure his posting had something sinister to do with what was happening on the continent. Almost everything these days, including the weather, seemed to be conspiring to make her restless and on edge—much more so, she realised, than Katy who, possibly because of her age, had never been quite so conscious of the evils of war as any of her elder sisters.

"I think I'll drive over to Bulbarrow and fetch Emily home now," May said, suddenly. "I don't know about you, but I could do with an early night."

In one way it was a relief to listen to her niece's cheerful unconcerned chatter on the way back: to hear of Helen's intention of taking a Domestic Science training now that she, too—a year later than her best friend—had passed School Certificate; to agree with Emily that it seemed unfair that she should be subjected to a driving test after she obtained her provisional licence at the end of November, whereas her aunt had been spared such an imposition; to discuss the possibility of buying a new car after Christmas.

For a few moments, May found herself quietly looking forward to the coming months. But as soon as she was in bed that night the fear returned. Unable to sleep, she could not help thinking how the future hopes of everyone could so easily be shattered. What might they all have to face, especially the young men she knew? John William, for instance; Bob Swayne and his brother, Tim; Edith's two eldest boys, Donald and Ernest, and the lance corporal who had so surprisingly and providentially married a pregnant Della; then there was Robert Farley's son, a fully-fledged solicitor yet, as May well knew, also a territorial. And what about her other nephew, Frank François, and even her own brother? Please God Henry would be too old for active service. But *surely*, no one in his right mind would let war happen again. The government would do *something*. Reason would prevail. Or would it?

Oddly—or perhaps not so oddly—enough, it was John William who was uppermost in her mind, rather than her own kith and kin. To May, he was such a splendid example of English manhood. She was aware that she was probably just a silly old spinster, but in her eyes he seemed well-nigh perfect: a kind of golden boy, with his dazzling good looks, irreproachable manners and irresistible charm. She had never dared to say as much to her sister, let alone her niece; but it always touched her that he came to call on them whenever he was in Netherford. This was more often than she had ever dared to hope for, because his grandmother had left him the Grange in trust until he came of age. Throughout much of that summer it had been closed up, but now a resident caretaker had been installed and, at the end of July, John had spent a fortnight there, together with a friend from Cambridge.

It went without saying that Emily could never visit the place unchaperoned when he was in residence, but one evening, while his guest had gone off somewhere or other by himself, they had entertained John to supper at the Hermitage and he and Emily had gone down to the river by themselves afterwards. May had watched them covertly for a little while from her workroom window: the boy, so tall and thin and graceful; the girl—her glasses temporarily abandoned—a little shorter, her figure somewhat given to puppy fat yet still beautifully proportioned, her rounded limbs bare and brown, her dark wavy hair falling thick and loose in the fashionable page-boy bob. For all the difference in their ages and background, May sensed that they found pleasure in each other's company. The very fact that her niece had been so reticent about the occasion afterwards somehow made her even more sure that this was the case. But, of course, she must remember that Emily was still so young, little more than a child, really. It was no good building castles in the air. She was behaving just as she had done over Katy and Maurice Fitzherbert and where had that got them all? One could not legislate for romance. Just because it had slipped through her own fingers was no reason for trying to resurrect it vicariously through others. Besides, love almost seemed to be something best avoided with the world in the state it was today.

When, nearly three weeks later, the European crisis deepened, May was never far from her wireless set. Throughout the Prime Minister's three visits to Germany, firstly to Berchtesgaden, then Godesburg and finally Munich, she and Katy waited with mounting anxiety. Knowing that there was an unbroken intercession for peace round the Unknown Warrior's tomb in Westminster Abbey, they often slipped into St. Mark's and said a prayer or two when they went to Wilhampton, where they would find others doing the same thing. One day they ran into Edith hurrying out of a side entrance, her face white and tense. On the last day of September, when Neville Chamberlain returned to England with his 'Peace with Honour' message, May wept.

Summer seemed loth to leave that year. Though the trees were tinged with yellow and there was definitely a nip in the misty early morning air, the heat of the sun soon broke through, dispersing the tiny sparkling cobwebs on the dew-drenched grass and bathing the Willon valley in calm, golden light. Sometimes, all three inhabitants of the Hermitage would rise early before Emily left for art school and go mushrooming at Sweetacres, a pursuit for which Robert Farley had long given them permission.

Once, a little later on in the day, May went alone to pick blackberries along the old Barbury turnpike. When she had gathered enough to make one of her specialities—blackberry and apple jelly—she sat down on the grass and contemplated the scene spread out below her, sharp and clear like a child's model toy. She knew and loved every inch of it: the Felt Mills with its tall black chimney, Bulbarrow away to the west, the grey spire of St. Mark's, the dark mass of yew trees almost, but not quite, hiding the Hall, the cluster of mostly thatched dwellings which made up Netherford, the distant town of Westonbury with its white-bright chalk-pit high on the downs behind; and then, as if it were somehow threading the whole tapestry together, lay the River Willon, peacefully shining in the autumn sun.

She was so lost in appreciation of all that she could see that she did not notice Robert Farley coming along the hedge until he was almost beside her. Gun under arm and Sweep, his black labrador, at heel, he smiled and wished her good-day. Then he, too, stood looking down on the view before them. She knew that he was a man who did not find it easy to express himself, but who probably felt a little as she did about the countryside where they were both born and bred.

"It's . . . beautiful, isn't it?" she said, simply. "It's days such as these that make one feel so grateful to Mr Chamberlain."

When he did not reply, she glanced up towards him and was astonished to find his previously genial expression gone, his eyes now hard, his jaw set. He remained silent for so long that she realised she must have upset him in some way.

At length, he said, quietly, "We let the Czechs down, May. You can't get away from it. It might be peace in our time, though I doubt it. But one thing I do know is that there's precious little honour attached to it."

This time it was she who remained silent. Sweep flopped down beside her and, absently, she stroked his ears. After a while Robert went on, almost as if he was talking to himself, "Besides, it wasn't right . . . a British Prime Minister flying *three* times, cap in hand. Chamberlain's never made a journey by air before. He's an old man. Sixty-nine. Hitler's twenty years younger. The boot should have been on the other foot."

33

"Telephone, Emily."

May laid down the receiver and watched her niece come hurrying across the garden. She had fined down since the previous summer—not without some careful avoidance of certain items in her diet, such as Wilhampton lardy cake, of which she was particularly fond. There seemed now to be a radiance about her—especially when she left off her glasses—not dissimilar, May felt, to Katy's during the year when she had first fallen in love with Philip.

Yet with Emily, there was a difference. May found it difficult to explain. Though more socially aware and certainly far better educated than her mother, she had a strangely disconcerting innocence about her. While she obviously attracted the opposite sex, she treated all the young men she knew in an artless, almost sisterly, manner, accepting their attentions with surprised pleasure which held them bewitched, but at arm's length.

There was Bob Swayne, for instance, who had twice taken her to the pictures, firstly to see Merle Oberon and Laurence Olivier in *Wuthering Heights*—which Katy and May had subsequently gone to by themselves—and secondly, Vivien Leigh and Clark Gable in *Gone With The Wind*. On both these occasions Helen, though older but still very much a schoolgirl, had kept tactfully in the background. One or two male students from the art school had also asked Emily out, Katy making it a rule, however, that she could not go anywhere with anyone unless they had first come to the Hermitage. Such stringent vetting—usually accompanied by a small glass of sherry—was something which the sisters enjoyed discussing afterwards. So far, each young man Emily had brought home had been perfectly presentable, although May sometimes wondered how her mother would have handled the situation if one had arrived of whom she did not approve.

May noticed that the responsibility for her daughter seemed to weigh more and more heavily on Katy's shoulders these days. Considering how emotional and highly strung her sister had been, she never ceased to be surprised at the way she appeared lately to have settled down. May loved her dearly, but she often felt that she did not altogether know her. Katy was well-informed, read assiduously, had become an active member of the local Red Cross Society—into which she had roped both Emily and herself—and had agreed to help organise, as well as exhibit in, the forthcoming Westonbury Show. But the word which invariably came into May's mind whenever she thought of her was: wasted.

Now, in order to leave her niece alone at the telephone, May went out to join her sister, who was carefully tying up a new clematis which she was training to grow against the thatched cob wall behind the herbaceous border.

"It's John William," she said.

"I thought it probably was."

"That's three times in the last fortnight."

"Yes."

"He's in love with her, Katy."

"But she's not in love with him. Or anyone, for that matter."

Katy turned round and pushed back a strand of hair which had escaped from the neat bun she wore nowadays, a style which May did not think exactly suited her. All at once, she realised her youngest sister was middle-aged. She was quite grey at the temples and her once-slim figure had definitely thickened round the waist.

"They're still children," Katy went on. "Far too young for anything serious."

"You and Philip weren't much older."

"Yes . . . but Emily's not really physically . . . well, mature. She's still very much at the romantic stage. They both are."

May was silent. They walked across the lawn and sat down on the old wooden seat which had once graced the garden of the Mill House. She knew her sister was right. The trouble was that she herself was a romantic. She had been one all her life. But since her unfortunate experience in the last war, she had always shied away from the thought of that ugly act in which romance presumably culminated.

"Besides," Katy continued, "however suitable it might seem from our point of view, the Moretons would never approve. They've probably got very definite ideas about the sort of background any future daughter-in-law of theirs would have to come from."

Suddenly a door slammed and Emily came running out of the house.

"John wants to take me to Lord's, Mummy."

"Lord's?"

"Yes. You know, the Eton and Harrow match. He adores cricket. His family always takes a box. Two days. In July.

"Is he waiting for an answer?"

"No. Apparently Lady Moreton has written to you about it. Her invitation's in the post."

There was a pause. Katy wondered how much difficulty John had probably encountered in getting his mother to do so. She supposed that, with his persuasive charm, he had managed to overrule any objection. "It would mean us staying in London," she said, at length.

"Couldn't we?"

It was May who, in not much more than a murmur, seemed to settle the question. "I could make her outfits . . . Sprigged muslin . . . would look lovely at this time of the year."

Her niece pulled her to her feet and, after a few protesting "chippatoos", waltzed her round the garden.

Early the following Saturday morning, Emily drove both her mother and aunt to Bournemouth. She had passed her driving test the previous winter at her first attempt and, although May and Katy occasionally remonstrated with her for going too fast, they knew that she was basically the best driver of the three. Having spent several hours in their favourite shop, they came away with everything they wanted. As such unanticipated requirements were quite beyond Emily's dress allowance, the cost was borne mostly by Katy, although May insisted on paying for various trimmings, including some artificial flowers with which to adorn her niece's two hats.

During the next fortnight she could scarcely have worked harder, or with more enthusiasm, had she been preparing for a wedding. Crisp white muslin billowed around her small sedate figure, as she sat threading black ribbon through neck, wrist and waistline. A white straw hat with a single red rose in the front lay perched on the top of her tailor's dummy. Then came the turn of some printed lilac-coloured chiffon on which, at her niece's request, she had promised to sew deep purple bows. "Like the tune," Emily said, as she herself began sewing imitation violets on to a lilac-coloured crown. "They're playing *Deep Purple* all the time on the wireless these days."

"Do you remember, Aunt Chip," she said, one evening after Katy had driven into Wilhampton on Red Cross business, "when I was a little girl staying at the mill, how you made a dress for my doll out of a remnant from the first dance dress you ever made Mummy?"

"I remember, Emily."

"And now you're making clothes for me to go to a . . . well, not a dance, but something almost more exciting."

"Yes."

"Aunt Chip. Why did you never marry?"

May took off her spectacles and laid down her sewing. She had not expected quite such a direct question, although she could recall Emily's mother having asked her the selfsame thing at round about the same age. But now, just as then, it was something she did not want to talk about. Why had she never married? She couldn't tell Emily—any more than she could have told Katy—about Major Walter Perkins . . . how, ever afterwards, she had known that she could never face the physical side of such a union.

"It's hard to say, my dear."

"But you'd have made a marvellous wife. Always doing things for others. It doesn't seem . . . right, somehow."

"It depends," May answered, guardedly, "how you look at it. I shall get a lot of pleasure seeing you go off to Lord's. I think you'll find even Lady Moreton won't be better turned out."

On the following Thursday, the three of them travelled up to London by train to stay at Brown's hotel. After the heat of the journey, its foyer seemed refreshingly cool and dark. Suddenly, Katy had a vivid recollection of the day when she had come there to meet Belle before going to the Private View at the Royal Academy. How long ago was it? Eight . . . no, nine years. So much had happened since then. Yet Brown's appeared just the same: solid, quiet and comfortable. Even the head porter's face was vaguely familiar. The only difference seemed to be that last time it was she who had been arriving so eagerly, "dressed up to kill", as Philip used to say; and today—or, rather, tomorrow—

it was the turn of her daughter. May had even made the child a smart lightweight cloak, just as she had done for her, in case the weather turned cold or wet.

But fortunately, it did not. She noticed John William give a start and then a look of admiration—even awe—come into his face when he called to collect Emily, arrayed almost entirely in white, the next morning. Then, as he shook hands with them all, he said something which once again jerked her back, not nine years but nineteen. He used the selfsame words which Maurice Fitzherbert had used when he had taken her to her first dance in Wilhampton town hall: "I've never seen a prettier dress." She watched Emily flush, saw the delight in May's eyes and, as the two young people went out of the door, hoped no one had noticed that she had been fighting to keep the tears from her own.

The sisters saw little of Emily that day or the next, for Sir Charles and Lady Moreton were taking a large party out to dinner on the Friday evening, in which she had naturally been included. Left to themselves, they mostly looked round the shops together, although on Saturday morning Katy slipped away for an hour or so and walked up through Berkeley Square and into Davies Street. She was surprised to find on reaching Number 51 that it was no longer a bookshop. Its window was filled with flowers. Somehow, she felt pleased. Mason and Son had ceased to exist rather as that part of her life had ended also. Just occasionally, as now, a few little bright hurting memories thrust themselves forward and played havoc with her determination to suppress them. She knew it was no use looking back, even though nowadays it was sometimes difficult, even scaring, to look forward. Only the previous evening, she and May had gone into Hyde Park and seen all the air raid shelters. She was aware that many of them had been there since the previous year, but it was obvious that fresh ones were being dug. She had walked back to Brown's, grateful that she was the mother of a daughter, not a son.

Late on Saturday night, when they were on their way home in the train, she listened to Emily's graphic account of all she had done. It was rewarding to realise how much the visit had meant to her and how well she had acquitted herself. Alicia Moreton had apparently complimented her on her clothes remarking, on being told how much May was responsible for them, that she had always known her aunt had genius. Even Phoebe had admired her hats.

"It was all so beautiful," her daughter prattled on. "Of course, I'm sorry Eton lost. It was the first time they'd done so for ages. I really don't understand much about cricket and, as I'd left off my glasses, it was difficult to see what was going on most of the time. But when the intervals came and everyone strolled out on to the ground, the colours were unbelievable. I'd love to have painted it. The only really sad thing was when some very old man came into the Moretons' box and started telling Sir Charles that there was bound to be a war. There won't be, will there?"

"I hope not, darling."

"If there is, John says he's going to leave Cambridge and join the R.A.F."

"The *R.A.F.*?"

"Yes."

The train was drawing into a station now and a news boy ran along the platform shouting "Late Night Extra", but the rest of his words was drowned in the sound of slamming doors and people greeting each other or shouting goodbye. A whistle blew, there was a hiss of steam, and slowly they started moving westwards again.

As their carriage drew level with the lighted entrance to the station, May noticed the news boy, this time standing beside a placard. The train had begun to gather speed but she could still read the headlines. They were large and clear: BRITISH PLEDGE TO POLAND.

34

Emily sat behind the wheel of the car at Wilhampton station. On its windscreen was a sticker denoting the number and sex of the evacuee children whom her mother—now out on the platform with a contingent of Red Cross helpers—had volunteered to house at the Hermitage. May had remained behind there, busy with last-minute preparations. "Girls," Emily remembered her aunt saying, a few days earlier. "Best ask for girls. You can come into my room, my dear, and we can put up two camp beds in your own." Dutifully, Emily had removed all her precious belongings, including books and drawings, from the bedroom which she had recently helped to redecorate in her favourite colour: pale mauve—the same shade as that of the dress she had worn on the second day at Lord's.

It was a warm evening—the first of September. Presently, having wound down all the windows of the new Ford Katy had bought soon after Emily passed her test, she decided to get out. But she did not move more than a few steps away. Drivers had been specially requested to stay by their vehicles. She had never seen so many people and cars milling about the station. It seemed as if the whole of Wilhampton had turned out in force. Helen and Bob Swayne waved to her from the other side of the yard, Helen in her mother's second-hand Baby Austin, Bob in the family milk van. It appeared that Dick and Dorothy were expecting, with their typical generosity, to care for at least four children, besides a mother and baby.

Away to her left, Emily caught sight of Frances Farley and Luke Ridley, the Fairfaxes' agent, as well as Mrs Morgan, the rector's wife, all parked next to each other. Presently, a cheer went up as old Mr Butt arrived, nosing his ancient Singer through the crowd, its windscreen proclaiming that he was willing to accommodate two boys over five years of age. Emily hoped that his housekeeper—prim Phyllis, as she was known—would be able to manage them. Ethel Sharman, not being a driver but having elected to house two evacuee schoolmistresses, was to be seen in a small group—including Edith, who had valiantly offered to have a child of either sex—standing anxiously beside one of the Parkers' taxis, which seemed to have a variety of stickers all over it. Every so often, Emily noticed the rector and Dr Fitzherbert going in and out of the station doors, yet there was no sign of Clare. Idly, she wondered whether, in spite of war appearing imminent, his wife was the only person in the whole of the little community who was being unco-operative or if a doctor's household was, perhaps, in some way sacrosanct. She felt rather excited, albeit slightly shamefaced about this. She was not sure how much it had to do with the strange unprecedented situation or the fact that John William was coming to the Grange in two days' time.

Suddenly, a bell rang. There was an instant hush while the stationmaster's voice gave out: "The train from Portsmouth is now arriving." She scanned the railway line through her glasses, on to which she had clipped the dark lenses she had lately taken to wearing for vanity's sake. Soon, she heard the familiar roar and stood watching while puffs of steam above the tree-tops came closer and closer, as the engine rounded the last bend and drew slowly to a halt.

After what seemed a very long wait, she saw her mother coming towards her with three little girls, wearing identification labels and gas-masks slung over their skinny bodies. They were dirty, dishevelled and in tears. Any previous feeling of excitement gave way to overwhelming pity.

"This," said Katy, "is Susan and Shirley and Pearl. Susan is seven and Shirley is six. They are sisters. Pearl is five and she has come all alone." The youngest child looked at Emily and held out her arms. She picked her up and in that one small moment it seemed as if she had left her own childhood behind her for ever. She helped them all into the car and drove away, Maurice Fitzherbert raising a hand in friendly salute as they passed. It was only now she was older that she had come to realise, with sadness, the extent of his carefully-masked devotion to her mother. She felt he would have made a wonderful stepfather.

There followed a busy thirty-six hours. The children, tired and disorientated, woke crying both on Friday and Saturday night. Rather to her amazement, Emily found that it was to her they seemed to turn. They kept asking for "Miss" and she got little sleep. On Sunday morning, she devised a way of keeping them quiet with paper and crayons while she waited with her mother and aunt for the Prime Minister's broadcast at eleven o'clock. There was a little light music being played on the wireless—an unusual occurrence for the Sabbath—and then silence, after which came Neville Chamberlain's voice: grave, regretful and final. Having received no reply to his ultimatum to Hitler to withdraw his troops from Poland, he informed the listening nation that he had no other option but to declare: "This country is at war with Germany."

Almost immediately, they heard the Felt Mills chimney let out an air-raid warning siren. It rose and fell in a hideous distant wail. Then, after a while, when no expected aircraft appeared in the sky, the all-clear sounded.

"Thank God," said May, "that Mother isn't alive."

At the mention of "Mother", the little girl called Pearl rushed towards Emily and began to scream. The two others followed suit. Sunday lunch was not an easy meal. All the inhabitants of the Hermitage were exhausted but fortunately, about two o'clock, the children were coaxed to sleep.

"Why don't you go and lie down too, my dear," May suggested to Emily. "You were up most of last night."

"I think . . . I'd sooner sit by the river," she replied. "It's as good a place to rest as any."

It was very quiet underneath her favourite willow tree, save for the sound of Fred Cutler calling the Sweetacres cows for their afternoon milking, and the occasional 'plop' as a trout or grayling rose to the surface of the Willon and then, as quickly, disappeared beneath the dark green undulating weeds. She leaned back, conscious of that special rivery fragrance she had come to love. She took off her glasses and closed her eyes. Soon, she too, was asleep.

He arrived so quietly that she had no idea how long he had been watching her when she awoke. She was vaguely aware that the shadows had lengthened and the cows had returned to the opposite meadow. He was lying sideways on the bank a little way away from her, his head propped up on one elbow.

"John!"

"Emily!" He smiled, got up and sat down beside her.

"When did you come here?"

"About an hour ago."

"An *hour*?"

"Yes, but I didn't want to wake you. Your aunt said you'd had a rough night. I thought the sleep would do you good."

"That was . . . very kind."

"You seem to have your hands full at the Hermitage."

"Yes."

"I'd like to have evacuees at the Grange, but I don't quite know who would look after them and I'm afraid the authorities have other plans for the place."

"Oh. What kind?"

"An army H.Q. I've got to see some general in Southern Command about it tomorrow."

"Will you," she asked, shyly, "be staying long?"

"I'm afraid not. You remember what I said at Lord's. I have an interview in London next Wednesday."

She turned to face him, suddenly apprehensive. "What kind of an interview?"

"You know. For the Air Force. They may not call me up just yet, but I don't want to hang around."

"I see," she answered slowly, and they lapsed into silence.

It was a good ten minutes before, diffidently, he took her hand.

"I like to think of you being in Netherford," he said, "whenever I'm away. Although I suppose . . . I mean, you might want to do other things now."

"I . . . really don't know." She hadn't thought. It had all happened so quickly. She still could not envisage a war, especially here, in these peaceful surroundings. But she supposed he was right. Somehow, painting pictures seemed quite out of the question at the moment.

"Emily." His hand on hers tightened. "There's something else I'd like to think. This war . . . it can't go on for ever. I'll be twenty-one next August. Will you marry me then, war or no war?"

She did not answer at once. She suddenly realised that she had known, all along, that one day he would ask her, but she had not expected it would be quite so soon. She would like to have gone on as they were. She felt that she was in love with him. It was wonderful to have him near her. She liked the feel of his hand holding hers. She was frightened for his safety and wished that he was not so set on joining the R.A.F. She longed for him to kiss her and had been disappointed that he had not done so on the night he had brought her back to Brown's after Lord's. But marriage was different. Marriage meant something else. If she did marry him, would he, perhaps, leave out that frightening part of it, at least until after the honeymoon?

When she still had not replied, he continued, "I thought . . . well, I hoped . . . that we could become unofficially engaged. In fact . . ." Here he broke off and searched in one of his pockets, suddenly producing a small, blue, jeweller's box. "It was my grandmother's," he explained, opening it. "I felt you might like to wear this little eternity ring."

She stared at it, almost uncomprehendingly. Then she said, softly, "Will you put it on, John?"

Carefully, he lifted up her right hand and slipped it over the third finger. It fitted beautifully. At last, he gathered her in his arms and kissed her, very gently, on the lips.

Then they remained, without speaking, watching the river flowing serenely past them, on and on through the golden September afternoon.